# THE RAVENS

**MINNESOTA TRILOGY**

*The Land of Dreams*
*Only the Dead*
*The Ravens*

# THE RAVENS

## VIDAR SUNDSTØL

Translated by Tiina Nunnally

**MINNESOTA TRILOGY 3**

University of Minnesota Press
Minneapolis

This translation has been published with the financial support of NORLA (Norwegian Literature Abroad, Fiction and Nonfiction).

Published by the University of Minnesota Press
111 Third Avenue South, Suite 290
Minneapolis, MN 55401–2520
http://www.upress.umn.edu

LIBRARY OF CONGRESS CATALOGING-IN-PUBLICATION DATA
Sundstøl, Vidar.
[Ravnene. English]
The Ravens / Vidar Sundstøl ; translated by Tiina Nunnally.
ISBN 978-0-8166-8944-6 (hc)
ISBN 978-0-8166-8945-3 (pb)
1. Murder—Investigation—Fiction. 2. Family secrets—Fiction. 3. Brothers—Fiction. 4. Minnesota—Fiction. 5. Mystery fiction. I. Nunnally, Tiina, translator. II. Title.
PT8952.29.U53R3813 2015
839.823'8—dc23                                          2015000051

Printed in the United States of America on acid-free paper

The University of Minnesota is an equal-opportunity educator and employer.

21  20  19  18  17  16  15                10  9  8  7  6  5  4  3  2  1

# 1

LAKE SUPERIOR had frozen over and was transformed into a desolate white wasteland. In Duluth the temperature hovered at a steady twenty below. No ships passed under the old Aerial Lift Bridge, although normally that would have happened several times a day. Now the bridge remained motionless all day long as the low January sun glinted off the frost-covered steel.

Inga Hansen was knitting. Only the faint clacking of her knitting needles disturbed the silence. From the walls stared so many faces from her long life: her husband wearing his police uniform, the two of them in their wedding picture, her grandchildren at various ages, her sons in high school photos. One picture showed a group of dark-clad people, maybe thirty or forty in all, both adults and children, formally posed for the photograph taken on the deck of a ship. Behind them steam rose up from the smokestack. In the bottom right-hand corner someone had written, "Duluth, October 3, 1902." In among the solemn-looking crowd were two young people who would become Inga's grandparents—a fact that almost brought her to tears whenever she thought about it. This was a response that had gradually emerged over the years. In the past she'd been able to bear anything at all without shedding a single tear. Nowadays it took very little to make her cry.

She looked at the newest photo of her granddaughter, Chrissy. With her neatly brushed blond hair forming a halo around her head, she looked like an angel, Inga thought. But Chrissy hadn't come to visit in a long time. Truth be told, they hadn't seen each other in over a year, although they'd talked on the phone a few times. No doubt that was what happened when kids became teenagers; suddenly there were things that were far more interesting than grandmothers. Even so, Inga had decided that the green-and-white scarf taking shape under her never-idle hands would be a birthday gift for Chrissy when she turned eighteen.

On the slope below the nursing home the houses and yards were covered with a blanket of snow. High overhead was the pale blue vault of the sky, looking as it had every day for nearly a month. And stretching out beneath it like the marble floor of a vast cathedral was the lake, once again frozen over. She couldn't look for very long at the white surface that extended eastward until it merged with the sky; the sight hurt her eyes. And she found it alarming that the entire lake looked exactly the same. So she tried not to dwell on it, although occasionally the thought would slip into her mind, unnoticed, until she suddenly pictured a place so far away that there was no land in sight in any direction; nothing but a dazzling whiteness with no shadows, because there was nothing out there that might cast a shadow. Yet the worst was imagining the total lack of sound. She imagined a piercing silence.

Someone was knocking on the door. Quickly she set down her knitting and smoothed out her skirt.

"Come in!"

One of the staff members opened the door.

"Hi, Inga. Postcard for you," she said, stepping into the room and holding out the postcard, as if it were a major event for someone to be writing to Inga Hansen.

"Is that all?" asked Inga.

"Yes. But it's nice to get a card in the mail, don't you think?"

Inga smiled politely as she set the card down without much interest. But as soon as the door closed, she picked up the postcard and eagerly read what it said.

"Oslo, Norway" was printed diagonally in big white letters across a nighttime scene showing a street decorated for Christmas. She turned the card over and read the few lines written in the familiar script.

*Dear Mom—*

*Having a good time in the "old country." Staying
at another hotel now, it's a little cheaper. Haven't
yet made it to Halsnøy but of course I will soon.
The Norwegians are nice, polite people, as you can
imagine. Won't be home for a while yet. It's really cold
here! Happy New Year, and say hello to everybody.*

*Lance*

The postmark showed that the card had been sent from Oslo on January 17, which was five days ago. The two other cards she'd received from her son had also been sent from there. It was back in November, right after the deer hunt, that he'd phoned to tell her he was going to Norway. She was glad that he'd decided to do something different for a change. Otherwise he spent all his free time immersed in those history archives of his.

Inga turned the card over again to look at the picture on the front. A long street gently sloping up toward a building painted yellow with a flag flying from the roof. The street was crowded with people. It was possible that some of them might even be relatives of hers. She liked that idea. There they were, her relatives, and all of them spoke Norwegian, just like her grandparents and the rest of the immigrants in the photograph taken on board the steamship in Duluth on that October day in 1902. When she was a child, she sometimes heard her grandparents speaking their native language to each other. She almost thought she could hear all those people on the street decorated for Christmas on the postcard. All those Norwegian voices humming on a winter evening in Oslo, where her son Lance was also walking around.

Inga put down the card and picked up her knitting. She couldn't sit idle for long if she was going to finish the green-and-white scarf in time for Chrissy's birthday.

Yet she soon found herself thinking again about the ice-covered lake, and she felt a shiver pass through her.

# 2

HE LUNGED OUT OF BED, striking his head so hard on the floor
that flames shot up in the back of his eyes, and he tore at his
pajama top, sending several buttons flying. It was pitch dark in
the room, and he was dying. His breath had stopped somewhere
between his lungs and his mouth, like an elevator stuck between
floors. Desperately he began flailing around in the dark, trying
to make something happen, although he didn't know what that
might be. Nothing was certain anymore except that he didn't have
long to live. His hand touched something that fell to the floor
with a bang and shattered into pieces. He inhaled with a gasp, as
if suddenly returning to the surface after making a lengthy dive.
He greedily drew in great quantities of air, noticing how the paralyzing fear slowly released its hold on his body. Maybe he wasn't
going to die after all.

   With trembling arms and legs he hauled himself into a sitting position on the edge of the bed and turned on the lamp on
the nightstand. His pajama top hung open, without a single but-
ton. His big white stomach gleamed in the faint glow of the lamp.
Fear was still circulating through the room like electrical pulses,
or like arrows shot from bows by thousands of little demons that
had descended upon him as he slept. A sob suddenly filled his
throat like a cork; it felt so tight that he didn't even dare swallow.
He knew that under the painful cork was a bottomless reservoir

of self-pity, and right now he was close to giving in to it, but he refused.

Anything but a nervous breakdown, thought Lance Hansen.

He stood up, still on the verge of tears, and caught sight of himself in the mirror. A fat, middle-aged man with tearful eyes, a white whale living in total isolation in a hotel room in a foreign country. The next moment he was over at the desk, swinging his right arm like a sledgehammer and slamming his fist down on the surface, sending scraps of food skittering across the floor. A beastly howl echoed through the room, and the jolt of pain reverberated all the way up to his shoulder, but he didn't give a shit. Again he pounded the desk with his leaden fist, this time splintering the wood. Oh, how good that felt! Lance turned around and jabbed the air with several left-right combinations, like a boxer just before a fight, throwing swift punches that would have knocked anybody out cold. "That's enough!" he shouted. "I won't stand for this anymore!"

HE MUST HAVE FALLEN ASLEEP AGAIN, and when he woke, there was no longer anything wrong with his breathing. He took a shower, got dressed, and went downstairs to the small room where breakfast was served. But he found no food and no people. The hotel seemed dead, and his footsteps echoed along the empty hallways as he went back to his room. He checked his watch, which he'd left on the nightstand. It was 5:10 in the morning.

Lance was ravenous and desperate for a cup of coffee, but it would be almost half an hour before he could get breakfast, and nowhere else was open this early. So he really had no choice but to undress and go back to bed, although he really didn't want to. He wanted breakfast and some strong coffee. Resigned, he sat down at the desk and looked inside the carton from yesterday's Chinese takeout. There was still a little food left. He used his fingers to stuff his mouth with the cold rice and sauce that had now congealed like butter. Then he remembered that several days ago he'd put a couple of rolls in one of the desk drawers. He had intended to eat them with dinner, but then forgot. He pulled out the drawer, and there were the rolls along with the old diary written by his grandmother Nanette. That had been one of the first things he'd packed when he decided to make this trip. The book was over a hundred and twenty years old and written in French. Inside were two sheets of paper with an English translation of a few pages. Lance ran his finger over the worn binding; it was so soft that it was almost like touching living flesh. The diary and the two sheets of paper contained quite a number of truths about him. That was probably why he'd brought them along when he left—to remind himself, here in this foreign land, of who he was and where he came from.

Lance closed the drawer and placed the two rolls on the desk. With his fingertip he poked at one of them. The roll was hard as a rock, but when he broke it in half, the bread was still edible; only the crust was too hard. After devouring the insides of both rolls, he finished off the meal with a couple of glasses of water from the tap. Then he began packing his suitcase.

# 3

AFTER DRIVING FOR A GOOD HOUR Lance stopped at a gas station to fill up the tank and buy a couple of hot dogs, a soda, and a cup of coffee. He paid with some of the foreign coins that he was slowly getting used to. Then he gulped down the coffee so greedily and quickly that the young guy behind the counter couldn't help staring.

He felt better after eating the food and finishing his coffee. Then he continued southward through a landscape that didn't change significantly. As he headed into the morning hours and away from the night, the traffic increased. When he encountered a semi on the road, the drifting snow was like a huge cloud of powder.

For two months he'd been living the same aimless life, like a prisoner. If he awoke in the evening, he would often just lie in bed until he dozed off again. Sometimes he would get up and go to the bar just down the street, but he never ate out, since he felt like everyone was staring at him, even though he looked no different from the local populace. For the most part he'd spent the past two months in bed in his hotel room. Fortunately they had American TV programs. Usually he ate in bed too. But mostly, he'd slept, always without dreaming.

THE CAR RADIO had stopped working. The only sound it made was a crackling, hissing noise that made him think of the desolate space and cold outside. He'd been driving for over three hours, but the landscape was still the same: snow-covered forests in between empty white expanses of varying size, concealing a tarn, a marsh, or a lake. He drove across narrow bridges with rivers or creeks underneath, but he never saw even a drop of water; the current flowed at least six feet under the snow and ice.

As he pulled out of a tight curve, he saw a wolf standing in the middle of the road. He stomped on the brakes and managed to stop twenty or thirty yards away. The wolf was wearing its best winter pelt, with a hint of frosty white in the gray. In the wolf's world, it was clearly the car that had to yield the right-of-way. The animal held its position with its head lowered in a threatening pose. In the background lay the carcass of a stag on which the wolf had been feeding. Lance let the car roll forward slowly until there were only a few yards between him and the wolf, but the animal didn't move, and he was again forced to stop. Then it bared its teeth, hackles raised. Yet Lance noticed that the wolf also seemed afraid, its body tensed as if ready to run off at any moment.

To put an end to the standoff, Lance honked the car horn. The wolf spun around and ran, but after only a few yards it stopped and stood still, facing the car. Lance honked again, but this time the wolf merely backed up a few paces, its ears lying flat. Even though he was sitting inside the protection of the car, Lance felt scared. The wolf couldn't hurt him, but there was something ominous about the completely irrational display of defiance and strength. The wolf possessed something to which no human being had access, and it seemed to consist solely of this incomprehensible otherness as it stood there, refusing to flee.

Another car appeared, coming from the opposite direction, and both Lance and the other driver honked. Only then did the wolf retreat. Awkwardly it backed up along the snowbank and then disappeared into the woods.

RIGHT AFTER THAT he drove through a small community and saw a bunch of kids, probably waiting for the school bus, standing in a shelter with their shoulders hunched and their faces buried in thick scarves. He imagined himself and his brother, Andy, on their way to school in the bitter cold, walking along as they'd done so many times in the past. Duluth in the 1970s, the town on the steep hillside with a view of the lake, the ships loaded with taconite, the old Aerial Lift Bridge—all those things that he saw and yet didn't see because they were there every day and always had been. What had they talked about on those mornings? He remembered only the heavy winter clothes, Andy's book bag that swung from side to side as he ran, the frosty vapor whenever he spoke.

Without his noticing, the highway had changed into a street, and he recognized the place from the time he'd driven in the opposite direction a couple of months earlier. He came to a traffic light and stopped to wait for it to turn green. At the end of the cross street, off to the right, he could see the smoke from the big paper factory on the American side of the river. As he approached the bridge over Rainy River, the line of cars got longer, until it almost came to a standstill. Otherwise the streets seemed deserted in the small town straddling the river. On the opposite shore the first low rays of sunshine broke through the smoke coming from the American factory, coloring that side of the river pink.

Thinking about the wolf, Lance drove across the bridge. This was the same border he'd crossed two months ago; it was even the same route he'd taken. But the border he'd crossed inside himself was different this time. When he'd left the States it was with the certainty that one day he would return. But there was no turning back from where he was now heading.

# 4

ELY IS LOCATED on the shores of wind-swept Shagawa Lake, within the Iron Range of Minnesota, and Lance decided that would be a suitable place to begin. He checked in at the Lakeland Motel and ate a slice of pizza at the local Pizza Hut. Afterward he bought some bread and lunchmeat and a pair of snowshoes at a store close to the motel. He flung the snowshoes in the trunk of the car with a feeling that they might come in handy.

The room was virtually identical to the one in which he'd just spent two months in Kenora, Canada. The bed was no better or worse than the other, but there was one big difference: it was in the United States.

Eirik Nyland was the person who had made the whole disappearing act possible. Lance had chosen some Norwegian postcards from his personal collection and written messages to friends and family, as if he were vacationing in Norway. Then he'd sent the cards to Nyland with instructions about when each one was to be mailed. As far as the Norwegian police detective knew, Lance was shacking up for a month with some woman he'd just met, and he didn't want his colleagues or family to start poking around and asking questions.

When he woke up, it was midnight. He went over to the window to look out. Even the old, faded shopping center looked beautiful in the light from the moon. Not a sound could be heard; the buildings and parked cars cast long blue shadows.

LANCE KNEW EVERY MILE of the road between Ely and the lake, and yet the landscape seemed transformed in the moonlight. There were bridges he didn't recognize, and big open expanses in the midst of the forested terrain. He wasn't sure whether they concealed water or marshes. At lengthy intervals a building or two would appear, but even those he was unable to place.

He'd started to wonder if he might have taken a wrong turn, when he suddenly found himself in the town of Finland. It was impossible to mistake the twenty-foot-high wooden sculpture of St. Urho, the Finnish American patron saint, as it stood there looking like some sort of totem pole.

Finland was wrapped in ice-cold slumber, not a single person was outside, and no movement was visible behind the curtains in the few houses where the lights were still on.

As he passed the town's only shop, the Finland General Store, where you could buy everything from sewing accessories to bread and milk to snow blowers, he realized why he'd driven to this particular place. Debbie Ahonen. They'd dated for a short time when Lance was twenty-five, but Debbie fell in love with another policeman and moved to California. He'd hardly recognized her last summer, more than twenty years later, when he'd unexpectedly discovered her sitting behind the counter ringing up his purchases. Only when she spoke did he realize who she was, although her voice, like everything else, was duller than he remembered. That voice of hers. In the past it had nearly driven him crazy. How many lonely nights had he lain awake, trying to conjure up the sound in his memory? But when he heard it again last summer, he'd noticed instantly that something was missing. He couldn't put it into words. A certain sweetness? Or was it simply her lost youth? In any case, it had no doubt disappeared from his own voice as well. If his voice had ever contained any hint of youthfulness, that is. Regardless, he had recognized Debbie the second she spoke to him. Her laughter, which men in the past would have killed to hear, was now merely a prologue to a smoker's cough of the very worst kind. He could hear the mucus laboriously making its way up her respiratory passages to land in her mouth, followed by the sound of her swallowing it again.

And yet she was still Debbie Ahonen.

Richie Akkola, who owned both the gas station and the grocery store, had to be close to seventy, and he'd been a widower for years. Now Debbie was living with him in an apartment above the station. What was it she'd said? Something about Richie taking care of her old mother. And it was because of her mother, who couldn't manage on her own anymore, that Debbie had moved back here. But now Richie Akkola was caring for her, and in return Debbie was living with him. Was that the arrangement? *In return?*

Lance stopped the car outside the gas station and sat there, staring at the windows on the second floor. It was dark up there, and the curtains were drawn. That's where Debbie is right now, thought Lance. He almost couldn't believe it was true. Like a sleepwalker, and without knowing why, he reached out to turn on the radio, which had been on the blink for nearly a week. Suddenly the car was filled with voices and laughter. His heart skipped a beat and a sharp taste, as if from metal or blood, filled his mouth. A light went on behind one of the windows above the gas station. Lance quickly put the car in gear and drove off.

The radio program he'd tuned in to was a repeat of the most recent *Car Talk*. The two hosts, who were brothers, had a man from Boulder, Colorado, on the line. "So your windshield wipers keep going on and off at random?" said one of the hosts in surprise. "Yeah. They act like they've got a will of their own," said the caller. "I have the same problem with my wife," replied the other brother.


HE PASSED the Whispering Pines Motel where Georg Lofthus and his friend had spent the last night before Lofthus was killed. No, not his friend, Lance corrected himself, his *lover*. Georg Lofthus and Bjørn Hauglie had been lovers who'd kept their relationship secret, since the Christian community to which they belonged was extremely judgmental. Even sitting alone in his car in the middle of the night, Lance had a hard time thinking about what was discovered during the autopsy of Lofthus's body. Hauglie's semen was found in his stomach. When Lance heard about that, he'd felt as if the last puzzle piece had fallen into place, and it was a puzzle showing him the all-too-familiar face of the man who had murdered Lofthus. Only a day after the murder, Lance had begun to suspect his brother. But why would Andy have killed the Norwegian canoeist?

When Lance found out that the Norwegians were gay, he instantly thought about the episode from high school involving a boy named Clayton Miller. Everybody knew that Clayton was gay, even though no one had ever heard him say so or seen any obvious indications of his sexual preference. It was just something they all knew. Even though Lance had spoken to the boy only once, he had a very clear memory of how Clayton looked. A lock of his raven-black hair, which was cropped close in the back, hung over one eye. He wore long, multicolored scarves that he had supposedly knitted himself. Lance shook his head at the thought. A boy who knitted!

Clayton Miller was like no one else at their school. He stood out. And that must be why Lance remembered his appearance so clearly more than thirty years later. And because of the one instance when he'd spoken to the boy. That was on a Saturday, when the schoolyard was deserted, and Clayton was lying on the ground with a punctured lung. Lance had been frantically summoned by one of Andy's friends. As he was walking across the schoolyard toward Clayton, he saw his brother suddenly come around the corner of the gym, holding a baseball bat in his hands. In Andy's eyes Lance saw the look of a person who was so alone that he didn't know what in the world to do with himself. It was a look that he'd never seen before. Lance hadn't hesitated. He went over to Andy and grabbed hold of the bat, saying, "Let go." He was not afraid of his younger brother. Not back then.

Andy had instantly released the bat and after stammering a few incomprehensible words, he fled the schoolyard. When Lance asked Clayton Miller how he was doing, the boy replied that he thought his lung was punctured. Lance remembered so clearly how the boy who was lying on the asphalt had carefully whispered his reply, as if scared that he might rip himself open if he spoke too loud. "Are you his brother?" Clayton whispered. And when Lance nodded, he said, "He tried to kill me." Those were the only words Lance had ever exchanged with Clayton Miller.

IT WAS 3:05 IN THE MORNING when Lance drove into Two Harbors. The light from the moon, which was now low in the west, made the signs in front of the Dairy Queen cast long shadows across the sidewalk. In the frozen landscape the ads for Blizzards and milkshakes seemed totally absurd.

Lance parked near the Lutheran church, then walked back to the Dairy Queen and headed down the road behind the building. The snow creaked under his boots, but otherwise it was utterly quiet in Two Harbors. Not even a police patrol car anywhere in sight. He walked slowly, as if trying to postpone what was coming. Finally he stood still and stared at the green, two-story house with the two cars out front: a brand-new Ford Freestar and an old white Chevy Blazer with a red door on the right-hand side. The house was a good fifty yards away, so there was still time to turn around.

He continued the rest of the way over to the cars and crouched down behind the Chevy. He listened hard, but not a sound came from the house, and only the outdoor light was on. After staying there like that for several minutes, he stood up and went over to the house to try peering through the living room window. But it was darker inside than out, and through a gap in the curtains he could make out only a TV, identifiable because of its red electronic light. He crept over to the kitchen window and looked inside. Here the moonlight was shining through another window so he could see the counter and table. The counter was covered with bottles, boxes, and a number of other things he didn't recognize. On the table he saw a coffee mug, a pack of cigarettes, and a lighter. Even though all the clutter and the cigarettes would not have been found in his own home, the sight of those items still stirred up emotions for him. Probably because this was the first home he'd seen in more than two months, his first glimpse of someone's private life.

A door opened. Fear raced through him like a paralyzing fluid. He hardly dared breathe as he waited for Andy's voice, but nothing happened. Had he just imagined the sound? No, he was sure he'd heard it. Feeling weak and sick with terror, he managed to move back to the cars and crouch down behind the Chevy again. From that position he saw a light go on in the bathroom.

After a few minutes it was turned off, but he didn't dare go back to the house. He couldn't keep moving about like this. Somebody was bound to see him, but there was something about the sight of a home that got to him, even if it wasn't the nicest. He was afraid of getting caught, but he felt such a longing to go inside. Or maybe not inside that particular house. Some other house where people were living out their lives.

The side window of the Chevy was coated with a layer of ice. Lance took off his right glove and scraped at the ice with his fingernail. He had an urge to leave something behind, something that would connect him to them. But what should it be? He couldn't simply write his initials.

In the end he scratched a tiny figure of a man in the ice.

# 5

LANCE GOT BACK IN HIS CAR and drove the back roads toward Finland, but without knowing why or where he was actually heading. No matter what, he couldn't let anyone see him. For instance, it would be unthinkable to walk into Our Place, Finland's only bar, and have a chat with Ben Harvey, the amiable owner of the place. It was Ben who had told Lance that Andy had spent a whole evening in the bar with Georg Lofthus and his friend. That was one of the many things Andy had never mentioned, either to his brother or to the authorities. And it was one of the many things Lance had never told anyone else either. But if it had been simply an ordinary meeting of three men in a bar, then why hadn't Andy reported it when one of the Norwegians was found murdered? He wasn't the only person in the area to have met and spoken to those two, and other people had been more than happy to talk to the police.

When he reached Finland, Lance pulled his scarf up to cover his mouth and nose. It was light enough that he might be recognized. Slowly he drove past the Finland General Store as he tried to catch sight of Debbie Ahonen through the window. It wasn't easy, since the Christmas decorations hadn't been taken down yet. In the town of Finland, Santa Claus was still on his way with a sleigh full of packages. The eight reindeer were prancing along, with competing red lights blinking from the sled, from Rudolph's nose, and from Santa himself. It was hopeless trying to see a Finnish blond through all of that.

Just outside of Finland five or six ravens rose up from the road to perch in a nearby tree and wait for the car to pass. They'd been having a real feast. The guts and stomach contents of a buck were scattered over a wide area. Maybe the wolf had been there too. As Lance drove past, some of the ravens flapped their wings to fly farther away, but two of them stayed where they were. They were so black that they didn't look real as they sat there in all that whiteness, as if someone had placed a couple of plastic figures high in the trees. Suddenly one of them shrieked, although for Lance it was a soundless shriek since he was enveloped in the noise of the car. But he saw the bird stretch out its neck and seem to eject the raven shriek from its suddenly opened beak. He could practically *see* the sound. Then he was past, and in the rearview mirror he saw that the ravens were once again landing on the carcass.

Ravens were among the few birds that stayed through the bitter cold of an entire Minnesota winter. Even their little brothers, the crows, would take off around New Year's, and about the same time the very last of the bald eagles followed the rest of the local birds south to the Mississippi valley. Those that remained were the nuthatches and brown creepers, chickadees, several types of woodpeckers, blue jays, gray jays, and a few owls; birds that were almost never seen except at bird feeders. And the ravens. They were the exception. Big and pitch-black, they flew through all that whiteness, enduring the cold and eating their fill on road-kill deer.

Lance turned on the radio, getting nothing but white noise, as usual. The fact that it had suddenly worked fine outside the Akkola gas station was obviously just a fluke.

WITHOUT REALLY INTENDING TO, he'd arrived in Duluth. He had no idea where he was headed, but he had no desire to drive through more forested land. Finally he parked outside the health-food store on Fourth Street and went inside. It would be very unlikely for Lance Hansen to meet anyone he knew in a health-food store. He sat down in the small café area with a serving of vegetarian lasagna that didn't taste half bad, a bottle of mineral water, and the latest issue of the *Duluth News Tribune*, which was available for customers to read free of charge. But he hadn't sat there long before a headline in the paper made him go both hot and cold.

"*Accused North Shore Murderer on Trial Soon.*" That was the text in big letters above a mug shot of a long-haired and scowling Lenny Diver.

Lance read the article, which first gave an account of how Georg Lofthus was found dead near Baraga's Cross the previous summer. It then stated that the trial of the accused Lenny Diver would start on February 28 in Minneapolis. According to the article, Diver continued to maintain his innocence, sticking by his explanation that he'd spent that night with a woman in Grand Marais, although he couldn't remember her name because he'd been extremely drunk. The article also mentioned the prosecution's trump card: the baseball bat that had been discovered in Lenny Diver's car. The suspect's fingerprints had been found on the bat, along with blood from the victim. Lance knew that the initials "A.H." were carved into the wood, and he was almost positive that the bat belonged to his brother. But he wasn't as certain how the bat had ended up in Diver's car and with his fingerprints on it.

He'd suddenly lost his appetite. This was the first time he'd seen the face of the man who was about to be sent to prison for life. Diver looked older than his twenty-five years. Probably because of a hard life, in general, and his methamphetamine habit, in particular. Yet in spite of how wretched he looked in the picture, there was something about him, a certain strength or energy that seemed to shine through everything else; the word "radiance" occurred to Lance.

He'd actually planned to sit here for a while, enjoying the feeling of being back in his hometown, but right now he felt miserable. The photo of the accused man had literally put a face on the injustice he had committed. The only person who could save Lenny Diver from prison was Lance, but he was not going to do it. The face in the newspaper kept on staring at him with that dark, imperious expression. Finally he couldn't take it anymore. He got out his cell and tapped in a number that he, as a police officer, had in his contact list. The phone rang for a long time before anyone picked up.

"Minnesota Department of Corrections. How can I help you?" said a morose male voice.

"This is Lance Hansen. I'm an officer with the U.S. Forest Service in the Superior National Forest. I would like to visit an inmate."

"And does this inmate have a name?" said the man sarcastically.

"Lenny Diver," replied Lance.

He could hear the guy in Minneapolis repeating the name to himself as he presumably searched his computer.

"Lenny Diver is in the Moose Lake jail. And your name again was . . . ?"

"Lance Hansen."

"Right. First we have to ask the prisoner if he wants to see you. We'll get back to you in a few days."

Lance thanked the man and ended the call.

Then he sat there, staring at the newspaper photo. What had he done? Was he really going to look the man in the eye and talk to him? That suddenly seemed impossible. It was probably best not to think about it anymore. Maybe they wouldn't even call him back.

He gave a start as he caught sight of a familiar face. Stepping into the store was Peggy Winters, the biologist at the Tofte Ranger Station. Her cheeks were rosy, and she had on her usual fur hat. Lance turned away. He hoped she wouldn't come into the café area! The instant she saw him, his bluff would be called. After a moment he took a chance and looked over his shoulder, but he couldn't see her so she must have gone farther inside the store. That didn't mean she wouldn't come over here after she'd made her purchases.

He needed to leave right now. Peggy's sudden appearance had given him a shock, and he felt a strong urge to find a dark place where he could sit all alone, nursing a beer. This time he went to the only place in Duluth where he could be a hundred percent sure that no one he knew would turn up.

# 6

THE KOZY BAR was a notorious gathering place for criminals and prostitutes. A good number of crimes had been committed over the years in the vicinity of this establishment. Yet Lance knew that the bar was completely harmless this early in the day, especially since he had a police ID in his wallet. He made sure the bartender caught a glimpse of it when he paid for his beer. The man briefly raised one eyebrow when he saw the ID. Lance kept his expression impassive as he picked up the pint glass and went over to a corner table to sit down. The Kozy was located half a flight below street level, and the narrow windows near the ceiling had green-tinted glass, which let in very little light. Aside from Lance, the only customers were two long-haired men at the other end of the room about thirty years old who looked like they might be American Indians. A cup of coffee sat on the table in front of each of them. There was something about the way they were slouched in their chairs that told him they'd been there a long time.

But that was none of Lance Hansen's business. He wasn't on the clock. Officially he wasn't even in the United States. With a certain reverence he raised his pint glass. This was no ordinary beer. During the two months he'd spent in Canada, he'd had to settle for Fort Garry Pale Ale, since that was the closest he could get to Starfire Pale Ale. But it was still a far cry from the original. This, on the other hand, *was* the original. He made sure that the bitter, reddish beer properly coated his taste buds before he allowed it to pass down his gullet. For a moment he was filled with pure joy. Oh, how he'd missed that taste! A moan of pleasure slipped out. The bartender looked in his direction and actually smiled. He probably thought he was dealing with an alcoholic cop who had just taken his first swallow of the beer he'd been yearning for all day. Lance laughed softly to himself as he sat in the dimly lit corner. "Welcome home," he murmured.

It occurred to him that he was, in fact, *enjoying* himself here in the Kozy, even though he figured that he wouldn't feel as comfortable in a few hours when the regular clientele began filling the bar. But for the moment, it was perfect. Two young women came in and sat down at the table with the two Ojibwe men, if that was what they were. They began talking, but so quietly that he couldn't make out what they said. Otherwise there was nothing going on in the place. The TV up near the ceiling was turned off, and the bartender wasn't playing any music. Nothing happened. He almost felt like he was asleep, except that he was able to drink Starfire Pale Ale while he was sleeping.

He closed his eyes. Instantly he saw the ravens flying up from the carcass on the road. When he opened his eyes, he saw that the four other customers were leaving. They stopped at the door to exchange a few words in low voices. A couple of them had cast brief glances at Lance. He felt uneasy at the thought that those people might be talking about him. Finally the men and one of the young women left. The other woman waited until the door had closed behind them. Then she walked through the bar and came over to Lance. He took a sip of his beer as he looked at her over the rim of the glass. She was younger than he'd thought, just a teenager, with a pretty face although it was much too pale. Only when she reached his table did he recognize her.

"Lance?" she said, staring at him in disbelief.

Andy Hansen's daughter had gleaming black hair, and she wore a black coat that reached to her knees. Her lips were a dark red outlined in black, and black liner rimmed her eyes. She had on black lace-up boots.

"Chrissy?"

"What are you doing here, Uncle Lance?"

He could tell how foolish his expression must be. Chrissy

burst out laughing. She laughed so hard that she ended up squirming like a kid who needed to pee, and every time she looked at him, she started laughing again.

"Okay, cut it out," said Lance, annoyed.

In a halfhearted attempt to apologize, she raised her hand, as if to signal that she'd try to get hold of herself. Lance noticed that her face remained deathly pale. Had she powdered her skin white?

"I'm sorry," he said. "I must look like an idiot. But I didn't recognize you either."

"You did look a little weird. It was just that I didn't . . . I mean . . . Jesus! The *Kozy?*"

She sat down at the table across from him.

"Yeah. I know," said Lance.

"Is this where you usually hang out?"

"No, are you crazy? Do you?"

Chrissy ignored the question. "I thought you were in Norway."

He didn't hesitate more than a second before coming up with an answer.

"I'm working undercover," he said.

His niece's expression indicated all too clearly that she didn't believe a word of it.

"But aren't you a forest cop?" she exclaimed.

"All right. Here's the thing," said Lance, pretending that he'd come to a big decision. "No one was supposed to find out. That's partly why I came in here, because nobody I know would . . . Well, regardless, I'm on an undercover assignment."

He could hear how stupid that sounded. Chrissy ran the fingers of her left hand through her gleaming black hair as she gave her uncle a skeptical look. An exaggerated skepticism, thought Lance. As if she were acting in one of those sitcoms on TV in which everybody was young and had complicated, chaotic lives that could make you laugh yourself silly if you enjoyed that kind of thing, which Lance definitely did not. But that was how Chrissy was acting. He hadn't noticed that sort of behavior from her before and wondered what it stemmed from. At the same time Lance sensed something unapproachable just below the surface. Was this something new?

"An undercover assignment?" she repeated. "For the U.S. Forest Service?"

"Of course not. I'm first and foremost a police officer, and I was the one who found the murdered tourist near Baraga's Cross last summer. I've been involved in the investigation all along."

Chrissy still had strands of hair twined around her fingers, but she'd stopped moving her hand. Her eyes were big and shiny. Was she on the verge of tears? There was something else about her look, something different, but maybe it was simply the fact that she was no longer a child.

"Does that mean they haven't caught the killer, after all?" she asked in a low voice.

"All I can tell you is that . . . there are a few, what you might call, *unresolved* issues in the case."

"Did they arrest the wrong man?"

"That's a possibility," said Lance.

"So is the trial going to be postponed?"

"Listen to me, Chrissy. I'm not supposed to discuss any of these things with you. Do you understand that?"

Chrissy nodded.

"The only reason I'm telling you about this is because you . . . well, you saw me. It's absolutely essential that nobody finds out I'm here. All right?"

"Okay."

"If anyone hears about this . . . I can't go into detail about what might happen, but we're talking about a murder case, a life sentence and everything, right?"

His niece nodded. She still had her fingers stuck in her dyed black hair, as if there were so many thoughts swirling through her brain that it had completely forgotten about her hand. Her other hand was lying passively on the table. Lance reached across to grab her hand as he stared into her eyes.

*"You can't tell anybody,"* he said urgently, keeping his voice low. "But if you do, keep in mind that you'd be breaking the law and you could end up in court. Do you hear me?"

He added the latter comment on impulse, based on the simple fact that Chrissy was here, in the Kozy Bar, where most of the regulars wanted nothing to do with the police.

"Jesus! Let go. I won't say anything," she replied, pulling her hand away.

There was something in the tone of her voice—partly indignant, partly resigned—that gave Lance a feeling that she was used to such things. Used to being grabbed and spoken to in such a harsh manner.

"By the way, what are you doing here?" he asked.

"Just came in to talk to a few people."

"Do you realize what kind of place this is?"

She gave him a withering look, as if what he'd just said was too lame to warrant a comment. Another example of the overacting that she'd displayed before, as if she had a repertoire of set facial expressions for every emotion: resignation, astonishment, despair, surprise, and so on.

"Don't you have school tomorrow?" asked Lance.

"Sure."

"But how are you going to get back to Two Harbors?"

"Drive, of course."

"You borrowed a car?"

"Yeah. The Freestar."

"Do your parents know you're here?"

"No. And they don't know that you're here, either," she said defiantly.

"You're not in some kind of trouble, are you?"

"What the hell, Uncle Lance? Why don't you just chill! Besides, I've got to go. They're waiting for me."

"So you're not going home?"

Chrissy took her cell out of her pocket and glanced at the display.

"It's five forty-five," she said. "Don't you think I can stay up a little later?"

"As long as you make it to school in the morning, I guess."

"Man, what's wrong with you?"

Abruptly she stood up, ready to leave.

"Sorry," he said. "I shouldn't be talking to you like that."

She gave him a conciliatory smile. Lance noticed again that there was something odd about the look in her eyes, something that hadn't been there before. But he couldn't put his finger on what it was.

# 7

THE NEXT DAY he was driving aimlessly through the streets of Duluth when he caught sight of the redbrick building that housed the Great Lakes Aquarium. The building drew his attention in an inexplicable way, luring and enticing him, as if promising that it contained something he needed.

After he bought a ticket and hung his jacket in the cloakroom, he stood in the middle of the huge hall, his mind blank as he looked around. The few other visitors who were present only served to make the place seem emptier; both their bodies and their voices seemed to disappear inside the space. Outside the windows on the east wall the white icy expanse stretched out until it met the blue sky at a razor-sharp divide. Only the small, dark figures of the ice fishermen broke the perfect barrenness out there.

The aquarium's three huge fish tanks rose vertically through the central part of the building, looking rather like giant test tubes filled with water and fish. Consequently, the middle of the building was open all the way up to the glass roof high overhead. In these tanks the fish swam in various layers through the water, clearly distributed according to the depth that each species preferred. At the very bottom were several sturgeon—big, prehistoric-looking fish, maybe five feet long.

Lance closed his eyes for a moment and listened. The whole aquarium was pervaded by the steady, bubbling sound of oxygen being pumped into the various tanks. The sound vaguely reminded him of being underwater. It was the lake that had lured and enticed him. Because the lake was inside here too, in the bubbling from the tanks, in a silvery fish flapping its tail fin in the light shining through the glass roof, and in the sensation that he was underwater. Lance knew that the moment he opened his eyes, he would see the lake's frozen nothingness stretching out toward the horizon.

When he did open his eyes, he felt a flicker of fear pass through his brain, and instantly began moving away from the center of the big, vaulted space.

There were no other visitors in the room with the model of the Great Lakes. Gratefully Lance sank down onto a chair at the western end and let his gaze wander over the huge display table, many square feet in size. On exhibit was an exact model of America's five Great Lakes and the surrounding terrain. The cities were marked by tiny houses and bridges. The old Aerial Bridge in Duluth, which was the town's most prominent landmark, was not depicted to scale; instead, it was larger than the tallest buildings. If Lance leaned forward and stretched out his arm, he would be able to touch it, but he didn't like the thought of touching his own world from above, as if he were some sort of giant in a comic book. A freighter was also included in the display, no doubt loaded with taconite. He could have picked it up between his thumb and forefinger to lift it high above the lake with water pouring in a steady stream off the hull, and then he could have tossed it against the mountain ridge, where it would have crushed a countless number of old wooden houses along with the people inside. Suddenly everyone who was outside would be craning their necks to stare in terror at the giant looming overhead in the sky. His hand alone was larger than the biggest building in town. The streets of his childhood would be filled with the sounds of panic. But wasn't there something familiar about that enormous face? It was so big and round and reached so high into the sky that it almost looked like the sun. Sooner or later someone would shout: It's Lance Hansen! Look how big he is! Yes, and how horrible, someone would add. Look how he's destroying our whole world. Why is he doing that?

Through the window at the other end of the room Lance could see the ice fishermen sitting next to the holes in the ice, waiting for something to bite. Their lines reached down into the depths, and no one knew what they might catch.

One time he had stood at the deepest spot in the lake, 1,332 feet below the surface, and felt the marrow in his joints start to freeze. During the nearly eight years that had passed since he'd had that dream, Lance had never awakened with even a scrap of a dream in his head. Not even with a feeling that he might have dreamed something but had simply forgotten what it was. For him, sleep was merely a big nothingness into which he disappeared every night. As he sat there studying the model of the five Great Lakes, and as the ice fishermen jigged their lines in the westernmost part of the real Lake Superior, Lance felt his inability to dream like a nutritional deficiency that was eating him up from the inside.

Lance got up, leaning his hands on the edge of the big display table and bending forward over Lake Superior. Even the rivers that emptied into the lake were depicted. There he saw the Temperance River, where he'd parked his car before starting the last drive of the deer hunt. And there the Cross River entered the lake. A tiny cross marked the place where Father Frederic Baraga had miraculously survived a storm in August 1846 when he was on his way to Grand Portage to help the Ojibwe who were suffering from smallpox. It was near Baraga's Cross that Lance had discovered the murdered body of Georg Lofthus. And it was there that he'd lain on his back a few months ago and listened to Andy topple backward into the underbrush after the shot was fired. Only a few inches farther along the shoreline was the Grand Portage Indian Reservation, marked by a canoe floating on the water. The canoe was as big as the freighter that was docked in Duluth, and when Lance leaned closer, he saw a man sitting in the canoe, holding on to a tiny paddle. That's Willy, he thought. He didn't know where the thought came from, but once it took hold, he couldn't get rid of it. Down there, paddling the canoe, was his former father-in-law Willy Dupree. Lance thought about the Ojibwe relationship to dreams and how it had always governed their lives. He leaned even closer to the canoe and the tiny man sitting inside. Willy couldn't see the gigantic face hovering above him, but Lance hoped that he would somehow sense it was there.

"Help Lance dream again," whispered the face.

# 8

AFTER TAKING a long and complicated route through the snow-covered forests and along icy waters, Lance pulled up in front of Willy Dupree's house in the Grand Portage Indian Reservation. It was almost midnight, but for safety's sake, he parked behind the garage so his car couldn't be seen from the road.

He felt a great warmth flood his chest when Willy opened the door.

"Come in," said the old man.

More than two months had passed since the last time Lance was here. That was back in November, and he and Andy had finished the first day of their deer hunt. What happened on the second day hadn't yet taken place. No ice storm, no shot fired in the dark, or the sound of Andy falling backward with icicles clinking all around. But as Lance took off his coat in the hall, he remembered that he'd had blood on his hands. He'd hit a cat as he was driving out to see Willy, and he'd been forced to kill it with a wrench. And the more he'd struck the poor animal, the more pleasure it had given him. His hands had been spattered with blood, and there were also drops on his face, like dark freckles on his nose and cheeks. Willy had pointed this out to him, but not until Lance was about to leave. During his entire visit the old man had sat there looking at the blood on his hands and face without saying a word or asking any questions.

When they were each settled in an easy chair, Lance dutifully ate one of the cookies that Mary was always baking, a painful reminder of the normal life he'd once lived. Then Willy clasped his hands over his stomach and gave his ex-son-in-law a solemn look.

"You might as well tell me the whole story, don't you think?" he said.

On the phone Lance had merely said that he wasn't in Norway but in Ely, and that he needed to talk to Willy.

"I can't."

"Then tell me what you can."

"Okay. So, I'll start with the obvious. I'm not in Norway. I didn't go there at all. And if I know myself, I'll never go there. Instead, I've been in Kenora, in Canada, and I spent two months there, lying in bed in a hotel room, watching TV. Finally I couldn't stand it anymore, so I came back here to the States. Right now I'm staying in Ely."

"But aren't you working anymore?"

"I've got tons of vacation days saved up. I could practically take off a whole year, if I wanted to."

"So you're actually on *vacation?*" asked Willy.

"Sort of."

"But why? Why the whole story about Norway? Jimmy got postcards from there. What exactly are you doing?"

"That's what I can't tell you. You just have to trust me, the way I trust you. You can't tell anyone about this, not even Jimmy. You're the only one I can trust, Willy."

"So what did you want to talk to me about?"

"I'm part Indian," said Lance.

Except for the ticking of the clock on the wall, the room was utterly silent. Lance stared at the two old photographs hanging on the wall over the sofa. A man and a woman with white hair and sunken, toothless mouths in furrowed Indian faces. Under them hung a dream catcher that was gray with age. Several minutes passed as neither Lance nor Willy spoke.

"What do you mean, you're an Indian?" Willy said at last.

"One of my great-grandmothers was Ojibwe."

"When did you find out about this?"

"Sometime last summer."

"And you haven't told anyone until now?"

"No."

"Why not?"

Lance paused before replying.

"I guess I'm afraid it will change things," he said.

"But you already know," said Willy. "And Jimmy is Ojibwe, no matter what. So who's it going to change things for? Your brother and his family? Your mother? Do you really think it would turn their lives upside down if they found out that this great-grandmother of yours was Ojibwe?"

"I know it sounds stupid, but . . ."

"Could it be that you're the one you're protecting by not saying anything?"

"Maybe that's what I'm always doing," Lance said. "Protecting myself by acting as if I'm protecting others."

"So what is it you wanted to talk to me about? Do you want to be made a member of the tribe?" Willy's shoulders shook briefly with soundless laughter.

"I'm just wondering whether it *means* anything," said Lance, feeling a bit insulted. "For instance, does it mean that I belong here in some other way than I previously thought?"

He could see that the old man gave the question serious consideration.

"Depends what you decide to make of it. The fact is there for you to use. Or not use. It's an opportunity for you to belong in a different way, but it's up to you."

It was comforting to listen to the soothing, familiar voice of Willy Dupree, to be addressed by someone who was older and knew more, and not have to bear everything alone.

"But there's something else bothering you, isn't there?" said Willy after a moment.

For a few seconds Lance was tempted to tell him everything, about the murder, about Andy, and about the shot in the dark on that Sunday in November. But he stopped himself. He wasn't sure that Willy would keep quiet about a serious crime. The most serious crime of all. For the first time in ages Lance felt himself waver. Maybe the only way out of this mess was to call the FBI agent Bob Lecuyer and tell him everything he knew; accept the probable punishment for withholding information, obstructing the police investigation, and so on. Let the whole thing run its course, and possibly send Andy to prison for life. Continuing on like this was no longer an option, at any rate.

"You're right," said Lance. "Something has been bothering me lately, but you won't believe me when I tell you what it is."

"What is it?" asked Willy.

"Are you superstitious?"

"What does superstition really mean? One man's superstition can be another man's faith. I trust people that I know I can trust."

"Am I one of those people?"

"Yes, even though you have a lot of secrets."

"Okay, well, here's one of them. On four separate occasions, I've seen Swamper Caribou."

Lance held up four fingers.

A look of boyish curiosity lit up Willy's face. "Where?" he asked.

"The first time was on Highway 61, near Silver Cliff. The second time he was sitting in a canoe not far from the lighthouse in Grand Marais. That was on the Fourth of July, by the way. Next time I saw him sitting on the lakeshore just north of Grand Marais. He was just sitting there, staring straight ahead. And the last time I saw him in the woods when we were out deer hunting in November. Also near the lake, between the Temperance and Cross Rivers."

"And how do you know it was Swamper Caribou?"

"I just know."

Willy nodded.

"Does he scare you?"

"What scares me is that I can see someone nobody else sees," replied Lance. "That makes me feel very alone."

"Lots of people have seen Swamper Caribou's ghost," said Willy.

"But nobody that I know."

"No, but other—"

"Ojibwe," said Lance.

"Yes."

"Do you think that's why I see him too? Because I have Ojibwe blood?"

"I don't know," said Willy. "I don't know enough about these kinds of things. But do you want him to stop appearing to you?"

"Yes."

"Have you tried thinking about him before you fall asleep?"

"I've tried that lots of times."

"Have you ever dreamed about him after doing that?"

Lance shook his head.

"No? Because it's possible to decide who you want to dream about. At least to a certain extent," Willy added. "I do that myself sometimes."

"But why would I want to see him in my dreams too?"

"Because that's the only place you can reach him. And when you meet him in your dreams, you can ask him what he wants from you. Why he's appearing to you. Then maybe you can put an end to it."

"Are you serious?" said Lance, in surprise.

"Sure. What would *you* suggest? Have you got his phone number or something?"

"No, but . . . the problem is that I never dream."

"Of course you do. Everybody dreams."

"I haven't had a single dream in almost eight years," said Lance.

Willy was about to say something, but he didn't. It looked as if something had started to dawn on him.

"Not even one?"

"No. And the strange thing is that I never used to care about dreams, but now I'd be willing to do almost anything to dream again."

"You can't live a proper life without dreaming," said Willy.

"Why not?"

"It's through dreams that the other world speaks to us. If you're in touch only with the visible world, you're only half alive. But it's important to find the right balance between both worlds; too much of either of them is never a good thing. I once heard a story about a man who was born without the ability to dream. As an adult he went to see a medicine man to ask for advice. Since he'd never dreamed, he didn't miss it, but he'd heard other people talk about their dreams, and he envied them. The medicine man instructed him to build a dream bed and gave him specific rules to follow as he fasted, and so on—all essential to dreaming the Big Dream."

"The Big Dream?" said Lance.

"It's the one dream that will tell you who you really are and how you should live your life. Few people do it today, but this happened long ago. The medicine man offered guidance, and soon the man was fasting and sleeping at his chosen spot in the woods. But after he'd been gone for a week, two of his brothers went out to visit him. They found him in a deep sleep, and it was impossible to wake him up. Between them they carried their slumbering brother back to the village. After that he became a popular attraction, and people came from far away to see him. He became known as the 'sleeping man.' I think he lived more than twenty years in that sleeping state. If he had any dreams, the story makes no mention of them. Personally, I don't know which would be worse—twenty years spent in the labyrinth of the dream world or twenty years in an unconscious state of sleep, as if he were already dead. It's hard to know, isn't it?"

Lance didn't know what to say to that, but he suddenly had an idea.

"So does it work?" he asked. "Fasting until you have the Big Dream?"

"Probably not for everybody, but it worked for me, anyway."

"You've done it?"

"My father coached me. I built a dream bed high up in a tree and began fasting. On the third night I dreamed the Big Dream."

"What was it like?"

"Well, it was a dream like any other, but it showed me my spirit guide, a figure in the spirit world that is always with me and that I can turn to in special situations. To ask for advice, for instance. But I guess this sounds like a lot of superstitious foolishness to you."

"Not foolishness, but very strange," said Lance. "Not that I haven't heard about this sort of thing before, because I have, both from Mary and other people. And I've read a bit about it too, but hearing you talk about it as something in your own life makes it seem even stranger and at the same time more real."

Willy nodded to show that he understood.

"It's real if you choose to make it real," he said. "It's totally up to you."

"I do want to dream again," said Lance.

"But the dreams won't come?"

"No. It's like a frozen faucet. Not a drop. Not even any rushing sound in the pipes. How do I go about fasting so I can dream again?"

"You just need to fast. It's as simple as that. You're actually supposed to build a dream bed, a platform up in a tree, so that you're lying high up under the open sky, but I wouldn't recommend it when the temp is twenty below. I'm sure you can do it just as well at home."

"Or at the motel?"

"Sure. Why not? Maybe you could still make some kind of dream bed by arranging a place to sleep on the floor so it's different from other nights. The important thing is to fast."

"But I won't be able to sleep if I'm hungry."

"Hungry?" Willy sounded annoyed. "Do you think this has anything to do with going to bed hungry? I'm talking about self-deprivation, Lance. Torture. You need to suffer until you have a vision."

"But . . . won't that cause permanent damage?"

"Not at all. You can survive for several weeks without food. Just be sure to drink some water. And take a few vitamins along with a little salt."

"Do you think it will work for me?"

"Yes, I do. But you have to *choose* to do this. And make it part of your reality. As I said, it's up to you."

Then there was a long pause—not the uncomfortable kind that clamors to be ended but a natural pause, as if the conversation were taking a break. Lance considered the idea of fasting, which was a foreign concept for him. He was not a Catholic, a Muslim, or an Indian; he was a Protestant American with roots in Halsnøy, Norway. His people did not fast. They worked hard, ate healthy meals, and went to bed early. That was how Lance had always lived, but if he had any hope of dreaming again, he needed to choose another way. He was convinced of that. And what would be more natural than to take the option that was part of his own past, Nanette's option? In spite of everything, she was also part of his ancestry, and he carried her blood, although perhaps not to the same extent as his Norwegian blood. Yet it was still just as real.

"But what a man of your age needs, first and foremost, is a woman," said Willy after a moment. "Then you wouldn't care about all these dream problems. Or Swamper Caribou. A young man like you should be thinking about completely different sorts of things. Oh, to be your age again! I don't mean to get too personal, but you really ought to find yourself a girlfriend."

"And why are you so certain that I don't have one?"

Willy threw out his hands, a small gesture that encompassed the whole situation. The two men sitting there at midnight, talking about ghosts and dreams while Lance's car was parked out of sight behind the garage, and no one was supposed to know that he was here in the United States.

"In fact, I do have a girlfriend," said Lance.

"Really?" Willy looked surprised.

"I think so."

"You *think* so?"

"No, I mean, I do."

"So she hasn't been seeing much of you lately?"

"She doesn't even know I'm interested," said Lance.

"Oh, come on, Lance! Have you considered getting one of her friends to ask her about you? You're not a schoolboy anymore."

"No. But I didn't even realize it myself . . . not until . . . but now I see that I've known for a while, without really knowing it."

"Right," said Willy, shaking his head with resignation. "And we're not talking about my daughter, are we?"

"No."

"Good."

"Good?"

"Well, I mean . . ."

"You wouldn't want to be my father-in-law again. Is that it?"

"I've always thought that you're a good man, Lance, but the

fact that you made up this whole story about Norway, no matter what your reason for doing so . . . And sending phony postcards to your son . . . I think Mary might be better off alone."

"I think she is. And I am too," said Lance.

"So what about this other woman?"

"We were together a long time ago, long before I met Mary. But only for a few months."

"Ah. An old flame." Willy chuckled.

"She dumped me."

"But you want to try again?"

"I don't know."

"You have to, Lance. This is much more important than fasting and dreaming. Don't you know anything, man?"

# 9

17 MARCH. *The boy arrived this morning. What a bitter cold he has endured! His face was like cold meat to the touch. His dreams are terrifying. He screams as we go about our daily chores. The children race anxiously past his bed every time they have to pass. My husband feels such great sorrow that it has not been possible for any of us to have peace in our hearts during this day. Thanks to God's mercy he is still among the living, but just barely. His thoughts merge with his dreams, and he speaks in delirium. Thank God that the children do not understand what he shouts in his dreams and feverish fantasies! Apparently he knows no English or French, but only the Norwegian language, which in my opinion can be learned only by a child who hears it sung at the cradle. A great and difficult task is now demanded of us. I promised Father François at the mission school that no lie would ever cross my lips. But when we removed all of his clothes, as we were forced to do, we saw two deep wounds in his right arm. I think that it is because of these wounds that he has lost most of his strength. My husband tried to ask him questions, but he would not tell us anything of what had happened to him.*

LANCE SAT ON THE EDGE OF THE BED and read the text typed on a couple of sheets of paper as he ran his fingertips over the old, leather-bound book lying on his lap. He had always thought of himself as a white American of Norwegian ancestry, but in between these worn pages he had discovered a different truth. When he received the translation of several pages from his great-grandmother's diary, the police had just arrested the young Ojibwe Lenny Diver for the murder of Georg Lofthus. And Lance had started to think that Andy might not be guilty after all. The most important evidence found at the scene of the crime was in the blood, which had to have come from an Indian, although not necessarily a full-blooded Indian. And that meant that Andy couldn't be the killer. Lance had felt that he'd been saved by the bell, because everything else had pointed directly to his brother.

But then there was the diary, the French Diary as it was called in his family. None of them had ever read it, for the simple reason that nobody in the Hansen family could read a word of French. The official story was that the diary had been written by Inga's paternal grandmother, Nanette, who was French Canadian. But when Lance got back several pages that he'd sent to a translation agency, he immediately realized the truth: they were part Ojibwe. So there was nothing in the police evidence to exclude Andy as the possible murderer.

Lance continued reading from the excerpts of the book that had been translated.

18 MARCH. *My husband does not think that his sister's son will survive unless we can bring a doctor here or take the boy to a doctor. But every time he mentions this, the boy is seized with a terror that seems worse than his fear of dying. He still refuses to say anything about what happened to him, but it seems clear to us that he was in the cold water and nearly froze to death. But it is easy to see that someone stabbed him with a knife to give him those wounds. He refuses to talk about that, and we think that is the reason he does not want to be treated by a doctor. Because the doctor would ask how he had acquired those two wounds, and if he did not answer, the doctor might mention it to the authorities. It is clear to us that this is what he fears. But I have given this a lot of thought on my own, both last night and during the course of this day, and I am struggling to decide whether to*

*tell my husband of my thoughts, because according to our beliefs, this is the work of the devil. What Nokomis taught me was not about the good, even though she was the most beloved, both then and forever. She lived in the darkness in which so many old people lived. But if I am now going to bring the boy back to health and save him from death, I will have to do as Nokomis taught me before I went to the mission school.*

IT ALL BEGAN on the day when Lance found the body of the Norwegian canoeist Georg Lofthus. Everything started that day. After the corpse had been removed, Lance and several other police officers had talked as they stood in the parking lot near Baraga's Cross. One of them wondered whether this might be the very first murder in Cook County. No one knew for sure, but when Lance got home, he'd done a search of the archives. A newspaper article from 1892 reminded him of an old missing-persons case that he'd actually heard about before, although it had taken the form of a legend. It had to do with Swamper Caribou, the local Ojibwe medicine man, who had disappeared without a trace, as if he'd been the subject of his own magic and had spirited himself away. Yet it was clear from the newspaper article that this was a real case of someone who had gone missing. The medicine man's brother, Joe Caribou, was also quoted as asking for help from the public. According to the paper, Swamper had disappeared from his hunting cabin near the mouth of the Cross River, meaning close to Baraga's Cross, *"at the time of the last full moon, meaning in the early morning hours of March 16."*

21 MARCH. *Thanks be to God that we have managed to keep him on this side of death. He is past the worst of it now. I made him a decoction to drink, as I remember Nokomis doing, and something to spread on his wounds. I have also committed the sin of making an asabikeshiinh for a person's dreams, because he screamed and flailed so much that none of us could get any sleep, not even the children, but now he is calm. May God have mercy on me, for I knew not what else to do.*

HE HAD IMAGINED that Swamper Caribou could have been murdered, although it was impossible to say with certainty what had happened to the medicine man. But that was before the other puzzle piece in the story had fallen into place. That happened one day as he sat in his mother's room at the Lakeview Nursing Home in Duluth, and they were talking about their ancestors, as they so often did. Inga had told him about Thormod Olson from Halsnøy, the nephew of Knut Olson and his wife, Nanette. The boy was just fifteen when he arrived at the North Shore under dramatic circumstances in March 1892. While attempting to cross the frozen bay, he had fallen through the ice into the water. This was in the middle of the night, and he was walking in the light of the full moon. It was so cold that it really shouldn't have been possible to survive a night in the woods in wet clothes, but early the next morning he had knocked on the door of the house where Knut and Nanette lived. When they opened the door, Thormod fell into the room, his body as stiff as a board and enclosed in an icy armor that shattered as he hit the floor. Ever since then, he had been the family hero.

"That's the stuff we're made of." Lance remembered his father saying that, and yet Oscar was not related to Thormod Olson by blood. The story was the family's primordial myth, and Lance had heard it told countless times before. Yet there was something about what his mother had said on that day in her room at Lakeview that had jolted him out of his habit of listening halfheartedly to the story. He already knew that Thormod was supposed to have fallen through the ice "somewhere close to the mouth of the Cross River," but suddenly he also knew when this happened. Because the boy had been able to keep walking at night, *in the light of the full moon.* And that was in March 1892. Near the mouth of the Cross River. Which meant that the disappearance of Swamper Caribou and Thormod Olson's accident had taken place more or less at the same time and in the same place.

Even though it could be just a coincidence, Lance had begun to wonder whether his ancestor might have killed the medicine man. Yet he didn't know for sure. That was when he'd thought about Nanette's diary; somewhere in those pages there had to be a mention of Thormod's arrival.

24 MARCH. *Today he sat at the table and ate with us! When we changed the bandages on his wounds, we saw that they were clean and without pus, just as the wounds of Old Shingibis were after Nokomis treated him when he was attacked by a bear when I was a little girl. I clearly remember when they arrived with Shingibis in the canoe. But even though this is a good sign, and my husband is now lighter of heart than I have seen him before, nothing can ever rectify what I have done. For that reason my heart is as heavy as stone. My husband says that we must never speak of this, just say that the boy fell through the ice and almost died from frostbite, but that we saved him with porridge and coffee. That is how we will speak of it in the future, also when we talk to the boy. We will never try to find out what happened to him. And here I have promised Father François that no lie shall ever issue from my lips.*

IT OCCURRED TO LANCE that these old diary entries conveyed an atmosphere of secrecy and deception that was similar to what he'd been experiencing the past few months. Deciding not to say anything was always the preferred solution to every problem; that was how it had been for as long as he could remember. This reaction was as natural for him as the air he breathed. Yet to see exactly the same pattern of response played out more than a hundred years ago made him feel incredibly sad. That in itself was nothing new. He often felt sad. But this was a sorrow that seemed to span generations.

# 10

CHRISSY HANSEN came walking through the school gate with another girl who was also clad in black from head to toe. Lance rolled down the car window and called her name. When she caught sight of her uncle, her first impulse seemed to be to run away. But then she said something to her friend, who continued along the snow-covered sidewalk alone as Chrissy went over to the black Jeep.

"Get in," said Lance.

His niece did as he said, although reluctantly. Once she was seated in the car, she stared straight ahead without saying a word.

"I thought we could have a little chat," said Lance.

No reaction. Her school backpack, which she'd set on the floor, offered a childish contrast to her mute figure, swathed in black.

"Is it okay if I drive somewhere else?" he asked. "I don't want anyone to recognize me."

A slight movement at the corner of Chrissy's mouth could be interpreted to mean anything at all. Lance chose to take it as a sign of agreement.

He drove north, away from the lake, and parked at a turnout a couple of miles outside Two Harbors. Neither of them spoke during the short drive. Now Lance opened his mouth to say something, but Chrissy beat him to it.

"I haven't told anyone," she said.

"Good."

"But if you say anything about me to Mom or Dad, I'll tell them that you're not in Norway. It's no skin off my nose."

"And if you mention that I'm not in Norway, I'll tell Andy that you hang out at the Kozy. That's no skin off my nose, either."

"Okay, but—"

Chrissy was interrupted by the ringing of her cell phone. She dug it out from under her long coat.

"Hello?"

". . ."

"Yeah. I know that."

". . ."

"But I'm with . . . fuck that!"

". . ."

"Okay, okay. I'm coming."

". . ."

"I said, I'm coming!"

". . ."

"See you."

Lance gave her an inquiring look.

"That was Mom," she said. "I promised to help her with something. You'll have to drive me home."

"Sure. But I want to talk to you some more later."

"Fine with me. Because there's something we need to talk about," she said.

"What's that?"

"I know something about the murder."

Lance grabbed her by the arm.

"What do you know?" he asked.

"I'll tell you later."

He tightened his grip.

"No. Tell me now," he said.

"Let go of me!" Chrissy shouted.

Lance instantly let her go.

"Sorry," he said. "Sorry, honey. I didn't mean to . . ."

"Just don't touch me," she told him.

"Okay," he said. "I promise."

"So drive me home. You can let me out at the gas station, and I'll walk from there."

"But do you really know something about the murder?"

"I'll tell you tonight."

"Where?"

"When you drive me to Duluth."

"Why would I do that?"

"Don't you want to hear what I have to say?"

"Of course I do."

"In that case, you can drive me to Duluth tonight."

"So you can go back to the Kozy?"

By now he had started driving back toward Two Harbors. Chrissy gave him a look loaded with scorn.

"Believe it or not, that's not where I'm going," she said. "It might actually do you some good to come with me. If it's not too late, that is."

"Too late for what?"

Chrissy laughed, but it sounded artificial.


AT SIX THIRTY he picked her up at the gas station, as they'd agreed. The minute she got in, he smelled the cigarette smoke on her clothes.

"What'd you tell Andy and Tammy?"

"That I was catching a ride with a girlfriend."

"To go where?"

"To a poetry reading."

Lance couldn't help laughing.

"You actually said that?"

"Yeah."

"So where are you really going?"

"To a poetry reading. What do you think?!"

She was clearly in a better mood than a few hours earlier. Lance gave her a skeptical look.

"You're not serious, are you?"

Chrissy laughed merrily.

"Sure. And you're coming with me," she said.

"Now wait a minute, I—"

"Otherwise I won't tell you what I know."

He glanced at her again. A barely visible smile was tugging at her mouth.

"It'll do you good," she said. "I bet it's been a long time since you've gone to a reading."

"You're right about that."

They passed the big white fiberglass rooster with the bright red comb and yellow feet, and with that they left Two Harbors behind.

"Every time I see that shitty rooster, I wonder why the hell I had to be born in this place," said Chrissy with a sigh.

Lance was about to admonish her for swearing, but he stopped himself.

"It's not that bad, is it?" he said.

"Yeah. It is."

He tried to recall what it had felt like to be almost eighteen. That was back when he decided to be a policeman, like his father. Maybe not the most exciting choice of profession, but he had never regretted his decision.

"So, what do you know about the murder?"

"I was out at the cabin that night. I told Mom and Dad I was going to spend the night with a girlfriend in Duluth, but we drove up to Lost Lake instead."

"You and who else?"

"Me and two friends. We were going to meet some other kids up there and party. So that's where we went. There were a few others that I didn't know. And two guys who just showed up. They told a story that sounded like it was straight out of *The Twilight Zone*. Everybody thought it was cool, but at the time we didn't know anything about what had happened that night."

"What did the two guys say?" asked Lance.

"They said they'd seen a bloodstained man with a baseball bat."

Lance felt his throat close up.

"Where?"

"Just outside Finland, near the river over there. That's the Baptism River, isn't it?"

"Right."

"They said he looked like he was on his way down to the river to get washed off."

The idea that someone had seen the murderer right after he'd killed Georg Lofthus had an overwhelming effect on Lance. He felt as if all the strength had drained out of him.

"Did they say what the man looked like?" he asked.

He didn't recognize his own voice. It sounded like it was coming from an old man.

"No. Just that it wasn't an Indian," replied his niece.

"Are you sure?"

"Yes. Because first they said the car was an old junker, and then somebody said the man was probably just drunk. That was supposed to be a joke. I thought it was a stupid thing to say, but . . . Anyway, they said the man they saw definitely wasn't an Indian. It was a middle-aged white guy. I remember that's what one of them said."

"But you didn't personally see this individual?"

"No."

"So what did all of you think had happened?"

"At that point we hadn't heard about the murder. Those two guys said they thought he must have hit some animal and used the bat to put it out of its misery. Maybe a cat . . . And that he was on his way down to the river to wash off the blood."

"A cat?" whispered Lance.

"Uh-huh. At any rate, we never dreamed that he might have killed somebody."

"Have you told anyone else about this?"

"No."

"Not even Tammy or Andy?"

"I never tell my parents anything."

"Okay. But what you've told me is now part of an ongoing investigation, so you can't mention it to anyone," said Lance.

He couldn't very well say that he didn't know what her father would do if he heard that someone had seen him that night.

"Do you have any idea the approximate time when this happened?" he asked.

"No, but it was really late by the time those guys arrived, in the early morning hours. And it must have been fairly light when they saw him. Light enough to see the blood on his clothes."

"So maybe around dawn?" Lance suggested.

Chrissy nodded.

"But when you heard about the murder, didn't you realize there might be a connection?"

"Sure. I thought a lot about it, and I was really scared. But then I read that the police had arrested an Indian, and the baseball bat that was used in the killing was found in his car in Grand Portage. So how could the other man with the bat have anything to do with it?"

"Then why are you telling me about all this now?"

"Because you said that you were still working on the case and that they might have arrested the wrong man."

"Huh."

They drove for a while in silence. Lance thought about all the times he had let his niece chase him through the house, from one room to the next, until she finally caught him and arrested him. Not all that many years ago either.

"I'd like to testify or something," said Chrissy.

"Testify?"

"Help out so the right man is arrested."

"But you said you didn't see him yourself. Why can't those two guys who saw the man come forward to tell their story?"

"I don't know who they are. They were just a couple of strangers who showed up, uninvited, to the party. None of us had any idea who they were. I think they were from somewhere on the Iron Range."

"We can try to find them through the local media, CB radios, and so on," said Lance. "It shouldn't be that hard."

"But you don't get it, Uncle Lance. These guys aren't the type to go to the police voluntarily. Not even if it has to do with a murder."

"Meaning what?" said Lance sternly.

"Well, they brought some . . ."

It suddenly occurred to him what she was talking about.

"Pot?" he asked.

"And meth."

As a police officer Lance was all too aware of what methamphetamine could do to a person. A drug that provoked extreme aggression, and users often lost their teeth, their hair, and their minds.

"Good Lord, what kind of people have you been hanging out with?" he exclaimed in alarm.

"I told you I didn't know them. None of us did," said Chrissy.

"But couldn't one of your girlfriends testify? There must have been others who heard the story. Why haven't they come forward?"

"Maybe because they don't have an uncle who's an undercover cop and who tells them that the police might have arrested the wrong man."

"Hmm . . . ," said Lance.

He was beginning to realize how impossible this situation was. If he allowed Chrissy to give a statement, her father might end up spending the rest of his life in prison.

"Well, we'll just have to see what happens," he said. "At least now I know the story. If it turns out to be important, I'll be sure to get in touch with you."

"But you do think they've got the wrong man, don't you?"

The question, which required no answer, hovered in the air between them. That they were even having this conversation was answer enough, along with the fact that Lance was secretly sneaking around the North Shore.

"So where are we actually going?" he asked as he exited Highway 61 and turned onto London Road.

"Third Avenue and Fifth Street."

"Okay. And what's there?"

"A whole different world," said Chrissy.

# 11

IT WAS AN ORDINARY-LOOKING BAR, equipped with a simple sound system and a microphone on a stand at one end of the room. Next to the microphone was a bar stool and a tall table with a pitcher of water and a glass. Lance noticed that Chrissy didn't seem to know anyone, or at least she didn't greet any of the other patrons. Yet there was something about the way she moved through the room that led him to believe she'd been there before.

They found a table at the very back and hung their coats over the backs of their chairs.

"I want something hot to drink," said Chrissy. "Want anything?" She was speaking in a lower voice than normal.

"A Diet Coke would be good. It's my treat," he said, handing her a five-dollar bill.

Chrissy took the money without a word and went over to the bar, where she got in line behind a few other customers.

Lance sat down, trying to look as unobtrusive as possible. A quick glance around the room told him that there were about thirty people present. At the very end of the bar, seated near the microphone, he saw two men and a woman, who he assumed must be the poets. They were middle aged, the woman possibly a bit older than the men, and they were all leafing through pages of text. One of the men had a ponytail and a neatly trimmed gray beard. Lance thought he looked like an artist. The other man looked totally normal, almost like a bank teller, while the woman was thin and elegantly dressed. She didn't look like any of the women that Lance usually associated with—women who, for the most part, were employed by the U.S. Forest Service. He was well aware that he didn't fit in with the rest of the audience. No doubt he looked like he'd just climbed off a snowmobile, while many of the others wore clothing that looked homemade, even though it had probably been bought in a shop and for a higher price than all of the insulating, weatherproof, synthetic fibers in which he'd wrapped his body—from the underwear made of knitted polyester with a quick-dry function to the enormous thermal jacket he'd draped over the back of his chair.

Chrissy wound her way between the tables carrying a glass of Diet Coke and a mug with steam rising from it. There was something about the way she walked that seemed so respectful, almost as if she were stooping forward a bit so as not to disturb the others. She was by far the youngest person in the bar, and Lance thought that maybe he ought to feel proud of his niece. But he noticed that several people cast an inquisitive glance in her direction as she walked past in those strange black clothes of hers, with the heavy eyeliner and the black lipstick. So when she set the tea and Coke on their table and sat down, he instead felt embarrassed. Did they think she was his daughter?

"Do I really have to stay here?" he said.

She frowned as if she didn't understand the question.

"How about if I run over to Lakeview and visit your grandmother in the meantime?" he went on. "Then I'll pick you up afterward. What do you think?"

"I think that's a bad idea, since nobody's supposed to know that you're here," Chrissy pointed out.

For a moment Lance had totally forgotten about that. His shoulders began shaking with suppressed laughter.

"Jeez, what a weirdo you are." Chrissy shook her head.

Suddenly he was afraid he wouldn't be able to stop laughing, so he stood up and gestured toward the men's room at the other end of the bar.

"Hurry up, then," said his niece. "They're going to start soon."

Having made his way across the room, Lance was relieved to be able to close the door behind him, safely out of view. After spending two months alone in a hotel room, he clearly wasn't used to being out in public anymore. He sat down on the toilet, propped his elbows on his knees, and buried his face in his hands. A thin film of sweat covered his brow. It wasn't simply because he was out of practice being in a roomful of people. There was everything else as well. For instance, the fact that he was lying to his own niece, whom he'd known all her life, making her think he was working undercover for the police, while in reality he was convinced she was living in the same house as a murderer. He thought about what she'd just told him about partying at the cabin. Her story fit with the discovery of the music magazine *Darkside*, which he'd found when he broke into their cabin in the summer. So Andy hadn't been there at all on the night of the murder. What had he been doing the whole time until he picked up Chrissy from her girlfriend's house in Duluth the next morning? All indications were that at some point, maybe around dawn, he had been standing in the ditch along the road outside Finland, holding a baseball bat and covered in blood. What had that boy said? That it definitely wasn't an Indian they'd seen standing there? But it wasn't that simple, because Andy and Lance were descendants of Knut Olson and his Ojibwe wife, Nanette.

He was about to go back into the bar when something caught his eye. Hanging on the door in front of him was a poster announcing the evening's "poetic master reading," as it was being called. A simple poster with no pictures, just a brief blurb about each of the three poets. And it was the last of the bios—or rather, the name at the very bottom of the poster—that had caught Lance's attention. At first he merely skimmed the words, but then he took a step back and read more carefully:

Clayton Miller (45): Professor of English at U of M, Twin Cities, originally from Duluth, has published a series of critically acclaimed poetry collections and has won numerous prizes and grants for his literary work. Latest book: *Siamese Wing Strokes* (Larsmont Publishing).

On the other side of the door he heard a woman's voice welcoming the assembled audience to the evening's master reading. If he didn't exit the toilet at once, he'd be forced to walk through the bar while one of the poets was in the middle of a reading. The very thought filled him with terror.

He stepped out, keeping his head low as he hurried past the poets and emcee to make his way over to Chrissy.

At that moment the emcee introduced the first of the poets. "A woman who has devoted a large part of her life to studying Lake Superior: Liz Brent!"

The slender, gray-haired woman with the gold-rimmed glasses read a series of poems in which Lance could find only scattered references to the lake, through phrases such as "lava rocks," "the ancient geometry of arrowheads," "the city, the iron, the water," and "the good woman and the bad woman standing on either side of the lake, shouting."

When she was done, he politely applauded as he tried to guess which of the two men was Clayton Miller. Both were tall, and it was his height that was practically the only thing Lance could remember about Clayton. Even so, he thought it had to be the man who looked like a bank teller, and he turned out to be right. When the emcee introduced "Clayton Miller, native son of Duluth," the man with the cropped hair got up and took a seat on the bar stool next to the tall table. Calmly and deliberately he adjusted the microphone, as if he were in the privacy of his own home and not in a bar where thirty strangers were watching his every move.

Then Clayton Miller began to read. These poems had nothing to do with the lake, at least as far as Lance could tell, but that was really the only thing he understood. Soon he stopped listening altogether and instead stared at Miller, envious at how good the man looked. From what Lance could recall, Clayton had been one grade behind him in school, which was one grade ahead of Andy, but he could easily be taken for ten years younger than either of them. This was the boy who had been lying on the ground in the schoolyard, actually not very far from this very location. "He tried to kill me," Clayton Miller had gasped after Andy had run away. That was the only time Lance had spoken to the man who was now sitting on a bar stool, whispering words into the microphone: "a mother-of-pearl heart on the mantelpiece, a knife, a peeled apple."

After the applause faded and Miller was once again sitting at the bar next to Liz Brent, Lance leaned over to his niece and whispered in her ear: "Do you think it'd be possible to talk to the authors afterward?"

"You want to *talk* to them?"

"Do you think I could?"

"Sure. They usually sell copies of their books after the reading. So, did you like it?"

"Yes, I did."

"Really?"

"Yeah."

"Clayton Miller?"

"Uh-huh."

"Jesus," she said.

The last poet was introduced, but the only thing Lance could think about was what he was going to say if he got the chance to talk to Miller. *Do you remember that time in high school when you got beat up real bad? Well, that was actually my brother who did that to you. So, how's it going?* No, he couldn't ask about the one thing he wanted to know. If he was going to try to do that, he'd have to get Miller to meet him somewhere else, in some other setting than this one, maybe go to a pub or something. But why would Professor Miller go to a pub with a guy like Lance Hansen? He wouldn't. But maybe with a girl like Chrissy? But wasn't Miller gay? At least that was what everyone had said about him in school. And besides, Chrissy was practically a child.

WHEN THE POETRY READING WAS OVER, the emcee announced that books would be for sale, and the authors would be happy to sign copies. The poets took seats behind a table with stacks of books. The audience members started getting up from their chairs. A few headed for the door, but most looked as if they planned to stay awhile longer.

"Are you going to buy a book?" asked Chrissy, looking at Lance.

There was something strange about the look in her eyes.

"Er, I don't know," he replied.

"But I thought you said you liked Clayton Miller."

"Sure, but what should I say?"

"If you give me the money for a book, I'll show you how it's done."

Lance hesitated but then shrugged and took out his wallet.

"How much do you think it costs?"

"Come on. We'll find out." She took his wallet from his hand.

Together they got up, grabbed their coats, and went over to the table where people had formed a haphazard line to purchase books and get them signed.

"It's not really necessary," said Lance, wanting to leave.

"But *I* want to buy a book," Chrissy insisted.

Lance pictured Andy finding a book by Clayton Miller on their coffee table.

"Okay," he said.

When it was finally her turn, Chrissy leaned forward as she held her long black hair back from her face. Miller looked up at her and smiled.

"Hi," she said shyly. "I'd like to buy a book."

"Which one?"

She pointed at one of them.

"That one," she said.

Miller picked up the slim volume.

*"Siamese Wing Strokes?"* he said.

She nodded.

"What's your name?"

"Chrissy."

He quickly wrote a greeting on the first blank page.

"That's twenty dollars."

Chrissy opened her uncle's wallet and handed a bill to Miller.

"Thanks for the poems. They're great."

The professor gave her a brief smile and then turned to look for the next customer as Chrissy slipped behind Lance. Suddenly he felt her hand pressing against his back. She pushed him forward to the table until he was standing in front of Clayton Miller, who looked up at him with an expectant smile.

"Hello," he said.

"I bring you greetings from an old acquaintance," Lance managed to say, feeling beads of sweat appear on his forehead.

"Oh, really? Who could that be?"

"It's a personal matter," said Lance in a low voice. "Do you think it'd be possible to have a few words with you in private afterward?"

Clayton Miller cast a quick glance at his watch.

"This is probably going to go on for a bit, and I also need to talk to the organizers before I can leave . . ."

"I'll wait," said Lance.

"Sure. Okay. If you like. But didn't you want to buy a book?"

"No, thanks."

Lance turned on his heel and saw Chrissy watching him from a short distance away, a tentative smile on her face. He hoped she hadn't heard what he'd said to Miller.

"You didn't buy a book?' she asked in surprise when he went over to join her.

"No."

"Why not?"

Lance merely grunted in reply.

"What?" said Chrissy.

"Listen . . . I arranged to have a little talk with him when he's done here. Could you go somewhere else, and then I'll pick you up later?"

"A talk with who?"

"With Miller."

"What?"

Lance nodded, trying to act nonchalant, as if it were perfectly normal for him to be having talks with professors and poets.

"But what do you want to talk to him about?"

"Poetry," said Lance after a slight pause.

His niece gave him an incredulous look.

"But why can't I stay?' she asked.

"Because it's . . . guy talk."

"About poetry?"

"Oh, can't you just . . . ," snapped Lance, annoyed.

"So why do you want me to get lost?" she shouted, starting to cry.

"Chrissy. Honey." Astonished, Lance reached out to put his hand on her shoulder.

"Leave me alone!"

Lance noticed that people were staring at them. Clayton Miller was too. Not to mention the gray-haired Liz Brent, who looked as if she were about to get up and come over to them.

"This is important to me," Lance whispered, urgently.

Chrissy looked at him with big, tearful eyes, her lip quivering.

"Let's go outside for a moment and I'll explain."

"Okay," she sniffled.

Shamefaced, he headed across the room with his niece in tow. People moved out of their way as if they were lepers. Outside on the sidewalk he put his hand on Chrissy's shoulder, giving it a cautious squeeze. Just once.

"I'm an idiot for talking to you like that," he said. "I'm sorry."

Chrissy smiled uncertainly.

"We were both acting like idiots."

"Yeah. Maybe so."

They laughed.

"So what is it you want to talk to him about?"

"Just some old stuff. You know that Miller is originally from Duluth, right? Well, we went to Central High together."

"You're joking," exclaimed Chrissy.

"No, I'm not. He was in the class behind me. We didn't actually know each other, but . . ."

"So that means he was a grade ahead of Dad?" she said.

"Right."

"Jesus! Do you think Dad knew him?"

"No, he didn't. Neither of us knew him. But there was something that happened between Miller and one of my friends . . . something stupid, something about a girl."

Chrissy's face lit up with curiosity.

"Tell me."

"I met a guy awhile ago, I hadn't talked to him in a long time, and we started reminiscing about the old days, high school and stuff like that. This is a private matter, you see, that's why I don't think I can tell you about it, but there was something this guy really regretted, something he'd done to Clayton Miller. So

I thought that since I happened to run into Miller now after all these years, I could . . . convey my friend's regrets."

"But don't you realize that I'd like to talk to Miller too?" said Chrissy.

"Sure, but what I want to tell him is something really private, also for Miller. I thought maybe you could wait for me someplace, maybe over at Uncle Louis's Cafe."

Chrissy gave him a resigned look.

"I'll sit far away from the two of you and close my ears," she said. "But I'm not going anywhere in this cold."

When they went back inside, the book signing seemed to be over. The three poets were talking to each other as they sat at the table with the stacks of books. Miller stood up and came over to Lance and Chrissy.

"So, there was something you wanted to talk to me about?" he asked.

"Yes, that's right," said Lance.

"Something about an old friend?"

"I'll wait for you over there," whispered Chrissy and went over to the bar. She sat down and began paging through *Siamese Wing Strokes*.

"Could we step outside?" said Lance.

"Sure."

As they headed for the door, he thought that this was probably the only chance he'd ever get to hear Clayton's version of what happened so long ago. It was important that he said the right thing and didn't make a mess of it.

"So?" said Miller impatiently as the door closed behind them and they stood outside in the ice-cold January night.

"Do you remember my brother, Andy Hansen? He was in the class below you in high school."

"Yeah?" said Miller, curtly.

"He was the one who beat you up that time."

"Yeah, I know. What's your point?"

By now Lance had figured out what he wanted to say.

"It has to do with my cowardice as a brother," he said. "As his big brother. I never talked to Andy about what happened. Of course I should have tried to help him, because there had to be something really wrong for him to beat you up like that. It's been bothering me more and more as time has passed, but after all these years, I feel like it's too late to ask him. He would never tell me anything now. When I realized that you were one of the authors . . ."

"So this is how you avoid the unpleasant task of talking to your own brother, is that it?" said Miller. "And by the way, weren't you the one who stopped him?"

Lance nodded.

"Do you realize that he wanted to kill me?"

"Do you really think so?"

"What do you think he would have done with that baseball bat you took away from him?" Clayton Miller shuddered.

"Well, um . . . ," said Lance.

"Actually," said Miller, looking as if he were searching for the right words. "Actually, it doesn't surprise me to hear that the two of you never talked about what happened."

"No?"

"But if this is about your 'cowardice as a brother,' as you said, then I don't see what good it will do to talk to me. Shouldn't you be talking to Andy?"

"You're right. But tell me this, did the two of you know each other?"

There was something about the way Miller had said his brother's name that made Lance react.

"Depends what you mean by 'know each other.' We hung out with the same bunch of kids for a while. But only during that one summer, I think."

"What bunch of kids?"

Miller smiled.

"Not your bunch of friends, at any rate," he said.

"No. I guess not."

"Andy was . . . I don't know. He just showed up and started hanging out with us. You know how kids are at that age, testing boundaries, trying to find out where they belong. Right? We used to sit around in Lester Park in the evening, listening to music, smoking pot . . . things like that."

"Andy smoked pot?"

Lance looked over his shoulder to see if anyone could hear them.

"We all did," replied Miller. "We were . . . what should I say? We were Duluth's belated beatniks."

"What do you mean?"

"Forget it." Clayton Miller laughed to himself. "By the way, it's getting really cold out here." He clapped his glove-clad hands and did a few clumsy hops, as if to underscore his point.

"I know," said Lance. "But could you just tell me what happened? It's important. I'd like to know."

Miller looked as if he was starting to tire of the whole story.

"He showed me something that he'd written."

Lance shook his head in disbelief. "Something he'd written?"

"Yes."

"Okay. And?"

"And I laughed at it."

"Was that all?"

"That was enough," said Miller.

"But Andy would never have tried to kill somebody because they laughed at something he'd *written*."

"Depends on what it was, don't you think?" said Miller. "But you'll have to ask him about that yourself. Right now I don't have time for this anymore. I've got a long drive back to Minneapolis."

Miller turned on his heel and went inside. Lance followed.

The poet immediately began packing up his books, putting them in a box. Feeling at a loss, Lance stood and watched until Chrissy came over to him.

"Done?" she asked her uncle.

Clayton Miller looked up from his books.

"Your daughter?"

"My niece," Lance told him.

"Oh, really? So she's . . ."

"Andy's daughter."

For a moment Miller studied the teenager in the black clothes and makeup. Then he nodded appreciatively.

# 12

THE WHITENESS was starting to fill up her mind, and she had begun to hear the terrible sound of silence in the middle of the lake. When she looked around, there was nothing to see, not even the shadow of her own body, only the endless white. There weren't even any compass points anymore.

Inga jolted upright in her chair, as if she'd been about to doze off. Was she dreaming? No, but she hadn't been vigilant about keeping tabs on her thoughts; she had allowed them to wander where they would. And lately that increasingly meant out to the vast, white space beyond the city. What was it really like out there? Because it was a real place, after all, and could be reached by snowmobile, for instance. Wasn't that something that young men sometimes did? Drove out to a spot where they could no longer see land in any direction, and where no one could see them? Making themselves invisible to the world. But they could still see themselves and their snowmobiles. That was the difference. When Inga's thoughts headed out there, she saw nothing but whiteness. She disappeared.

Oscar looked at her from the photograph on the wall. That same handsome policeman smile all day long, yet it hadn't always been that way. What was it about him? she wondered. She hadn't thought about that in a very long time. When he was alive, especially when the boys were still small, she would sometimes lie awake, listening to her husband snoring, alone with everything that he never even noticed. What was it about him? she would then think. Now she had the same thought: What was it about Oscar? And suddenly she realized what it was. Oscar had understood so little about what went on—both between the two of them and with the boys. Not because he was unwilling or uninterested, but because he was just plain *stupid*. He simply didn't get it. She had to laugh at this sudden insight. A bold and stupid cop—that was the man she'd fallen for! And she wondered what that said about her.

"Oh, Oscar," she whispered into the empty room.

Her knitting lay on the little table next to her chair. She couldn't remember setting it down, but she must have done so. There lay the green-and-white scarf she had started knitting for Chrissy. Should she ring for the staff and ask for a cup of tea? No, she didn't want to be a nuisance. They had so much to do, not only here at Lakeview but also dropping off their children and picking them up again, cleaning house, and cooking meals. They had friends to visit and lives of their own, about which she knew only a tiny bit, a mere speck.

She decided to reread the three postcards from Norway. This time she would read them even slower than before.

# 13

LANCE DROVE SOUTH from Ely through the same kind of snow-covered, forested landscape where he'd spent the past two months. Yesterday's events had shaken him, both the surprising encounter with Clayton Miller and, in particular, Chrissy's story. Had a blood-spattered man holding a baseball bat actually stood on the side of the road outside Finland? If that was true, it had to have been Andy. But there was something surreal about the story, as if it had been taken from an episode of *The Twilight Zone*, just as Chrissy had said. Except for the fact that such a series of coincidences was even less believable. Was it really plausible that a couple of dopers would have made up a story about a blood-stained man with a baseball bat standing along the road on the very night that someone had his skull bashed in with a baseball bat only a short drive away?

Something huge and dark opened inside Lance, filling him completely. For several seconds he felt like he consisted of nothing but this cold, dark void, like a starless night over the lake. Then he was back in the car, bewildered by what had just happened. He slowed down in case it occurred again, but the only thing he noticed now was that his heart was beating faster than normal. Could it have been a panic attack like the kind he'd suffered at night in Kenora? But no. On those occasions he hadn't been able to take in enough oxygen, and each episode had centered on his breathing. This was different. As if his brain no longer wished to function and had simply switched off, taking a break, abandoning him to a rushing, dark nothingness. It was the thought of the bloodstained man at the side of the road that had unleashed this feeling. He had pictured the man as Andy. Seen Andy's face after the murder. This scenario had suddenly become possible because someone else had seen it. For some reason this seemed worse than anything else. The fact that his brother had been seen! Not that there were any actual witnesses to the killing, and for that Lance was grateful. But someone had seen Andy when he had the face of a murderer, and that made him visible to Lance's inner eye, in all his blood-spattered loneliness. That was what his brain had at first refused to acknowledge.

HE LEFT THE CAR IDLING as he got out and went over to the door. The cold tore at his nostrils. For a moment he hesitated, his hand on the door handle. Then he took a deep breath and went inside.

Behind the counter Debbie Ahonen lifted her eyes without interest from the magazine she was reading, just as she no doubt always did on those rare occasions when someone opened the door to the Finland General Store. At that instant, in that moment of almost ingrained habit, when she was barely aware of herself, Lance recognized the Debbie that he had been so in love with twenty-five years ago.

"Lance?" she said in surprise, putting aside the magazine.

He smiled.

"It's been awhile," said Debbie.

"Yeah. I've been . . . busy."

"Oh? Doing what?"

He threw out his hands.

"Oh, you know," he said.

"No, I don't."

"All sorts of things."

"Ah. Sounds hectic," said Debbie. "Never a dull moment for the forest sheriff, huh?"

"What do mean 'forest sheriff'?"

"That's what Ben Harvey calls you. I thought it was funny."

Lance realized that his presence wasn't going to be a secret for much longer. Debbie and Ben would be talking again soon. He ran Finland's only bar, and she worked in the only store. And Lance wasn't going to be able to convince her—this woman whom he'd met only once in the past twenty-five years—that he wasn't actually here in the States at all. No, that whole charade was over now. Much to his relief.

"So, what can I get you?" asked Debbie, looking at him.

Was there something flirtatious about her expression? Oh, that eternal question: What did a woman really mean? It had been years since he'd given it any thought, but here it was again.

"A soda," he told her.

It was the only thing that came to mind.

"Sure. You can really work up a thirst in this heat," said Debbie.

Lance laughed.

"My God, what a winter," he said.

"And all the clothes you have to keep putting on and taking off," said Debbie. "Layer after layer. It's like peeling a fucking onion."

For a moment he pictured Debbie peeling off the layers, all the way down to her winter-pale, Finnish American skin.

"So what do people do here in Finland, if they're looking for some fun?"

"They move," said Debbie.

They laughed, and he recognized something in her laughter, something he couldn't put his finger on, but he heard it before her smoker's cough took over. She finally managed to cough up the phlegm and then swallowed it again.

"I need a cigarette," she said. "If you want to come in the back room we can see if there's any coffee left."

"What about the store?"

"I'm not exactly expecting a big rush. Besides, there's a window so I can see if anyone comes in."

She got up and came around to the front of the counter. This was the first time in more than twenty years that Lance got a real look at her. He was overwhelmed because he'd just pictured her peeled down until she wasn't wearing a stitch of clothing.

If Debbie's face couldn't exactly be said to be untouched by the tooth of time, her body was exactly the same. Here stood the slim and stately Debbie Ahonen that he'd never entirely stopped thinking about. A bit wider in the hips, but otherwise more or less unchanged. Lance was immediately conscious of his own big, ungainly body, which so clearly showed how much he'd neglected it, especially during the past two months in Kenora.

In the back room they sat down at a table with a Formica top that was covered with brown rings from years of countless coffee cups. Lance thought the table had to be as old as he was.

"Okay," said Debbie as she set two mugs in front of them. "It's been sitting around for a while, but I hope it's still drinkable."

She filled both mugs. The table stood under the room's only window, which faced the deserted aisles of the store. Looking farther, beyond the Christmas decorations, Lance could see part of the white parking lot and the equally white road. No cars or people disturbed the arctic stillness out there.

He took a sip of coffee, which was no longer hot.

"Mmm," he said with pleasure.

The coffee had thickened over the course of the day, and the consistency reminded him of soy sauce. He noticed a pen and a Yahtzee score card on the table. Did she play Yahtzee with herself?

"The coffee doesn't stay hot in such a cold room," Debbie apologized.

"It really is cold in here," said Lance.

"Is there anyplace that *isn't* cold?"

A small space heater under the table was the only source of heat in the room, which had no furniture other than the table and chairs. Against one wall was a sink with a bar of soap and a blue towel hanging from a nail, and in the corner stood a plastic bucket with two mops hanging over the edge. The calendar on the wall was a year old.

Debbie took out a cigarette and lit it. After a few puffs, the smoke prickled his nostrils, but he didn't complain. It had been a long time since he'd had a cup of coffee with a woman, and this wasn't just any woman, as he reminded himself.

"So, how's life been treating you lately?" she asked.

"Oh, fine . . . been pretty quiet."

He didn't even attempt to tell her the truth.

"What about you?"

Debbie grimaced.

"That bad?"

"Oh, you know, coming back here . . ."

Lance nodded.

"So how was it out there?" he asked. "In California."

"Warmer, at any rate. That's for sure. Otherwise I guess it's pretty much the same everywhere."

"Is it?"

"Isn't it?"

"I've never been anywhere else than here."

"Didn't you live in Minneapolis for a while?"

"Yeah. When I went to the police academy. But that's still Minnesota."

"Right."

"So how was California?"

"For me, California was first and foremost a bad marriage. Or at least that's what it ended up being. A bad marriage that I finally managed to escape from six years ago. By then Pattie was thirteen. She moved here to Minnesota with me, but now she's back in California. Couldn't take the cold."

"Is she a student?"

"Uh-huh. She's taking a night course. Accounting, I think. And she works in a shop during the day."

"Where?"

"In Santa Barbara. She lives with her father."

"Oh."

"And you married . . . who was it?"

"Nobody you know. Her name's Mary Dupree. From Grand Portage. Ojibwe."

Debbie raised her eyebrows.

"But that wasn't the problem," Lance went on. "At least I don't think so."

"So what was the problem, then?" asked Debbie, stubbing out her cigarette in the ashtray.

"I guess she just wasn't the right person for me."

Lance was so nervous that his mouth had gone dry. He took

a sip of coffee and tried to catch her eye, but she was staring past him.

"I realized that after a while," he went on, "but there was Jimmy to think of, our son . . ."

"And now you're divorced?" Debbie was still avoiding his eye.

"Yes."

Silence settled over the cramped, smoky room. Lance realized that he was standing at a crossroads. If he retreated now, it would be over before it even began. Then he could take a deep breath, get in the car, and drive back to Ely, or wherever he was planning to go now. On the other hand, if he took even the smallest step in Debbie's direction, it meant that he would be moving into open terrain, presenting himself as a man who had sought out an old flame and who no longer wanted to be alone.

"I've never stopped thinking about you," he said.

He felt his cheeks flush, but at least he'd said it. Even though it wasn't entirely true, it felt true here and now.

Debbie smiled her gentlest smile but still didn't look at him. From sheer nerves, he picked up his mug and took another gulp of the bitter, tepid coffee.

Finally she shifted her gaze and looked him in the eye.

"Don't you think it's too late?" she said. "I mean, *much* too late?"

"It's never too late," said Lance.

"Then you don't know what you're talking about."

"Maybe not."

"It's possible that I made a mistake back then, but it's not something that can be corrected twenty years later," said Debbie.

"Why not?"

"Because we're not the same people we were back then. Those two might have been able to . . ."

"But not us?"

Debbie shook her head.

"Does this have something to do with Richie Akkola?" asked Lance. "Last time you said that the two of you were living together."

Her face closed up.

"I mean, he's . . . Richie is . . ."

Lance couldn't get himself to say the word "old." That would be more of an insult to her than to Richie.

"I've gotta get back to work," she said in an ordinary tone of voice, and Lance didn't know where that came from. "It was nice chatting with you. Maybe we can have another talk again soon."

Debbie stood up and opened the door to the store, which was just as deserted as it had been all along. Without waiting for him, she went back to her place behind the counter and picked up the magazine that she'd been reading when he came in. She began leafing through the pages.

Lance closed the door to the back room and went over to her.

"Weren't you going to buy a soda?" she asked.

"What?"

A quick smile was all he got before she went back to her magazine. The sort of smile that was a dime a dozen.

# 14

IT WAS 2:10 IN THE MORNING, and Grand Marais, which was the administrative hub of Cook County, seemed dead in the cold. Up on Good Harbor Hill, just outside the town, a black Jeep Cherokee was parked with the engine running. It had been there quite awhile. Spread out before Lance Hansen was one of the most beautiful views in all of Minnesota. With the snow and moonlight, and with the vast expanse of the starry sky displayed above Lake Superior, which was completely white and endless, the view was even more beautiful than usual, bordering on something supernatural, as if it were on a planet that merely resembled ours.

He'd taken the one step that he never thought he'd dare take, and he'd ended up getting shot down like some young, inexperienced buck on the first day of hunting season. Now only the butchering remained. Every time he thought about it, he felt like someone was sticking a knife in him, slitting open his abdomen so his guts came pouring out, visible to all the world. What an idiot he was! To come slinking back to a woman who had dumped him more than twenty years ago, to see if it was possible to find a few crumbs that somebody else had left behind. What a loser he was.

He'd played all the cards he was holding without accomplishing anything other than to be left sitting there, empty handed. Debbie was beyond his reach, and soon everyone would know that he wasn't in Norway after all. He might as well show himself.

And say what? That he'd fooled everybody into thinking that he was in Norway? What a mess he'd made of things. But then he had an idea, and before he'd even thought it through, he got out his cell phone. Provided there wasn't any postcard currently in transit between Oslo and Minnesota, he could simply tell Eirik Nyland that his assistance was no longer needed—no more postcards from Norway. Then he could make his appearance here and say that he was back from his Norway trip.

He calculated that it must be just past nine in the morning in Oslo. So he tapped in Nyland's phone number. The criminal investigator answered on the first ring. He must have been sitting there with his phone in his hand.

"Nyland," he said.

"This is Lance Hansen."

"Hi."

"Am I interrupting your work?"

"No, not at all."

Lance thought the voices and footsteps, which he could hear in the background, were probably as close as he'd ever get to Oslo in real life.

"You know those postcards?"

"Yeah?"

"You don't have to send any more of them. They've done the trick, you might say."

"Okay. So you're back from . . . Where was it you went?"

"Arizona."

"Right. How'd it go with you and the girlfriend?"

"Not bad. But the situation's still a bit uncertain."

"You're still together?"

"Sure. But you don't need to send any more postcards."

"Okay."

"There aren't any on the way, are there?"

"Postcards?"

"Uh-huh."

"No, I don't think so. So how are things going over there? Has the trial started yet?"

"It starts on February twenty-eighth."

"There can't be much doubt that he'll be convicted," said Nyland. "What was his name again?"

"Lenny Diver."

"Oh, right."

"Tell me something," said Lance. "Did you think the whole time that I might have something to do with the murder?"

There was a pause before Nyland answered.

"I have to admit that I had a feeling you were holding something back."

"Like what?"

"I don't know. I couldn't come up with anything concrete."

"So you never thought I knew who the murderer was?"

"No. Did you?"

"Of course not," said Lance with a laugh.

A lengthy pause ensued. An uncomfortable silence.

"Is everything okay?"

"Sure," Lance replied automatically.

"Just let me know if there's anything else I can do to help. More postcards, more women. Whatever you need."


UP ON THE RIDGE the house stood in darkness, closed in on itself in the winter night. It was now past 3:00 a.m., and the traffic on Highway 61 wouldn't pick up again until people began leaving for work around six. Lance put on his snowshoes outside Isak Hansen's hardware store, where he'd parked, and began walking up the snowy road toward the house. It was only right that he should arrive home under cover of night, heading for a cold, dark house with the starry sky overhead, wading through the powdery snow on snowshoes like a fur trapper or an Indian. It was right because he was still a fugitive. Only when he was once again inside his own house would it be over. He was now putting behind him the last few yards of his exile.

Then he was standing on the top step, where he'd stood on that night in November after having walked the whole way from Baraga Cross Road. Back then he'd had to use his rifle to break off the three-foot-long icicles that were blocking the front door.

The lock opened easily, as always. Through his glove he felt the cold from the iron as he pressed down the latch and opened the door. Without even thinking about it, his hand sought the switch in the dark and turned on the light. There were his coats hanging on their hooks, his shoes and boots lined up on the floor. But there was an unfamiliar and subdued air about everything. Without further hesitation he opened the next door and turned on the light in there too. He found himself standing right in front of the photo of him and Andy kneeling on either side of a big buck. Each brother held a rifle in one hand while with the other they grasped the impressive antlers. He couldn't help thinking about the last time he'd stood here, when he was about to leave for Canada after having set up the ruse about taking a vacation in Norway. Because of what happened during the deer hunt, he hadn't dared stay here any longer. Those two brothers who had posed so proudly for the photo on the wall had ended up hunting each other instead of a deer. He had taken aim at Andy, and his brother had turned around and seen him do it. But I wouldn't have shot him, Lance thought now. Yet how certain could he be about that? Finally he had hidden in some dense thickets while his brother came closer and closer. *"You're a dead man, Lance,"* Andy had whispered, only a couple of yards away. The next second Lance's rifle had gone off by accident. The last Lance heard of Andy was the sound of his body as he toppled backward through the ice-coated thicket. It later turned out that the shot hadn't hit him. And that could only be called a miracle.

Ever since, Lance had lived in fear of his brother.

As he went from room to room, switching on the lights and turning up the heaters that had been left on the lowest possible setting the whole time, he noticed that the whole place had an unfamiliar smell, as if the house had its own smell that had grown stronger during his absence. It would take time for him to feel at home here again, if ever. Yet he continued his solitary nightly rounds through the rooms, turning on the faucets, opening the kitchen cupboards, studying the cups and glasses and stacks of plates, running his hand over the tabletop where he'd eaten so many meals both alone and with his small family.

After a while he went into the living room and sat down on the sofa, in exactly the same place where he'd sat on that long night after the deer hunt. Now the circle was complete. But had anything really changed during the past ten weeks? As if his body were answering the question, he felt a dull pain pulsing in his right hand. That was what had happened, and that was why he was even here in the U.S. at all. He'd had enough and had slammed his fist on the table in the hotel.

"I won't stand for this anymore," he said in a low voice.

He looked at the photos of Jimmy hanging on the wall. What sort of father was he, lying to his son as he had? And hiding the truth about something as serious as a murder. He needed to clear things up, for the boy's sake if nothing else.

HOW COULD HE HAVE BELIEVED that it would be over once he was inside these rooms again? His exile had nothing to do with this house; he had been shut out from the *people.* He got out his cell phone and clicked through the list of contacts. There they were: Inga, Andy, Mary, Becky Tofte, Ranger John Zimmermann, Bill Eggum, Sparky Redmeyer, and many more. All of them were under the illusion that Lance Hansen was on vacation in the "old country," that the inveterate local historian and genealogy re-searcher was at this very minute exploring his roots on the other side of the Atlantic. Not until he stood before them would his exile be over.

His gaze fell on the photograph hanging in the hallway. The one of him and Andy on a deer hunt twelve or thirteen years ago, out by Onion River. Could he keep that picture there if he sent Andy to prison? Could he stand to see it every day if that happened? Lance went into the hall and stood in front of the photo. His brother was smiling under his Minnesota Twins cap, while he seemed worn out, his face flushed. He knew that was due to problems with the camera's timing device. He'd run back and forth several times between the buck and the camera, which he'd set on a tree stump. But could he keep this picture hanging on the wall? No, not if he turned Andy in. Then he'd never be able to look at that smiling, proud face of his again, remembering how it had felt to be out in the woods with his brother. The mere thought of an outdoorsman like Andy locked up in a prison cell was sheer torture. Then he reminded himself that an innocent man was sitting in that cell right now. Even so, he left the photo where it was. For now, he thought.

He went back into the living room and pulled the heavy curtains aside to look out at the familiar view: Isak Hansen's hardware store, founded by his paternal grandfather more than eighty years ago, a segment of Highway 61, and below the road an endless white plain that disappeared into the blue of the moon: Lake Superior. All this he would have to reclaim. The fact that he even stood here was the first step. Tomorrow he would make some calls to let people know he was back home. And even though he had no intention of phoning Andy, it wouldn't take long before his brother heard the news.

# 15

AFTER BREAKFAST THE NEXT DAY Lance sat down in his easy chair to call his mother. It took only a few seconds for her to pick up.

"This is Inga," she said.

He felt a lump form in his throat the moment he heard her slightly quavering voice. He had to clear his throat before he could say anything.

"Lance?" she said. "Is that you?"

She'd recognized who it was from the way he cleared his throat.

"Yes, it's me, Mom."

"Oh, it's wonderful to hear from you, my boy! How are you?"

"Fine."

"And how's Norway?"

"No, I'm back home again."

"Oh, my dear," she exclaimed. "When did you get back?"

"Last night."

"You must be tired."

"You're right about that."

And he actually felt a great weariness flood over him. Probably because of all the lies that he'd already told her, and all the lies he was going to have to tell her in the future. She would want to hear about his Norway trip for a long time to come. Most likely for the rest of her life, he thought. From now on, every time he saw her she would want to talk about her son's visit to the old country. Which meant that he would have to lie to her every time they saw each other.

"So how are you?" he asked.

"I'm fine, but it's been awfully quiet here without you," she told him.

"Hasn't anyone come to visit you?"

"Awfully quiet."

"What about Andy?"

"He's got so much on his mind."

"But you talk to him on the phone, don't you?"

"Sure, but it's been at least two weeks now. He was really interested to hear what you were doing in Norway."

"What did you tell him?"

"Oh, looking for ancestors, that sort of thing."

Lance thought there was something about her voice that sounded different than before. A certain flatness.

"The lake is completely frozen over," she said.

"Yeah, I know."

"Oh. Did they hear about it over there too?"

"The Internet, you know."

"Oh. Right."

"So what else did Andy say? Did he say anything about me?"

"No, I don't think so. He was just wondering why you left for Norway so suddenly."

"Did he mention anything about the deer hunt?"

"No, but I heard that you didn't get anything."

"That's right. We didn't."

"Did you get caught in the ice storm?"

"Partly."

"That must have been scary."

"No, not really. It was fine," Lance said.

He could hardly open his mouth anymore without lying. Not because he wanted to lie, but because every lie gave rise to another, which gave rise to two more, and on and on.

"I've tried to call you several times, but a voice said that your phone was turned off, or something like that."

"That's because it's not possible to call my phone when I'm

out of the country. I can make calls, but I can't receive any." Another lie.

"Oh."

"Is he feeling okay? Andy, I mean."

"I think so," said Inga.

"He hasn't been sick?"

"Sounds like you've missed your little brother."

"Not really."

"Then why are you asking about him?"

"Okay, I guess I did miss him a bit."

"You two boys," said his mother, sighing.

"What do you mean?"

"Oh, I don't know. It's just that the two of you . . ."

A lengthy pause ensued. Lanced tried to think of something important to say that was also the truth, but he couldn't come up with a thing.

"Did you meet any of our relatives?" Inga asked at last.

"No, I didn't."

"But didn't you go to Halsnøy?"

"The roads were closed."

"The whole time?" She sounded surprised.

"Yeah."

"But why?"

"Snow."

"Oh."

"So it was all kind of foolish," said Lance.

"What did you do in Norway then?"

"I had a vacation."

"But you were gone so long!"

"I was just there—okay?" he snapped in annoyance and instantly regretted it.

"Okay, okay. When are you going to come and visit me?"

"I don't really know. There are a number of things that I need to take care of after being away for so long. But I'll come as soon as I can."

"Is everything all right?" His mother suddenly sounded worried.

"What do you mean?"

"There's nothing wrong, is there? Nothing serious?"

"Why do you ask?"

"Oh, never mind. Sorry. It's just me being old and confused."

For a moment he thought she was going to cry.

"Don't say that," he told her. "I'll come and visit you soon."

"Oh, I can't wait!"

"Me neither. But I've got to hang up now. I've got a lot to do."

"It's good to have you back home."

"It's good to *be* home. See you soon."

"Bye."

"Bye," said Lance, and ended the call.

Afterward he sat with the phone in his hand, staring straight ahead. He thought about how he always used to take it for granted that he never lied. Previously it had simply been part of what he thought of as good manners. Only now was he beginning to realize how destructive lying could be. It was like a poison that was destroying him from the inside.

# 16

"HEY, SON!"

"Dad!"

Jimmy threw himself into his father's arms. Standing on the porch, Mary smiled as she shivered in the cold. Lance smiled back over the head of their son.

"Did you have a good time in Norway?" she asked.

"No, it was boring."

"Feel good to be back home?"

"Definitely! I'll bring him back in a couple of hours," said Lance as he set Jimmy down on the ground.

"Have fun."

Father and son both gave her a wave before she turned on her heel and went back inside the house.

As they drove the short distance to Grand Portage Lodge and Casino, a big modern-looking building made of wood and glass, Jimmy talked nonstop about what he'd been up to lately, telling Lance about school and his grandfather and a mink that had come all the way up onto the porch and almost inside the house.

"I don't think it knew how to find food on its own," he said.

"Maybe it wanted to have dinner with the two of you," said Lance.

"We had fish cakes."

"See? What'd I tell you?"

FROM THEIR TABLE they could look right into the gambling hall where a number of people were sitting in front of the slot machines. Lance thought the sound from the machines had something disproportionately childish about it, considering that most of the gamblers looked to be retirement age. Occasionally they also heard an avalanche of clattering coins followed by a shrill squeal if the winner was a woman; the men merely looked over their shoulders when they won.

Father and son were both eating ice cream. Outside the windows ice crystals glittered on the parked cars.

"What was it like in Norway?" Jimmy wanted to know.

"Cold."

"Like here?"

"Yeah," said Lance.

"So you could just as well have stayed home."

"You're right."

"But now you're back."

"Yes, I am. Have you visited your grandma while I was gone?"

Jimmy shook his head as he ate.

"Would you like to go see her sometime soon?"

He nodded.

"Maybe you and I could take a drive down to Duluth together someday."

"Sure. Can we go to the aquarium?"

"We'll see."

"Do you remember those big fish we saw there?"

"Sturgeon," said Lance.

Then they both turned their attention back to their ice cream, but he noticed that the boy kept casting brief glances at him.

"Dad?" he said after a moment.

"Yes?"

"Are you tired?"

Lance put his spoon down on the napkin and looked at his son.

"Do I seem tired?"

Jimmy nodded.

"Well, I guess I am."

"Do you have jet lag?"

"Do you know what jet lag is?" Lance was surprised.

"Uh-huh. It's when you come back home from the other side of the world and take a dump like you're . . ."

Lance had to laugh.

"But that's what Dan Proudhom said."

"Who's that?"

"He goes to junior high."

"Do you know him?"

"No. He's Chad's brother."

"And you know Chad?"

"Uh-huh."

"And what did Dan Proudhom say about jet lag?"

"He said that you take a dump like you're on the other side of the world. In China, for example. Is that true?"

"Yeah, I take a dump like a Chinese guy now."

Jimmy laughed so hard he almost fell off his chair.


AFTERWARD they drove around Grand Portage for a while, which was one of Jimmy's favorite things to do. Just rolling quietly through the narrow streets between the high snowbanks made by the plows. Lenny Diver was from here. That was the thing about Grand Portage—for those who came from here, was it less likely that the dice would roll in their favor on the day when it really mattered?

A white pickup came slowly toward them when they were almost back at Jimmy's house. Lance noticed that it stopped a short distance down the road.

After making sure his son was safely inside, he drove back the same way they had come. The white pickup turned and again slowly approached. When they were almost level with each other, the driver stuck his arm out the open window and signaled for Lance to stop.

He pulled over and rolled down the window. There were two suspicious-looking men with long hair inside the truck.

"Are you that forest cop?" asked the driver.

His tone of voice was harsh, but he avoided looking Lance in the eye, as if he didn't dare show his face.

"Yeah," said Lance after a moment's hesitation.

"The guy who found the Norwegian?"

"Huh?"

"At Baraga's Cross?"

"Yeah. That was me."

The man deliberately raised his index finger and slowly moved it from side to side, in a warning gesture.

"What is it you guys want?"

"You know," he said.

"No, I don't."

Lance could hear how confused and pitiful his voice sounded.

"You can save Lenny," said the other man, partially hidden behind the driver.

"Lenny?"

"Lenny Diver. You can save him. If you don't, you'll be cursed for all eternity. You and your whole family."

The driver nodded, as if to underscore that they were serious. Then he rolled up his window and drove past.

# 17

WHEN HE WOKE UP, Lance thought at first that he'd dreamed something, but he couldn't remember what it was. Bewildered, he sat up in bed and looked around. The bedroom didn't seem familiar, as if he'd gone into the wrong house and fallen asleep in someone else's bed. Then he remembered: the white pickup. But that was no dream. His heart began pounding at a hollow, uncomfortable gallop. He got up and pulled open the curtains. The dazzling light stung his eyes.

The clock radio on the nightstand said it was 10:41.

He put on his bathrobe and slippers and then shuffled out to the kitchen and switched on the coffeemaker. The house had warmed up since the heaters had all been going full-blast for hours, but the rooms still had an abandoned air about them, as if they hadn't quite woken up from a long slumber.

Carrying his coffee cup, he went into the living room and sat down in his favorite chair. There he sat, squinting at the intense glitter coming off the snowy landscape outside the big picture window. Cars were soundlessly rushing past on the road below. His own Jeep Cherokee was parked in front of the red building that housed his cousin Rick's hardware store. The road up to his home had been newly plowed. His cousin must have done it while Lance was asleep.

He took a few sips of the piping-hot coffee and felt an inkling of well-being start to emerge, but then he happened to think of those two men again.

*"If you don't, you'll be cursed for all eternity. You and your whole family."*

Only now did the full consequences of what had happened dawn on Lance. Someone had threatened his family. Sick with worry, he got up and hurried down to the basement, where the ice-cold air nearly took his breath away. He unlocked the gun cabinet and took out his service pistol and some ammunition. Then he relocked the cabinet and ran back upstairs. For a moment he paused in the hallway, not sure what to do. Too many thoughts were lined up inside his head, like cars in rush-hour traffic, unable to move forward. Finally he put the gun and bullets on the little table in the hall and then went into the bathroom to take a shower.

THE CRUSH OF THOUGHTS had not diminished when he came out. He picked up his gun but then caught sight of himself in the mirror: a stark-naked, overweight man holding a gun in his hand. It was not a pretty sight, so he put the gun down and went into the bedroom where he got dressed without paying any attention to what he put on. When he sensed that he was fully clothed, he rushed back to the hall and again picked up the gun and ammunition. A quick glance in the mirror as he filled the magazine showed a man wearing heavy woolen socks, suit trousers, and a mossy green sweater that appeared to be on backward.

As he slammed the magazine into place, he heard the sound of a car coming up the hill toward the house. He cocked the gun; a bullet slid into the chamber. Then he checked to make sure the safety was on before he tucked the pistol into his waistband in front and pulled the loose sweater over it.

The car had stopped outside, but the engine was still running, and he hadn't yet heard any car door open or close. He paused in the cramped front entryway to listen, but all he heard was the sound of the engine idling outside.

Lance turned the lock and opened the door.

Andy was sitting in his white Chevy Blazer only a few yards away. The two brothers hadn't seen each other since that Sunday in November when Andy, who was standing on the bare rock near Baraga's Cross, turned around and saw Lance taking aim at him. And later, the shot in the dark, when Lance's rifle unexpectedly fired—although for Andy it must have seemed like a deliberate attempt to kill him. So here he now sat, right out front, with a hint of a smile on his face. Or was it a sneer? Lance felt the pressure of the gun against his stomach. He tried to think rationally, but couldn't do it. He merely stared at his brother, who stared back with that same little sneer on his lips. It was as if the world had suddenly become real again, boiled down to its purest form, and they knew it. They both did.

Calmly Andy raised his index finger and pointed it at his brother standing in the doorway. Lance waited for him to pull the trigger, as if firing an imaginary gun, but that didn't happen. Andy simply lowered his finger and drove out of the yard, down the hill to the highway.

THE FIRST THING Lance did after his brother's brief visit was phone Chrissy. His niece was probably in the middle of a class at school, but he hoped that she'd call him back during a free moment when she saw that he was trying to get hold of her.

She picked up after a couple of rings.

"Hello?" she said tentatively.

"Chrissy?"

"Yeah?"

"It's Lance."

"Huh?"

"Uncle Lance."

"Oh."

He could hear music thudding in the background.

"Are you at school?"

"What do you want?"

"I need to talk to you."

"Again?"

"It's important."

"Is this about the murder?"

"Yes."

"I don't know anything except what I already told you."

"But I do."

"Oh."

"When are you done with school?"

"Er . . . now."

"Could I pick you up at the gas station again?"

"But aren't you back from vacation? Officially, I mean?"

"So you heard about that, huh?"

"Grandma called."

"Right. Well, I'm back, but what I'm working on is still secret. In fact, it's even more secret. You didn't tell anyone that you'd seen me, did you?"

"No, I didn't."

"Good. Shall we say that I'll pick you up in two hours?"


THE LAKE was there the whole time. Occasionally it would disappear behind a stretch of woods, but soon it reappeared, endless and white in the dazzling sunshine under the blue sky. For the first time in ages he was able to drive along Highway 61 in broad daylight, and in spite of the difficult situation in which he found himself, Lance felt a sense of liberation, as if he'd returned to life after living a shadowy existence for more than two months. He felt with every fiber of his being that it was here he belonged, on the North Shore of Lake Superior, and nothing could make him leave again.

As a forest cop Lance Hansen had approximately the same relationship to his service pistol as to his uniform—it was something he put on each day before he went to work. It was part of his uniform, in fact. A few times he'd used it to put injured animals out of their misery, but that was all. Right now the gun was in the glove compartment of his own car, ready to be used in self-defense, if necessary.

He was not a free man.


CHRISSY AND LANCE said very little to each other on the drive to Duluth. He assumed that was where she'd want to go. Or maybe to the Twin Cities, but that was too far. She seemed sullen and withdrawn, as if preoccupied with something else entirely. Lance wondered why she'd even agreed to meet him.

"The Kozy?" he asked, teasing her as they drove into the city.

"God, no," groaned his niece.

"How about Fitger's?"

"Okay."

They parked and went inside the big brick building that still housed the legendary Fitger's Brewhouse, although on a smaller scale than in the past, when it had been one of the largest in the region. These days it was a restaurant, yet it still had its own brewery that produced many of the types of beer available locally.

Lance and Chrissy found a table in a dark corner at the back of the pub, which was already more than half full.

"What'll you have?" he asked her.

"What are you going to have?"

"A beer."

"Then I'll have one too," she said.

He didn't bother to reply, just stared at her, as if she still hadn't answered his question.

"Okay, a Diet Sprite," she said with a sigh. "I'm going to the restroom."

Lance ordered her soda and a pint of Starfire Pale Ale for himself. Then he took them back to the table and sat down. He sipped the beer as he looked around the pub. Even though the place was fairly new, it looked as if it had been there since before World War II. Tons of supposedly old knickknacks and advertising posters adorned the walls, which appeared to be gray with smoke, even though it was unlikely that a single cigarette had ever been lit on the premises. Lance was impressed by how authentic the whole place looked.

When Chrissy came back, she seemed in a better mood.

"So, what did you want to talk to me about this time?" she said with interest as she leaned forward across the table.

"Yesterday I was stopped by two guys who threatened me."

"Threatened you?"

She opened her eyes wide, feigning one of those exaggerated looks of surprise that she favored.

"They said that I could save Lenny Diver, and that if I didn't, my whole family and I would be cursed for all eternity, or something like that."

"Jesus!"

"Do you have any idea who they could be? It seems like you know people from more walks of life than most of the other family members do. Everything you tell me will be confidential, just between the two of us."

"The only people I know in Grand Portage are Mary and Jimmy."

"But when I saw you at the Kozy, you were with a girl and two guys who looked like they were Ojibwe."

"Oh, them. No, Suzy was the one who knew them. I'd never seen them before."

"What about the guys from the party at your cabin? The ones who saw the bloodstained man with the bat? Do you think they know Lenny Diver?"

"I doubt it. I think they're from somewhere on the Range," said Chrissy. "But what did those men mean when they said you could save Lenny Diver?"

Lance hesitated.

"It's a long story, and I've never told it to anyone before. It actually started thirty years ago, here in Duluth. But for my part, it began last summer, on the night before the Norwegian tourist was killed. I'd gone to visit Inga. I was on my way home when I saw a guy I know driving down Baraga Cross Road."

"Who was it?" asked Chrissy.

"Nobody you know. Apparently he didn't recognize me, but he has a very distinctive appearance, so it's impossible to mistake him for anyone else. I didn't give it much thought, although it seemed a little strange for him to be driving down to Baraga's Cross that late. It was around ten at night. The next day I found the body of the Norwegian only about a hundred yards away from the parking lot, and later in the day, when the news of the murder reached the media and everyone and his brother had heard about it, I saw that same guy again. He made a point of telling me that he'd spent the whole night at his cabin over by . . . well, I don't remember where he said it was. But he said he hadn't been anywhere near the lake and Baraga's Cross. And I knew that was a lie."

Lance paused to take a big gulp of his Starfire Pale.

"So you think he's the one who did it?" asked Chrissy cautiously.

"Yes, I do."

"But it sounds a bit vague, don't you think?"

"Weren't you the one who said that a man covered in blood and holding a baseball bat was seen outside Finland on that night?" said Lance.

"Yes, but . . ."

"A middle-aged white guy with an old junker for a car?"

"Uh-huh."

"Well, the guy I'm talking about drives an old beater. I'm a hundred percent sure that he was driving down toward the cross at about ten that night, and for some reason he decided to lie about it and claim he was somewhere else."

"That does sound suspicious," Chrissy admitted. "But why would he kill a Norwegian tourist?"

"I think I know that too," said Lance. "Remember I said that this story actually started here in town almost thirty years ago?"

"Uh-huh."

"I was a senior in high school. Your father was a sophomore. And the man I think is the murderer was a junior along with Clayton Miller."

"*Clayton Miller?* What does he have to do with all this?"

"Nothing really, and yet he has everything to do with it," Lance said. "As I was saying, they were in the same class, and the guy . . . let's just call him the 'murderer' . . . he was gay. It's not easy to talk about this, Chrissy. I'm very old-fashioned, but the murderer was in love with Clayton Miller, who was a very special kid."

"Special in what way?" Chrissy interrupted him.

"He knitted his own scarves."

"Huh?"

"Yes, he did. So of course everyone thought he was kind of strange. They all thought he was gay."

"But Clayton Miller has a wife and kids," said Chrissy.

"I know. They were wrong. It was the murderer who was gay, but of course he thought Miller was too. Everybody did. And one day the murderer wrote a note to Clayton. I don't know what it said, but maybe it was some sort of declaration of love. And

Clayton Miller, who was not gay, laughed at what he'd written. And then the murderer attacked him. He knocked him down and kicked him as he lay on the ground. Punctured his lung. Kicked out his teeth. And then he went to get a baseball bat and came back to Miller, who was lying on the ground defenseless. But someone else showed up. An older boy. And he took the bat away. It was an extremely violent assault. I have no doubt that it would have ended in murder if the older boy hadn't stopped it."

"Was that what you wanted to talk to Clayton Miller about?" asked Chrissy.

"Yes. I wanted to ask him what could have provoked such anger. And that's what he told me. But he refused to say what the murderer had written in the note. Did you know that the murdered Norwegian and his traveling companion were both gay?"

Chrissy raised a hand to her mouth in surprise.

"Lenny Diver has consistently maintained that he spent the night of the murder with a woman he met in a bar in Grand Marais. But he was so drunk he can't recall what her name was. It sounded like a pretty implausible explanation, but what if it's true? If that's the case, then he was also drunk enough that the killer could have planted his fingerprints on the baseball bat and then hidden the bat in his car. And that's what I think happened. The murderer just happened to come upon Lenny Diver. It must have seemed like a gift from heaven. Maybe the killer found him sleeping it off in his car the next day."

"My God," whispered Chrissy.

"But there's more," Lance went on. "Only a few days before the tourist was killed, this man that I'm calling the murderer was seen with the two Norwegians in a bar. They spent several hours together. These two gay guys and a middle-aged man who was also homosexual but who had spent his whole life in the closet. He has a wife and child, you see. But deep inside . . ."

"And so he got laughed at again?" said Chrissy.

"Something like that. And with the same result, except that this time no one came to take the baseball bat away."

Lance tried to hide a sob by taking a big gulp of beer, but it didn't work. This was the first time he'd ever put his thoughts about Andy into words.

"Are you feeling bad about this?" his niece asked.

"Yes, I am."

"Is it because you know the murderer well, or something?"

"Not anymore, but I used to know him a long time ago," replied Lance.

"And you haven't told this to anyone?"

"As I said, I know who the man is. I know who his wife is. And his daughter. He has a daughter your age. But last night my family and I were threatened. And if those two guys are friends of Diver's, I have to say that I understand where they're coming from, even though I don't know how they could know about all this. Regardless, that doesn't change anything. I can't put my family in danger. Not Jimmy . . ."

"Does that mean you want me to testify?" she asked, her voice quavering.

Lance nodded. Suddenly Chrissy's shoulders began to shake. She was crying silently, but Lance couldn't bear the thought of creating a scene in the crowded pub.

"Pull yourself together," he said in a low voice. "You don't have to do anything if you don't want to."

"But I do want to," she said, her voice thick with tears. Her big dark eyes had lost any trace of childishness.

At that moment a thought occurred to Lance.

"You have brown eyes!" he exclaimed.

A smile appeared on Chrissy's tear-stained face.

"Is this the first time you've noticed?"


AS THEY DROVE NORTH, she started crying again, but since they were alone, Lance didn't try to stop her.

He thought about what he'd told her about the "murderer." How could he even think that Andy was gay? But there was no way around it—all indications led to the same conclusion. What a tragedy this whole thing was. His family's insistent silence had destroyed everything. Their whole world was based on the simple fact that certain things were just not discussed, under any circumstances. There were no rules designating which subjects were taboo, but everyone who belonged to the same world as

Lance knew intuitively what topics to avoid. The fact that nobody had talked about what Andy did to Clayton Miller came under the big category of taboo topics. This tragedy might have been avoided if the members of the Hansen family had been a different sort of people.

"Brown eyes suit you," he told his niece, who had stopped crying.

"Thanks," she murmured.

"And it makes sense, since you're Ojibwe."

Chrissy didn't say a word, but out of the corner of his eye Lance saw her mouth open, and her face turned even paler than before, only to flush a bright red, all in a matter of seconds. She started gasping for breath, and for a moment he thought she was having some sort of seizure, but then she regained control. Partially, at least. Her voice shook when she spoke.

"What do you mean?"

"One of your great-great-grandmothers was Ojibwe," he explained.

As soon as he said that, it was as if something let go inside her.

"Is that true?" She looked at him with an eager glint in her brown eyes.

"Yep! And I think you and I are the only ones in the family who know that."

"But how . . . ?"

Then Lance told her the whole story about Nanette's diary, how he'd had some pages translated, and how she'd written that she made an "asabikeshiihn," a dream catcher, for the seriously injured Thormod Olson, who was having nightmares. And several times she'd mentioned "nokomis," which meant "grandmother" in Ojibwe. Finally he told Chrissy about his own investigation into the disappearance of Swamper Caribou, and the fact that he believed Thormod, for some reason, had killed the medicine man the night he arrived on the North Shore.

# 18

THE THOUGHT of a bloodstained Andy standing by the side of the road kept Lance awake. Only one other image had made as big an impression on him: the sight of the murdered Georg Lofthus with a row of white teeth visible in all the red, even though he was lying on his stomach in the woods. Once these two images had merged in his sleepless brain, it was impossible for Lance to separate them again. Previously he'd had in his mind only the picture of Andy driving toward the cross at around ten o'clock at night, after which he'd turned up at the ranger station on the following day and lied to everyone. Now Lance had a picture of his brother out in the vast darkness *between* these two time periods. Some kids drive past him outside Finland just before dawn. He's standing on the shoulder, next to his car, spattered with blood and holding a baseball bat in his hand. Maybe he's on his way down to the river to wash off the blood.

Chrissy said the guys who saw him thought he'd hit an animal, possibly a cat, and had been forced to kill it with the bat. Lance suddenly remembered the weight of a big wrench in his hand and a white cat howling as he struck it. And as he lay in bed, unable to sleep, Lance wondered whether at that moment he had looked just like Andy who stood at the side of the road outside Finland, holding not a wrench but a baseball bat. When he thought about that, he almost felt like he and the murderer had merged.

Lance got up, put on his bathrobe, and went out to the kitch-
en, where he poured himself a cup of coffee, since he wasn't going
to sleep anyway. He took the coffee into his home office. Everything was just as he'd left it. On the wall hung an old black-and-
white photo of his ancestors from Halsnøy, taken on the deck of
the steamer *America* in Duluth in October 1902. His desk was
covered with papers and loose photographs. On a bookcase that
filled an entire wall was the archival collection belonging to the
local historical society. The materials had been largely accumu-
lated by the society's founder, the teacher Olga Soderberg. When
she died, young Lance Hansen had taken over, and he was still
the chairman even though there were no longer any active members. A small handful of individuals, including Willy Dupree, still
paid dues, but it was pointless to schedule any meetings since the
members were all too old to show up.

Lance pulled out the chair and sat down at his desk. In the
midst of the clutter was a picture of the brother of Swamper
Caribou, the medicine man who had disappeared. "Joe Caribou
on the path leading to his mother's house, 1905." That was the
caption written in Olga Soderberg's florid schoolteacher handwriting on the folder in which the photo had been placed. In the
picture Joe Caribou looked like his brother's ghost, which Lance
had now seen four times—the last time during the dramatic deer
hunt in November when the medicine man had stood before him
in the woods, soaking wet, as if he'd just emerged from the lake.
Water poured out of his sleeves and dripped from the brim of
his hat. After a moment he had stretched out his hand toward
Lance with a pitiful expression on his face, like someone pleading
for something. As far as Lance knew, there were no photos of
Swamper Caribou. The picture of his brother taken in 1905 was
the closest he was going to get, and this was not the first time
he noticed the similarity between the man in the photo and the
ghost of the missing medicine man. Was it possible that the ghost
was actually some sort of *tangible thought* that arose in his sub-
conscious and that it had simply taken its face from the closest
thing, meaning the photo of his brother? Yet, according to an old
story that Willy Dupree had told, the two brothers had supposedly looked so much alike that shortly after Swamper vanished a

man thought he saw Swamper's ghost, while in reality it was the very much alive brother, Joe Caribou, who was walking about.

The room made him feel depressed. In the weeks following the murder, what had made him think he was any sort of detective? Most discouraging of all was that soon afterward he had started investigating something entirely different, a missing-persons case from 1892. That was so typical of Lance. Had he ever done anything that required him to look forward instead of back? He immediately thought of Jimmy, but didn't it seem like even the boy had started to belong to the past? Part of what once existed, the little family that would never return.

He looked at the archival materials that reached from floor to ceiling. It was true that he loved history—how he felt couldn't be described in any other way. He loved the distinctive feeling of opening a folder, which was like opening a landscape, to see how things used to be. Or driving along a paved road and knowing where the invisible cart road veered to the right and where the Indian cemetery had once been and still was. That was the sort of landscape in which Lance lived. And he couldn't live in any other kind. But when it came to his son, only the future was important. That was why he was doing these things now, such as shamelessly exploiting his niece, Chrissy, and getting her to collaborate in her father's downfall and imprisonment. All so that Jimmy wouldn't grow up and live his life in an atmosphere of secrecy and lies, as Lance had done. That's the stuff we are really made of, he thought. Secrecy and lies.

# 19

THE NEXT AFTERNOON he rang the doorbell of Andy's house. Tammy opened the door. She let out a little squeal that sounded genuine, but Lance couldn't tell whether it was prompted by enthusiasm or alarm.

"Back from Norway?" Her voice quavered slightly.

"A couple of days ago. Can I come in?"

Tammy stepped aside and opened the door wide.

"Andy?" she called over her shoulder. "Your brother's here."

Lance didn't hear anything from inside the house except for some muted but throbbing music coming from Chrissy's room on the second floor. He took off his boots and his heavy jacket and went inside. Andy looked over his shoulder and gave him a quick glance before turning away. Lance sat down on the sofa right across from his brother, who was wearing jeans and an open flannel shirt over the same T-shirt he'd worn when he showed up at the ranger station the day after the murder. The word "baseball" was printed on the front.

"Back from Norway," said Lance before his brother had time to ask.

"We know. Inga called to tell us," shouted Tammy from the kitchen, where the teakettle had already begun to whistle. Her famous instant coffee was coming right up.

Andy merely sat there, looking at his brother with a trace of that scornful smile on his lips. Lance was suddenly filled with a feeling of solidarity toward his younger brother. No one else was allowed to enter the space that contained the ongoing, silent dialogue between the two of them. It had always been that way, but lately the conversation dealt with murder and guilt and a prison sentence for life.

"So how was it over there?" asked Andy at last.

"Well, er . . ."

"Just like here?"

"More or less," said Lance.

"Not especially warm people, from what I've heard."

"About like us."

"Right," said Andy.

Tammy came in with three steaming mugs, which she set on the coffee table.

"Have you gone out to see Inga?" she asked.

"Going to do that later today."

"She sounded so happy to have you back."

"Uh-huh. She said it's been pretty quiet while I was gone."

Tammy made sure there was ample space between her and her brother-in-law as she sat down on the sofa and crossed her long legs. Lance remembered that she had actually been quite an attractive girl when she was young.

"What a winter," he said.

Tammy sighed in agreement.

"Didn't think you would have noticed," said Andy. "I mean, because you haven't been here since November."

"The winter was exactly the same over there. Just as cold."

"It sounds like you could have just as well taken your vacation on the Range, huh?" said Andy.

"Not really the same thing, you know."

"Oh, right. Because you got to meet the relatives."

"Actually, I didn't. The roads were closed."

"The roads were closed?" Andy feigned surprise.

"The roads to the west coast. Because of all the snow."

"What rotten luck," said his brother.

"Yeah." This wasn't how Lance had imagined things. He'd pictured making use of the surprise factor to go on the offensive and unsettle his brother. That was what he liked least about

Andy's brief visit—that he'd been caught off guard. But now it turned out not to be as easy as he'd thought to regain the initiative Andy had seized by being the first to put in an appearance.

"Do you remember that we talked about your baseball bat when we were out hunting?" he said in a new attempt to take the upper hand.

"Not that bullshit again," said Andy, sounding resigned.

"What?" asked Tammy, looking curious.

"Oh, just that I no longer have a bat, but I was thinking of hitting a few balls with Jimmy. So I asked Andy if I could borrow his, but apparently he *forgot* it somewhere."

"I know where it is," said Tammy, getting to her feet.

"No, you don't," Andy protested.

"Yes, I do. It's in the garage, where it's always been."

"Good Lord, who plays baseball in the middle of winter, anyway?" Andy was obviously annoyed.

"But he can still borrow your bat, can't he?"

Tammy left the room, and they heard the front door slam behind her. Then it was just the two of them, like it was on that Sunday in November.

"Do you think she'll find it?" asked Lance.

"No."

"Why not?"

"Is that why you tried to kill me?" said Andy. "Because of the baseball bat?"

"It was an accident."

"I know what I saw. You were aiming at me."

*"You're a dead man, Lance,"* he said, mimicking what Andy had said.

"I will defend everything that is mine. If that means I have to kill you, then I will," said Andy.

Lance reached out his hand to pick up his coffee mug and held it to his lips, blowing on the hot liquid. He peered at Andy and blew on the coffee again before taking a noisy sip. Then he set the mug back on the table. The whole time Andy kept his eyes fixed on Lance, as if expecting his brother to slosh the coffee onto the table because his hand was shaking, or in some other way reveal his nervousness. But instead Lance carried out a series of one-hundred-percent controlled movements under his brother's intense stare. When he was done, he leaned back against the sofa and looked at Andy. As if in another world, they heard the front door open and close. Tammy huffed and puffed as she bent down to take off her boots in the hall.

"You know what?" she said to Andy when she came in. "It's gone. Where could it be?"

Lance raised his eyebrows and gave his brother an inquiring look.

"Somebody must have taken it," mumbled Andy.

"Taken it?" Tammy seemed genuinely surprised. "But nobody else knows where you keep it."

At that moment Chrissy appeared in the doorway. Dressed in gray jogging pants and a yellow T-shirt, she looked more like the niece Lance remembered. She wasn't even wearing any makeup. Her hair was the only reminder of the Goth girl that he'd seen lately. And the brown contact lenses. He was positive that she hadn't heard any of their conversation about the bat.

"Oh. Hi, Uncle Lance," she said in surprise.

"Hi, Chrissy."

"Back from Norway?"

"Uh-huh."

"By the way," she said. "There's something I want to show you. Wait here."

They heard her bounding upstairs, as if she were ten again. None of them spoke as they waited. After a few seconds they heard her come running back down, and then she was standing there holding Clayton Miller's book. She handed it to her uncle.

"Do you remember him?" she said. "Apparently you guys both went to Central High at the same time."

Lance pretended to study the photograph on the back cover as he thought about her question.

"Clayton Miller," he said. "You're right. There was a boy who . . . Wait a minute! Hey, Andy, wasn't he the kid who knitted his own scarves?"

"Dad couldn't stand him," said Chrissy before her father managed to say anything.

"Really?" Lance looked at Andy in surprise. "I didn't know you knew each other."

"I didn't. But there was something sort of disgusting about him, something *girlish.*"

"So being a girl is disgusting?" said Chrissy.

"Only for menfolk," replied Andy.

She sat down on the sofa between her mother and Lance. She smelled of smoke. Lance thought her parents had to be aware of it, but clearly they didn't care. Had they simply given up on her? Could it be that the little he'd seen, for example, when he visited the Kozy Bar, was only the tip of the iceberg? He'd confided so much in her lately, and now he was suddenly afraid of what she might tell her parents. For instance, the story he'd told about Andy and Clayton Miller, although Chrissy didn't know it was about her father. Not to mention the two boys who had seen a bloodstained man with a baseball bat standing at the side of the road on the night of the murder. If it really was Andy they'd seen, what would he do if he found out?

"It's nice to be together once in a while," said Tammy. "As a family. It happens all too seldom."

Chrissy made a face.

"Your mother's right," said Andy. "In difficult times, family members are the only ones you can count on, unconditionally. Right, Lance?"

Lance nodded.

"My dear brother knows that only too well," Andy went on. "But even in this case, he's strongest *in theory.*"

"Andy," warned Tammy in a low voice.

"You're quite right, sweetheart. We should all be friends. Lance and I are brothers, after all. We still go out deer hunting together, for instance. I'm already looking forward to next year."

Lance stood up.

"I think I'd better be going," he said. "I'm planning to drive to Duluth to visit Mom. Guess it's been awhile since she had any visitors. Not since I went out to see her. Hope you all have a good day."

Chrissy and Tammy stood up too, but Andy didn't move.

"Could I go with you?" asked Chrissy.

"You're staying here," snapped Andy.

"But Dad . . ."

"Go upstairs to your room!"

"Honestly, Andy," protested Tammy.

Andy jumped to his feet, and for a moment Lance thought he was going to hit his wife. Instead, he grabbed Chrissy by the neck of her T-shirt and twisted the fabric.

"Go. Up. To. Your. Room."

He carefully enunciated each word in an icy voice. Chrissy's face crumpled, and she started breathing hard. Lance didn't know what to do, but Andy abruptly released his hold on his daughter, and she stormed upstairs. Her sobs could be heard through the whole house.

Lance, Andy, and Tammy were standing uncomfortably close to each other.

Tammy opened her mouth to say something but refrained when Andy looked at her. Then he turned on his heel and left the room. Lance and Tammy listened to the sound of him putting on his boots and jacket in the hall. The front door opened and closed, a car door slammed, and the engine raced a few times before they heard him drive off.

Lance hadn't said a word or lifted a finger during the whole scene.

"What was that all about?" he asked.

Tammy sank onto the sofa. She was sniffling.

"Is he abusive?"

She shook her head.

"But Chrissy just asked if she could . . ."

"Exactly," said Tammy. "Chrissy. He's completely crazy when it comes to that girl. Won't even let her leave the house anymore."

"Do you know why?"

"It started with the murder at Baraga's Cross. At first I could understand it; I even agreed with him. A murderer was on the loose, you know? But the suspect was arrested long ago. Wasn't he?"

"Yeah."

"And he's in jail?"

"Uh-huh," said Lance.

"And they've got the right man?"

"I'm sure they do."

"But Andy refuses to let Chrissy go anywhere alone. Or even with you. And all she was going to do was visit her grandmother!"

"But she's been . . ."

Lance was just about to say that Chrissy had already been out with him the past few days, but he stopped himself in time.

"You mean she spends all her time up in her room?" he asked.

"I try to let her go out now and then. But it's sheer hell every time. Like a few days ago, when she went to a poetry reading in Duluth. I mean, *poetry?* Who the hell worries about his daughter listening to poetry? That's like saying that he's scared she'll die of boredom. Andy had a fit when I told him. Sat up and waited for her to come home. She had that book with her, by that . . . I can't remember his name. The guy who went to high school with the two of you."

"How did Andy react to that?"

"To what?"

"The book by Clayton Miller."

"Why should he react at all?" asked Tammy, surprised.

"I don't know."

"No, Chrissy is the only thing on his mind. As if his sole purpose in life is to protect her. It's not healthy," she said.

# 20

INSTEAD OF DRIVING STRAIGHT TO DULUTH to visit his mother, as he'd planned, Lance headed north again. When he reached the turnoff for Baraga Cross Road, he exited the highway and drove down to the parking lot, where he stopped the car and got out. It was early afternoon, but the sun was already low in the sky. He put on the snowshoes he'd bought in Ely, climbed over the snowbank, and headed into the birch forest. After a few minutes he caught sight of the cross between the tree trunks. In the deep snow it looked shorter than he remembered, but that didn't make it any less impressive. It seemed as if all lines in the landscape met at the juncture of those two axes. Lance went over to the cross, took off his right glove, and pressed the palm of his hand against the ice-cold granite. He'd imagined that he'd feel something, some sort of contact with the cross and this place, but all he felt was the cold. He could hear muted, hollow sounds coming from rippling water. At this point the Cross River flowed into the lake, but not even a drop of water was visible.

The expanse of rocks sloping down toward the lake was covered in a thick snowdrift, but only the very top layer was loose and powdery. The snow underneath was packed solid and able to bear Lance's weight, as long as it was evenly distributed on the long snowshoes that he wore. Without looking back, he kept walking.

After a while he noticed that the ground underfoot began

to change. Bluish-gray ice seemed to stretch out forever in front of him, broken only by long, windswept streaks of snow, which indicated the direction in which the wind usually blew out here. The ice itself was not a uniform color, varying instead between a cold gray, which comprised most of the ice, to patches of a darker gray tone; that was the ice that scared him a bit. He couldn't possibly be in any danger, since the temp had hovered around minus twenty for several weeks, and the entire lake was frozen over. Yet there was something about those darker patches that gave him a feeling that he was uncomfortably close to the water and its vast depths.

Lance took off the snowshoes, carrying them as he continued on. With only his boots on his feet, it felt like walking across a parquet floor, even on the darker spots. But they still scared him. In an attempt to conquer his fear, he stopped on a dark patch and proceeded to jump up and down. Each time he landed, the ice emitted a sound, as if a giant were flicking his finger at a delicate crystal glass. A clear, resonating tone that shot across the ice and disappeared. He knelt down on the snowshoes and then leaned forward to press his forehead to the ice. How thick could it be? Probably no more than one or two feet of ice separated him from the dark embrace of Lake Superior. Wearing these clothes and heavy boots, he would sink slowly but irrevocably down through the water until his lifeless body ended up on the bottom. Wasn't that how it would happen? Or did a corpse float back up to the surface after only a short time? In that case, he would ram the ice overhead and then sink down again. In the long run, he would undoubtedly lie on the bottom. What did it look like down there? Old trees, perhaps; the thick trunks of pine trees from long before the first white settlers arrived here. Giants that were thousands of years old, dark and sleek, well preserved in the nutrient-stripped water of the lake. And among the ancient trees the forest's sheriff.

It was the cold that finally forced him back on his feet. When he turned around, a gleeful shiver passed through his body. He couldn't see where the white lake met the white land—everything was white. But he could glimpse the cross like a tiny dark speck amid all the white. With some reluctance he started back toward the cross.

# 21

SHE COULD PHONE, but that would give the impression that she was desperate for a visit, and she wasn't. Her biggest concern was whether he was all right. Something was making her uneasy, though she couldn't put her finger on what it was. Just that it had something to do with Lance.

She put down her knitting and slowly stood up, her knees aching. Then she went out to the corridor. Lakeview Nursing Home was a place for senior citizens who had good health insurance, for instance, from the retirement package of a deceased spouse. So it was no accident that the widows of four police officers lived here. This was the place for those who could no longer live in their own homes, or who chose not to. Inga Hansen was not one of the residents who *had to* live here; she had chosen to move in instead of continuing to live alone with her bad knees in the big house on Fifth Avenue.

A staff member waved to her from the kitchen as she passed the open doorway. From the smell she knew they would be having fish for dinner. The food at Lakeview was good, and she didn't have to cook for herself. All her adult life she'd cooked meals for the three hungry men in her family at least three times each day, while she herself had barely had time to sit down and take a few bites before she had to clear the table and do the dishes. So why would she want more of the same in her old age? No, she was not about to make even a sandwich unless she absolutely had to.

At the end of the long corridor she paused under the portrait of Albert Ringstrom, the founder of Lakeview. Why exactly was she out here in the hall? This happened to her frequently. Here she stood again, with no idea where she was going. Had she intended to take a walk? No, that couldn't be it. She wasn't dressed for the wintry cold.

Not wanting to draw attention, she continued a bit hesitantly to the next corridor leading to the other wing of the building, which she rarely visited. She had the impression that those who lived there were in failing health and would no longer be venturing anywhere at all. While she herself . . . well, where exactly was she going? She had no reason to be in this part of the building, at any rate. Even so, she continued her slow plodding along the deserted corridor. Here too she could smell dinner, but where was the kitchen? She felt like she was on a little field trip and wished she could find someone to talk to, preferably the kitchen staff. But all the doors she passed were closed, and she couldn't bring herself to open any of them.

Finally she caught sight of a door that was ajar. Maybe there was someone in there she could talk to. It would be nice to sit down and have a cup of coffee. But when she went over to the door, she saw that it led to yet another corridor. The smell of food seemed to be coming from there, so that meant there had to be people around. Inga walked down the next corridor, which looked exactly like all the others. The same green linoleum that always felt a bit sticky under the soles of her shoes and made a faint sound every time she lifted her feet. And here was the same portrait of Albert Ringstrom.

Her knees were starting to ache again; it didn't take much for them to give her trouble. Suddenly she realized that she had an acute need to sit down, but there wasn't so much as a straight-backed chair in the long corridor, and the closed doors were no help either. She didn't want to intrude on someone else's private space.

Why had she started on this long walk in the first place? Something about Lance? She'd been thinking about him right before she left her room; she was sure about that. She didn't need to use the toilet, did she? She paused for a moment. No, everything was fine. Regardless of the reason, she was standing halfway along a corridor that she'd never seen before, although it was identical to the one outside her own room. And her knees were hurting so bad that she couldn't even imagine making it back to her room without first taking a rest.

She stopped outside a door and looked around, but there was no one in sight. Then she hesitantly lifted her hand and knocked. No response from inside. Again she knocked, as loudly as she dared, but still nothing happened. Slowly Inga pressed down the handle and opened the door.

It was a janitor's closet. She was so relieved to find the room deserted, but with the comforting smell of soap and scouring powder. She was surrounded by brooms, mops, plastic buckets, rubber gloves, scrub brushes, and dust rags. She found the wall switch and turned on the light. Then she closed the door, and she was alone in the small space. In a corner stood a single stool that the cleaning lady probably used when she needed to take a break. Inga went over and finally was able to sit down and rest.

She leaned against the wall and closed her eyes.

# 22

THE NEXT DAY in between classes Chrissy phoned Lance to ask whether they could drive to Grand Portage and visit "Jimmy's grandfather," as she called him.

"Do you know Willy?" asked Lance.

"Do I have to know him if I want to talk to him?"

"No."

"Good. But it's a little hard for me to get away. I mean, you saw for yourself what things are like."

Lance could hear that she was on the verge of tears.

"Yeah. Not the best situation."

"I told them I've got dance practice at school tonight."

"Wouldn't you rather go see Jimmy and Mary if you're planning to go to Grand Portage?"

"No."

"But why Willy?"

"I've thought a lot about what you said about my great-great-grandmother. That she was Ojibwe."

"And what did that make you think about?" he asked.

"Just that I'd like to talk to someone who's Ojibwe," said Chrissy.

"I've already told him about it, and he wasn't particularly interested. It's pretty common up here."

"Oh, okay." She sounded disappointed.

"But of course we could still take a drive and go visit him," Lance hurried to say.

"Really?"

"Sure. Shall I pick you up in Two Harbors?"

WHEN THEY PASSED SILVER CLIFF, which was where he'd seen Swamper Caribou for the first time, Lance reached across his niece to open the glove compartment. There lay the gun. Without comment, he took out two little heart-shaped chocolates and then closed the glove compartment. Chrissy's expression didn't change. Maybe she hadn't noticed the gun, or maybe she thought it was normal for a forest cop to be armed, even when driving his own car.

"Want a chocolate?" he asked.

"Dove?"

They both took off the foil wrappers that covered the chocolate hearts.

"You have to read what it says inside," Lance told her.

She smoothed out the foil and looked at the words.

"Oh, right," she snorted.

"What does it say?"

" 'A smile is the best workout.' "

Lance looked at the deathly pale girl with the black makeup and laughed.

"Cute," she said. "So, what does yours say?"

He held up the foil wrapper but had to read the small text several times before he could make out the words.

"What does it say?" his niece asked again.

"It says, 'Love is for those who are tough.' "

Chrissy tried to suppress a giggle.

Lance sank into his own thoughts. If Andy really was the murderer, why would he be afraid to let Chrissy go out alone? It didn't make sense. According to Tammy, her husband's protective behavior had started when the body was discovered near Baraga's Cross. And she couldn't fathom why he was still acting like that after the killer was arrested. If Andy merely wished to protect his daughter from a murderer on the loose, it would mean two things. Number one: Andy couldn't possibly be the killer. And two: He had to be aware that Lenny Diver wasn't either. But Lance couldn't convince himself of this. There had to be another reason why Andy would hardly let Chrissy leave the house anymore. Then Lance remembered that father and daughter had come home together in the afternoon on the day after the murder. Andy had picked up Chrissy at the home of a girlfriend in Duluth, yet Chrissy had said that she'd spent the night of the murder at the cabin on Lost Lake. Maybe she'd gone back to Duluth with her friend the next day, so that Andy could pick her up as agreed, without realizing that the girls had spent the night somewhere else. That seemed plausible. And that would also mean that Andy thought it was okay to lie about having been at the cabin. Lance based all of these speculations on information that he'd gleaned from Tammy. He believed her because she was the only one of the three who had been home on the night of the murder. What Lance hadn't thought about before was that he had to take her word for it.

"All that stuff yesterday with Andy," said Lance. "What was that about, really?"

Chrissy uttered a sound that was a combination of a sigh and a whimper.

"Dad is fucking crazy," she said through clenched teeth. "He won't let me do anything. I've got no freedom at all. It's like living in a prison."

"But you've gone out driving with me."

"That's because he was away, or because Mom had a huge argument with him first, like when we went to the poetry reading the other night."

"So Andy didn't want to let you go to the reading either?"

"If it were up to Dad, I'd spend the whole time sitting in my room."

"But why is he acting this way?"

"God, it's so stupid."

"You don't want to talk about it?"

"He thinks I'm running around with boys."

"Well, aren't you? You're seventeen, after all."

"He's thinks I'm the kind of girl who . . ."

"What?"

"He thinks I'm a whore!" she shouted and then hid her face in her hands.

"Now come on, honey," said Lance, shocked. "What are you talking about?"

Chrissy began sobbing, and the sound was heartrending. After a moment it became almost a wail. When Lance saw a parking space, he pulled off the road and stopped. Then he got out of the car, just to get away from the howling. He quickly realized that they were at exactly the same place where he and Inga had stopped last summer. That time he'd seen Swamper Caribou sitting at the water's edge, wearing the worn, round hat on his head, with his knees tucked up under his chin. That was the second time Lance saw him. The medicine man had sat there, staring across the Kitchi-Gami, the Big Water, as the lake was called in his language.

Lance couldn't imagine that it would ever be summer again. Winter no longer felt like a season of the year but rather a place from which he could never escape.

Lance heard Chrissy open the car door and come toward him across the creaking snow. For a moment they stood side by side, looking straight ahead without saying a word. He thought about all the times he had played with his niece when she was little. Chrissy had been the closest he'd come to having a child until Jimmy was born.

"How I hate it," she said quietly.

"What?"

"All this."

Her small voice defied the vast space around them.

# 23

LANCE WAS EATING A COOKIE that reminded him of Jimmy's first year and the sweet smell of his hair.

"Here, have something to drink," said Willy, pouring Coke into the only glass on the table.

Chrissy gave him a strained smile and took a sip. Lance saw her looking at the old dream catcher that hung underneath the photos of Willy Dupree's parents.

"A dream catcher," said Willy.

She blushed, as if caught in the act.

"It was made more than a hundred years ago, for a little child who wasn't sleeping well," Willy explained. "And it's been in the family ever since."

"One of the things that gave Nanette's Ojibwe heritage away was the fact that she made a dream catcher for Thormod Olson," said Lance. "He was having nightmares and screaming so loud that the children couldn't sleep. So she made an asa . . . asabi . . ."

"Asabikeshiinh," said Willy. "A web spun to catch bad dreams."

"Does it work?" asked Chrissy.

"What do you think?" Willy challenged her.

"Me?"

"Yes, you."

Chrissy paused to consider.

"I think it does."

"Why's that?" asked Lance.

"That's just what I think."

Lance wondered whether Willy actually believed in such things: dream catchers, the Big Dream, the ghost of Swamper Caribou . . . although the latter was something Lance himself believed in. Or did he? Well, he believed Andy was gay, so why not believe in ghosts?

"Oh, how I wish I had a dream catcher," exclaimed Chrissy. Her shyness seemed to have vanished. "Not one of those trashy things that tourists buy, but one that—"

"One that works?" said Willy.

"Uh-huh. Does anyone still make real ones?" she asked eagerly.

"There are still some people who live according to the old beliefs. I'm sure I could get you a real dream catcher if you really want one."

"What do you mean by a real one?" asked Lance.

"One that's made by someone who has contact with the spirit world."

Lance gave his ex-father-in-law a skeptical look.

"Or who at least thinks he does," the old man added.

"Would you really do that for me?" Chrissy seemed about to take the old man up on his offer.

"Of course."

"Promise?" she insisted.

"Yes, I promise."

Lance noticed that his niece was looking at Willy with admiration, and it occurred to him that the old man was undoubtedly savoring the situation.

"Do you think it's strange that we have Ojibwe blood?" she asked.

"Well, you have beautiful Indian eyes. But when it comes to Lance, it's a little harder to believe," said the old man, smiling slyly.

"They're just colored contact lenses," said Chrissy. "I actually have blue eyes, like Lance."

"Why did you decide to change the color?" asked Willy.

Chrissy looked down, as if embarrassed.

"I don't want to talk about it."

"Oh. All right."

"But I have a good reason. A very good reason," she hurried to add.

"What did Andy and Tammy say when you came home wearing brown contacts?" asked Lance.

Chrissy rolled her eyes.

"I'm sure you can imagine. Dad went ballistic."

"But you stood your ground?" said Lance.

"Yup."

Willy and Lance both laughed.

"Have some more Coke," said Willy.

Lance wondered why Chrissy had asked him to drive her up here. There must be something particular she wanted to talk to Willy about. Or did she just want to meet him?

"But what does it really mean to be part Ojibwe?" Chrissy asked as she dutifully took another sip of her Coke.

"I don't think I know. At least not any more than you do," replied Willy.

"It's not like we can be members of the tribe, or whatever it's called. Right?"

Willy chuckled.

"I'm afraid that would require a little more than a great-great-grandmother. But that doesn't make your ancestry any less important. Your Ojibwe great-great-grandmother is just as much a part of you as your other great-great-grandparents. Or just as little. But what it does mean is that you come from a people who were here long before the whites arrived. So it's up to you to decide what to do with that knowledge. It means whatever you choose to make it mean."

"But where I come from . . . ," said Chrissy. "Two Harbors. It's not someplace where you can really belong. So I was thinking that maybe . . ."

"That you could belong here?" Willy finished her sentence for her.

She nodded.

"Don't be sad if you feel like you don't belong. That just means that your opportunities are elsewhere. Maybe you're one of those people who creates her own world as she goes along. Otter Heart was like that. Have you heard of him?"

Lance and Chrissy both shook their heads.

"Otter Heart was a young man who plays a role in lots of stories," said Willy. "He's always traveling, and new worlds appear along the way. I remember a story my mother used to tell me when I was a boy. It was about Otter Heart, the great hunter."

Willy sipped at his coffee and settled himself more comfortably in his chair. His eyes took on a distant look, as if he were listening to his mother's voice.

"One day Otter Heart was out on a long hunting expedition in the woods to the northwest," he began. "That night, while he slept, wrapped in his blanket under the stars, he dreamed that he had a wife and a son, and that his life with them was the best life any Indian could have. When he woke up, he was happier than he'd ever been before. But that lasted only a few seconds. Then he realized that what had seemed like an entire lifetime had been only a dream. Because that's how some dreams are. Right?"

Lance thought he noticed Chrissy's lip quivering slightly, but it was so faint that he couldn't be sure. He wondered whether Willy was telling this story especially for her.

"All day long Otter Heart walked around with a heavy heart because he would never again see his wife from the dream," Willy went on. "As dusk fell, he came to a beaver dam where he killed two grown beavers and a baby, but even that didn't put him in a better mood. Then he noticed the smell of smoke. If there was a campfire, there would be other Indians. And after a while he came to a birchbark teepee with smoke swirling out of the vent at the top. Otter Heart didn't know who lived there. It might be an evil sorcerer, for all he knew, so he crept over to the teepee to look through a crack. Inside sat a young woman doing handwork in the light of the fire. Since the situation didn't seem dangerous after all, he made his presence known. It turned out that the woman lived alone, and she welcomed Otter Heart as her guest. She invited him to stay the night but apologized for not having any food to give him since it was difficult for her to get hold of any meat. Then Otter Heart went out and brought back the three beavers that he'd killed earlier in the day. If she would prepare and cook the food, he would make sure there was meat. Then the young woman blushed, because it almost sounded as though they were already man and wife."

At this point Willy winked at Chrissy, whose serious expression didn't change. And now Lance could swear that her lower lip really was quivering slightly.

"And you know what?" Willy looked from Lance to Chrissy. "Now Otter Heart saw that this was the same woman he'd dreamed about the night before. It hadn't taken more than a few hours to find her again in the waking world! He was so happy he asked her right then and there to be his wife, and she nodded and smiled as she sat in the light from the fire. 'What's your name?' he asked, because he hadn't yet learned her name. 'My name is Sad Water,' replied the young woman."

"Sad Water," whispered Chrissy.

"Yes, Sad Water," repeated Willy. "She prepared the beaver meat, but only after first carefully examining the three beavers for a long time. She looked at their eyes and held up the big paddles of their tails to study them. When the food was ready, she made sure Otter Heart ate the biggest and fattiest pieces, which is what a good Indian wife always does for her hunter. She refused to eat any herself, no matter how much he coaxed her. No, she said, she preferred to eat at another time, and he shouldn't mind her. During the night Otter Heart was awakened by some strange noises. It sounded like an animal gnawing on something somewhere inside the teepee. In the faint glow from the fire, he thought he saw Sad Water sitting on the ground, bowed forward and gnawing on several twigs. But when he woke up the next morning, he was sure that he must have dreamed what he saw.

"His young wife served him warm beaver meat for breakfast, but she still refused to eat any herself. When Otter Heart was done eating, he asked her why she had examined the three beavers so thoroughly the night before. 'To make sure they weren't members of my family,' she said. Otter Heart thought he now knew what those gnawing sounds must have been. Sad Water must have turned herself into a beaver. But when he asked her, she said it was more complicated than that. Her father had been a chieftain in a village about a day's journey from there. One day a powerful medicine man had come to the village. The chieftain had had no choice but to invite him in and ask him to spend the night, even though he distrusted him. The medicine man, who was old and very evil, fell in love with Sad Water. He asked the chieftain for permission to marry her. But the young woman's father refused. He would rather die than see his daughter married to such an evil man. As punishment, the medicine man turned the chieftain and his whole family, including Sad Water, into beavers, so that they would be forced to work and toil all their days. For no animal works harder than a beaver."

Willy paused to stuff a cookie in his mouth. Little crumbs sprayed from his mouth as he chewed. Lance tried to make eye contact with his niece, but she had lowered her gaze and refused to look at him, even though Lance felt sure she knew he was staring at her. After finishing the cookie, Willy slowly raised his cup to his lips, his hand shaking, and noisily slurped at his coffee before slowly and unsteadily setting the cup back on the table.

"Well," he said, wiping his mouth on the back of his hand. "Where were we?"

"The evil medicine man had turned the whole family into beavers," said Chrissy quietly, still without raising her eyes.

"Exactly," said Willy. "They settled near a creek, where they built a dam and transformed a marshy area into a big, fine lake. Here they eventually built several beaver lodges. And since they still remembered many of the things they'd learned while they were human, they soon became the most powerful beaver family in the area. They could still speak the human language, and one day a highly respected medicine man came walking past the lake. The beaver father, who was the former chieftain, immediately recognized the man and began talking to him. Since this was a great and mighty medicine man, he was not surprised to meet a beaver that could speak the human language. He had undoubtedly seen these kinds of transformations before. The beaver father asked whether his magic would be strong enough to change them back into humans. But the medicine man said that wasn't something he could do since evil magic had been used, and he himself was not an evil medicine man. But he could give one family member the chance to become human again. 'Oh, then let it be Sad Water!' exclaimed the beaver father. This was fine with the medicine man. He met the little beaver that had once been the chieftain's daughter. He told her that she could become human again, but it would happen only if someone who had never seen her dreamed about her. And now this had finally happened. 'Because you dreamed of me, didn't you?' asked Sad Water.

"'I dreamed that I was married,' replied Otter Heart. 'I had the most beautiful, kindest wife that any Indian ever had. How happy I was! And then I woke up and realized that it was only a dream. This was yesterday. All day I walked along with a terrible ache in my heart. Then I noticed the smell of smoke coming from your tepee. And here we are. Sad Water and Otter Heart.' But Sad Water told him that there was one more stipulation. The medicine man had impressed on her that she must never get any running water on her feet. Rainwater was fine, as was the water she used for cooking. But she must never set foot in a creek or a river. 'I will build a bridge for you over every river we have to cross,' promised Otter Heart. 'And every creek too?' asked Sad Water. 'Yes, every creek too,' he assured her. 'You will always have dry feet. I will make sure of that.'

"Winter came, and they lived happily together. He was a brave hunter and she was an excellent wife, quiet and industrious, the way beavers are. She became accustomed to eating meat again, but she refused to touch beaver meat, and Otter Heart declined to kill any more beavers. In February she gave birth to a son, and on that very day Otter Heart made a bow for the boy. Sad Water shook her head and reminded him that it would be many years before the boy could use the bow. But in his joy at having a son, Otter Heart created one castle in the air after the other, each bigger than the last. Oh, how little it would take for those castles to come tumbling down!"

Willy took another break. Lance had begun to wonder whether this story was intended more for him than for Chrissy. He had married Willy's daughter, after all. The old man gave him an inscrutable look over the rim of his coffee cup, which trembled in his grasp.

"Soon Sad Water decided they ought to pay a visit to her village," Willy said as he set his cup down. "She had many friends there, and everybody knew who she was. She would be able to tell them what had happened to their chieftain and his family. Otter Heart didn't like this idea. They'd been living such a good life in this remote tepee ever since they'd met, and now he feared things would change if they went out into the world and met other people. But no man of sound mind would refuse to visit his wife's friends.

"The day arrived, and they set off, with Otter Heart in the lead. Sad Water followed, carrying their son on her back. Since it was still spring, the creeks and rivers were swollen with meltwater, and the waterfalls and rapids were white with foam. But Otter Heart kept his promise. Each time they came to a creek or a river he would fell some trees and build a bridge so that Sad Water could cross without getting her feet wet. Then, late in the afternoon, as they neared the village, Otter Heart came to what was little more than a watery path, maybe a foot wide. Whether it was because he was lost in his own thoughts or because he simply didn't want to fell another tree for such a small stream . . . whatever the reason, he merely stepped across and continued on as before. Soon he could no longer hear his wife's footsteps or his son's babbling. When he turned around to have a look, the narrow stream had become a wide, frothing river that could not be crossed, and on the opposite bank sat two beavers, one adult and one baby.

"Otter Heart realized at once what must have happened. Tired from walking so far and from carrying the boy on her back, Sad Water had tried to cross the narrow stream, but she stepped in the water and was transformed into a beaver again. The same thing happened to their son, who now sat next to his mother, both of them beavers. This was what the medicine man had warned. Otter Heart called to his wife to swim over to him. Then he would find another medicine man who could change them back into humans. But his wife replied that the only one who was powerful enough was the evil medicine man who wanted to marry her. But she would rather live her life as a beaver. 'There was only one thing I asked of you,' she then said. 'I asked you to build a bridge for me over every creek and river so that I would never get my feet wet. But you couldn't do even that simple thing for me. From now on, the little one and I will live in the deep rivers and the shallow creeks.' And the two beavers slid into the river and disappeared underwater while Otter Heart shouted his despair."

IT WAS LATE by the time they drove back south. Lance persuaded Chrissy to phone home and say that her dance practice had been delayed because the instructor's car had refused to start in the cold. He was careful to emphasize that she shouldn't tell her parents she was with him. He thought Andy was the one who answered the phone. It was impossible to make out his words, but the harsh, annoyed voice was unmistakable.

"Good God, I said I'd be home in an hour."

Chrissy groaned as she stuck her cell back in her jacket pocket.

"He thinks I'm with some guy," she sighed.

"Oh?" Lance was genuinely surprised.

"Just because I put on makeup and dress the way I do," she went on. "But you know what? I've only had one boyfriend, and what I miss most is holding someone's hand."

"Lots of people miss that," said Lance.

"You too?"

"Sure."

"Do you miss Mary?"

"I don't think this is a topic the two of us need to discuss right now."

"You mean love?" said Chrissy.

"Uh-huh."

"Isn't it the most important topic of all?"

"But you're my *niece*."

"So what?"

"My seventeen-year-old niece."

"Almost eighteen."

"Regardless, it's not appropriate," said Lance.

"You know what I think, Uncle Lance?"

"No. What?"

"I think you're scared."

"Scared of what?"

"Scared of girls."

Lance laughed loudly, but he could hear how false it sounded. In the uncomfortable silence that followed, he sensed that Chrissy was sitting there in the dim light with a triumphant little smile on her face. He tried to come up with something that would put her in her place, but suddenly all he could think of was girls.

Just after they'd passed through Grand Marais, his cell phone rang. Lance felt his anxiety rise like an ice-cold wave as the man on the other end of the line said he was calling from the Lakeview Nursing Home in Duluth.

"Is something wrong?" Lance hurried to ask.

"Nothing serious. Just the fact that your mother set off on a little expedition last night and went missing."

"What are you saying?"

"Well, we found her after a while. It turned out that she'd gone into a janitor's closet."

"What was she doing in there?"

"That's the question," said the man.

"Is she all right?"

"She's fine. But when we found her she was a little confused."

"And this happened yesterday?"

"Yes. Yesterday evening."

"So why didn't you call me before?" said Lance.

"It was an oversight on the part of a staff member. You should have been notified earlier today. I apologize."

"Okay. I'll drive down to visit her tomorrow."

"That would be good. I'll let her know that you're coming."

"But she's all right now?"

"Oh, yes. It was just a temporary confusion."

Chrissy didn't say anything when Lance ended the call. He allowed a few minutes to pass before he spoke again.

"That was Lakeview," he said. "Apparently Inga decided to hide in a janitor's closet."

Chrissy burst out laughing but quickly regained her composure.

"So is everything okay with her now?" she asked.

"Yeah."

"What really happened?"

"A temporary confusion, they said. Probably nothing to worry about."

# 24

AT THE TOFTE RANGER STATION everything was the same as always. Up near the ceiling the same bald eagle floated from its invisible strings, the big wolf over by the public entrance still had its tongue hanging out of its mouth, and the receptionist, Mary Berglund, had set the usual paper cup of coffee on the counter in front of Lance.

"Did you go to Haugesund?" was the first thing she wanted to know.

He shook his head.

"My great-grandfather came from there. The one who drowned, you know."

"He drowned?" said Lance.

"Uh-huh."

"I didn't know that."

"He fell overboard and drowned in Lake Superior during a storm. I'd like to see Haugesund someday."

"Me too," said Lance with a sigh.

"When are you coming back to work?"

"I'm not really sure. That's what I was planning to talk to Zimmermann about."

"He should be here any minute. He said he just had to make a quick stop at the post office."

"There he is," said Lance.

Through the window they saw John Zimmermann park

under the big birch, and shortly after he was standing in front of them.

"Lance Hansen," he said in surprise.

Lance smiled.

"Rested and ready for work?"

"Well . . ."

"Come into my office and we'll have a chat, okay?"

SITTING FOR THE FIRST TIME IN AGES under the big map on the wall of District Ranger Zimmermann's office, Lance felt a strong urge to pretend that nothing had changed. As far as he could see, his ruse hadn't been discovered. The only people who knew he hadn't been in Norway were Willy and Chrissy, and he could probably rely on both of them not to tell. So if he could just manage to put certain items out of his mind, things could go back to the way they were before. For the most part. It wasn't too late. Maybe not even with regard to Debbie. Suddenly he felt like he had a whole life ahead of him, and all he needed to do was forget. In theory this was entirely possible. His family had spent a century perfecting the art of forgetting—that was proof enough. But Lance had become someone else during the seven months that had passed since he found the body of Georg Lofthus.

"So . . ." Zimmermann fumbled with a stack of papers. "When were you thinking of coming back to work?"

"Not quite yet," replied Lance.

"But you've been out for—"

"I haven't been out. I've been on vacation. Vacation days that I've been saving up for years. And I'll use as many of them as I like."

Lance wasn't sure where that self-confident tone of voice had come from.

"Excuse me," Zimmermann ventured.

"No, excuse *me*—" Lance interrupted him as he stood up. "There are actually a few things that I need to be doing. Even though I'm still on vacation."

"You could at least tell me when you plan to be back on the job," said the ranger.

Lance paused to consider.

"When I'm ready," he replied, and then walked out.

HE'D LEFT HIS CELL PHONE IN THE CAR. When he was about to drive out of the parking lot in front of the ranger station, he saw that he'd received a call from Andy's landline.

He called back, and Tammy answered at once.

"What's going on?" asked Lance.

"Chrissy has disappeared," she said, out of breath.

"What do mean 'disappeared'?"

"When we got up, she was gone. The front door was unlocked. She must have left sometime during the night."

Lance tried to remember if he'd noticed anything special when he dropped her off at the gas station shortly after ten o'clock last night. But she'd immediately started walking home, and he couldn't recall seeing anyone else around.

"Did she go out yesterday?" he asked.

"Only to dance practice at school."

"When did she get home?"

"Ten fifteen, I think."

"Have you tried calling her cell?"

"Of course, but it's turned off. And that's not like Chrissy at all. Oh, I'm so scared!"

"Do you want me to get the police to search for her?" Lance suggested.

"No."

"She's probably just gone to see a girlfriend."

"In the middle of the night? When it's twenty below?" shouted Tammy desperately.

"Hmm . . ."

"You've got to find her for me."

"I'll do what I can, but if she doesn't show up sometime today, we'll need to search for her."

"No," Tammy again protested.

"But you must realize we need to do that," said Lance.

"Just find her," she pleaded.

THE FIRST THING he did after taking off his jacket was to try Chrissy's cell number, but a voice told him that the phone was either turned off or located in an area with no coverage. The latter was unlikely, since that would mean she'd have to be in the woods, far away from people. She'd probably switched off her phone in order not to get any calls. But he thought sooner or later she'd turn it back on to check for text messages.

"Call me if you want to talk. I won't tell anyone what you say," he texted and pressed "send." Then he sat down to wait for her to reply, but only a few minutes later he realized how hopeless that was. And he couldn't just sit here all day. He had to go to Lakeview to find out how his mother was doing.

Once again he got into the car and headed south, this time driving past the ranger station. As he passed the turnoff to Baraga Cross Road, he thought about Andy's voice shouting on Chrissy's cell last night. How angry he'd sounded. And Lance remembered what Chrissy had said afterward: "One day I think he's going to kill me." She must have reached a point where she couldn't stand things anymore. So instead of putting up with more accusations and the constant reprimands, she'd called one of her girlfriends and asked her to pick her up someplace nearby. Then they'd either driven over to the friend's house or gone to see someone else Chrissy trusted. Considering the world he was driving through, which was glittering white and almost unbearably cold, maybe he should have been more worried about his niece. But he didn't believe that Chrissy would have wandered off in the cold alone, without any plans. He was fairly certain that she was either in Duluth or Two Harbors. If he wasn't able to get hold of her sometime during the day, he would have to instigate a police search, after all.

When he reached Two Harbors, he decided to stop and have a talk with Tammy. Maybe she knew more than she'd said on the phone.

Lance rang the bell, and his sister-in-law promptly opened the door.

"Did you find her?" she asked hopefully.

"No, but I don't think there's any reason to worry."

Her face fell.

They went into the living room, and before Lance even sat down, Tammy had lit a cigarette. He could tell by the smell that she'd been sitting here alone, smoking and worrying about her daughter for most of the morning, while Andy, as usual, was chopping down timber somewhere in the Superior National Forest.

"So," said Lance as he sat down in an easy chair. "You haven't heard from her either?"

Tammy merely shook her head, her face lined with worry. She looked like someone who had seen very little of the world, and yet had seen more than enough.

"I'm sure she's staying with a girlfriend," he said, trying to reassure her.

"I hope you're right."

Lance waved away the smoke as discreetly as he could.

"Did anything special happen when she came home last night?" he asked.

Tammy lowered her eyes so fast that he knew he'd struck a chord.

"Yes. There was an incident."

"They had a fight?"

"She came home a lot later than she was supposed to. Something about the dance teacher having car trouble, or something. Andy went through the roof and grabbed hold of Chrissy."

"How hard?"

"Hard."

"Did he hit her?"

"No, but she's probably got bruises today."

Tammy buried her face in her hands and burst into tears. Lance didn't know what to do. He couldn't just sit here and do nothing. Finally he stood up, went around the coffee table, and sat down next to her on the sofa. He put out the cigarette that she'd dropped into the ashtray.

"Tammy," he said. "You can tell me what's wrong. Don't cry."

He tentatively placed his hand on her bowed back.

"There, there," he murmured, hesitantly stroking her back.

"Oh, God," Tammy managed to say between sobs.

Lance didn't know what else to do, so he kept on patting her back. She was wearing a thin sweater, and through the material he could clearly see her bra straps.

"There, there," he said again. Sitting so close to her made his voice husky with desire.

Tammy had started to lean toward him so that she was practically lying in his lap, with her head pressed against his chest. Lance put his arms around her thin torso and pulled her close. He felt something inside her dissolving and softening. Without thinking he ran his hand over her hair, and when she didn't say anything, he kept on doing that, slowly and calmly as he noticed her breathing change, and he felt an urge to hold her even tighter.

Then she abruptly sat up.

"What a life," she sniffled and went out to the kitchen. Lance could hear her tear off a paper towel to blow her nose.

It had been years since he'd held someone so close, and he was still feeling dizzy.

"When's Andy due back?" he asked.

Silence in the kitchen. Then she appeared in the doorway, red-eyed and pale.

"Why?"

"Somebody has to talk to him."

"What do you mean?"

"About the way he's been treating Chrissy."

"Don't you think I've tried?"

"Someone else, I mean. And I guess I'm the most likely person to do it."

"I'm not sure that's such a good idea, Lance."

"Is it better just to let things go on like this?"

Tammy closed her swollen eyes and sighed.


THE FIRST THING Lance did when he got to Duluth was go to the Kozy Bar, which had just opened. Not that he had any real hope of finding his niece there so early in the day, but if he stayed for a while, maybe she'd show up.

He ordered a Mesabi Red from the same bartender as last time and then sat down at the same corner table. The only other customer was a woman about Lance's age who was sitting at the very end of the bar. She was a platinum blonde, wearing faded jeans. Lance sincerely hoped that she wouldn't come over and join him, so he avoided looking in her direction.

As soon as he'd taken the first sip, he realized that it was too early in the day, even for Mesabi Red. He pushed the glass away and thought about what had happened with Tammy. Had anything really happened? Other than the fact that she'd started to cry and he'd tried to comfort her? He didn't even like her. He never had. But when she leaned against him like that . . .

Suddenly it wasn't too early after all. He took a long swig of beer. Tammy Hansen. Good Lord. Or Tammy Swenson, as she was called before she got married. That skinny, cranky woman. He drank more beer and thought with horror about how wrong things could have gone, there on the sofa. At the same time he wished it had happened. No, no. Not with Tammy!

Just then he heard the sound of a text message arriving. It was from Chrissy. "Everything's OK. Just needed to get away." Lance called her at once.

"Hi, Uncle Lance," she said, sounding guilty.

"Hi. So everything's all right?"

"Yeah."

In the background he could hear voices and traffic.

"Where are you?" he asked.

"With a girlfriend in Duluth."

"But don't you realize Tammy and Andy are upset?"

"They don't care about me."

"Of course they do."

"When I got home last night, Dad was furious. I've got bruises all over. And Mom is too scared to say anything. I don't want to go back home."

"You've got to, Chrissy. You're not eighteen yet, and you can't just run away from home."

"But Uncle Lance, I don't dare live in the same house with Dad. Not the way he is now."

A thought occurred to Lance. As simple and effective as a spear.

"Listen to me," he said. "I can guarantee that Andy will never lay a hand on you again."

"And how can you do that?"

"Just trust me."

"What if he does anyway?"

"He won't."

"But what if?"

"Then I'll help you run away," said Lance, completely serious.

"But how are you going to—?"

"Leave it to me. Just make sure you're back home sometime tonight."

Chrissy paused to think. Lance could tell she was trying to make up her mind. At the same time, he realized there was something about the background noise that didn't seem right, but he couldn't pinpoint what it was.

"Okay," she told him then.

"Good."

"But I'm counting on you."

"He's not going to touch you again," Lance said.

After ending the call, he downed the rest of his beer, nodded to the platinum blonde, and left the Kozy Bar. As he was standing on the sidewalk, it occurred to him what he'd noticed about the background noises as he was talking to his niece. They were not the sounds of Duluth. Lance had grown up in the city, and he knew what it sounded like. What he'd heard on the phone had a faster tempo and was louder than what would be heard here. Chrissy was in a bigger city than Duluth.


ABOUT HALFWAY between Duluth and Two Harbors, at a place called Stony Point, Lance turned off the road and headed down toward the lake. There he parked and phoned Tammy, who started to cry with relief when he promised that Chrissy would be home by evening. He was taking a chance, but it was hard to imagine that she'd gone any farther than Minneapolis.

"You're an angel, Lance," was the last thing his sister-in-law said.

He opened the glove compartment, took out the gun, and made sure the bullet was still in the chamber.

"Right. An angel," he muttered to himself.

The sound coming from the snow-covered ice was so intense that he thought he could see figures appearing and disappearing out there. The hazy, slightly trembling shapes of men who were on their way toward him. He raised the gun and aimed at one of them. "There," he said quietly, signaling the intended shot with a slight pressure on the locked trigger. It had been a while since he'd fired a pistol, but he'd always been good at it and felt confident that he could defend himself if necessary. *I will defend everything that is mine.* Wasn't that what Andy had said? *If that means I have to kill you, then I will.*

Lance sat there in the car, staring at the dazzling whiteness where the shadowy figures kept making their way toward him.

TWENTY MINUTES LATER he pulled up in front of the house in Two Harbors for the second time that day. Now Andy's old Chevy Blazer was parked out front. Lance took the gun out of the glove compartment, checked that the bullet was in the chamber, and stuck the gun in his waistband.

It took only a few seconds after he rang the bell for Tammy to open the door.

"She's not back yet," she said, looking worried.

"She'll be here," he assured her. "Give her a few hours. But I need to talk to Andy. Could you ask him to . . . ?"

Tammy went back inside. Lance heard her say something and then Andy's deep voice replied, but he couldn't hear what they were saying. Andy spoke again, sounding annoyed. Lance heard him approaching, and a moment later they were facing each other. Andy stood on the threshold to the entryway while Lance, dressed warmly because of the cold, stood outside on the porch.

"What do you want?" said Andy, a scowl on his closed face.

"I need to talk to you."

"Go ahead and talk."

"I think you should come outside and close the door behind you. You won't want Tammy to hear what I'm going to say."

Reluctantly, Andy put on a pair of boots and came out to the porch. Lance took a step back.

"Well?" said his brother after closing the door.

"You know that Chrissy is coming back home later this evening, right?"

"Yeah. I guess I should thank you."

"Not necessary. I didn't do it for your sake," said Lance. "But there's one thing I want to say to you. If you ever lay hands on Chrissy again, I'll make sure that she and Tammy and the rest of the world find out exactly who you are."

A slight flickering in Andy's eyes showed that he'd hit home.

"I met Clayton Miller, and he told me what you wrote to him back then. I know what you are, Andy. And if you leave even one bruise on her body, I'll make it public."

Andy opened his mouth but closed it again. He cast a quick glance over his shoulder, as if to make sure that the door was still closed. Then he opened his mouth again, but closed it without uttering a word. He looked as if he were searching for a phrase that would give him a way out, a key that might unlock the trap into which he'd fallen.

With a feeling that he'd won, Lance turned his back on his brother and calmly walked over to his car.

# 25

THE KITCHEN WAS FAINTLY LIT by the winter night outside the window. His long absence still hovered over the room. Two months of silence and stillness. Dust that had slowly settled and remained undisturbed. As if the whole house were as yet untouched by the fact that he was back. He recognized the old feeling of being one of the dead visiting the world of the living, incapable of having the slightest effect on it. Someone who couldn't even stir up the dust.

On the counter the coffeemaker was gurgling like a drowning man. He went over and filled a mug. When he switched on the light in the hallway, he caught sight of himself in the mirror: a big man in his bathrobe with a face that was gray with winter and long hours spent indoors. Behind him he saw the dimly lit living room and someone sitting there. Lance dropped the mug on the floor, and the piping hot coffee splashed up his calves. He let out a scream. Swamper Caribou was sitting in the easy chair, staring at him, the whites of his eyes gleaming under the brim of his big hat. Terrified, Lance turned around, but the chair was empty. He stood there peering into his own empty living room at three in the morning, screaming at the top of his lungs. He felt like he would explode with fear, but the medicine man was gone. He became aware that he was still screaming so violently that it could probably be heard far beyond the walls of his house. He fell to his knees and sobbed. After a while he collapsed forward, resting his forehead on the floor, and there he lay for several minutes until he stopped crying.

I'm completely nuts, he thought as he struggled to regain control. For a man who was lying on the floor and weeping in the middle of the night because he'd seen a ghost, there was no way back to normal. I need to dream about him, Lance thought. Willy was right. The world of dreams was the only place in which Swamper Caribou and Lance Hansen could meet as equals—neither of them more a ghost than the other. What he had to do was find an opening into that world he'd been unable to enter for almost eight years.

He opened the curtains but didn't switch on the light. After turning the chair to face the window, he sat down with a shudder. This was the same chair the medicine man had just occupied. It felt cold, and there were no dents in the cushion. What was it I saw? thought Lance as he stared at the winter-blue night outside the window, his own reflection swaying weightlessly and phantomlike over Lake Superior. What *exactly* did I see?

As he sat there, something began to dawn on him. He pictured Swamper Caribou sitting in the chair, and the more he thought about it, the more convinced he became that the Indian was holding something in his hands, something that had been partially hidden in the darkness. But no matter how hard Lance tried, he couldn't summon up the image from his memory. He hadn't seen what it was—only that something was definitely there. Swamper Caribou had been holding an object in his hands, as if he'd come to give something to Lance.

WHEN IT WAS A FEW MINUTES PAST SEVEN, Lance got out of bed for the second time, even though he'd been unable to go back to sleep. He made himself breakfast and then went out and started the car. He realized he wanted to drive north, even though he had no reason for heading in that direction. It was much too early to visit anyone, but since there was no point in going in any other direction either, he would go north.

Except for a narrow strip of light in the east, the vast night sky over Lake Superior was still intact. The myriad twinkling stars and the seemingly endless snow-covered expanse beneath them comprised a world that no one should stare at for long if he wanted to maintain his sanity. Here all distances were erased, and any kind of shape might emerge and perish without revealing whether it was real or not. Lance stared into the void as he drove. It didn't matter because he had no sanity to maintain. Or rather, he'd lost his former state of sanity, which might have been damaged by too much contact with all of this. His new state of sanity was concerned with very different things, such as the visit of an Indian medicine man who had disappeared in 1892.

As he drove through Grand Marais, he saw a man filling the gas tank of his car, clouds of icy white vapor issuing from his mouth. Clad as he was in a one-piece snowmobile suit, the man looked like an astronaut on assignment in frigid outer space. In front of Gene's Foods, a green forklift stuck its two spikes under a pallet loaded with canned goods and lifted it up. The driver was visible only as a dark, shapeless lump inside the cab. This was the world that Lance needed to return to. People who got up early and went to work every day whether the job interested them or not. A world, when viewed from outside, that hardly seemed to contain anything at all; yet in reality it could contain a whole life, as long as the person was immersed in it, as Lance had been until he found the body of Georg Lofthus. It was then that he began to fall, and by now he'd fallen all the way out of this world in which the man in the forklift was living. Yet it was there that he wanted to go.

When he reached Hovland the sky had paled considerably, and he had to concentrate hard to see the stars. It took less than a minute to drive through the little hamlet. In 1888 two Norwegian families had each built a log cabin in the woods here and spent the winter in the deep snow, with no neighbors besides the Indians. Several years later it had become a whole settlement, with a boat-building business, a school, post office, and telephone exchange. Nowadays very few people still lived there.

At the top of the long ridges beyond Grand Portage he stopped at a rest area. From here he could see a portion of the lake that was marked by big, forested islands and narrow bays that cut into the surrounding land, which was no longer flat and uniform but instead had steep slopes and deep valleys. A few miles farther north, the Canadian border station was visible as a small, dark patch in all the whiteness. The border itself followed the Pigeon River, which he couldn't see, hidden as it was under snow and ice, with snow-covered woods on either side.

As he sat there like that, looking at the borderland, he thought about everything he carried inside him. Black-clad fishermen from Halsnøy who dreamed of having their own boats and a good future for their children. Winter nights spent in smoke-filled birchbark dwellings, so far back in time that any connection with the past that he normally regarded as his heritage had vanished; the only possibility was to seek a different past, other dreams, a whole different beginning and end. And the story about Otter Heart and Sad Water was part of it. Had Willy told that story for his sake? In spite of everything, he was Willy's ex-son-in-law. He'd done everything for Mary, building a bridge over even the smallest creek. Yet it was never enough. No matter what he did, Mary's dissatisfaction soon returned. The worst part was that in the end she started using their son against him. "You're so wrapped up in the past that you don't even notice your own son," she told him one night. No, she had screamed the words, her face flushed with anger and sorrow, while their whole world collapsed all around them. That was how the last period had been, a whole world coming unhinged and falling apart. A unique world that could never be resurrected because it existed only in the interaction between Lance Hansen and Mary Dupree.

He felt so sad as he thought about this. But then he remembered Debbie. Beautiful Debbie Ahonen had come back from California to settle down once again in the town of Finland. She had rejected him when he appeared before her as the lonely man he was, rejected him for the second time. But if another chance should present itself, he would not only build bridges over even the smallest creeks, he would also carry her over those bridges. Never would a single drop of water touch Debbie's feet, if only he could have her.

Something was about to change. He just hadn't noticed it until now. What he had thought was a mountain chain far north in Canada was in reality something he hadn't seen for weeks: a dark cloud bank stretching across the horizon to the northeast.

He typed a text message and sent it to Chrissy.

"Back home?"

He quickly received a reply. "Yes, but at school."

"Andy didn't kill you?"

"What did you do to him?" replied his niece, followed by a row of smiley faces.

"Told him to shape up," texted Lance. Then he sent another message: "What were you doing in Minneapolis?"

This time it took longer for her to answer. "What do you mean?" wrote Chrissy.

# 26

BIG, WET SNOWFLAKES drifted past outside the window. Lance was sitting in his easy chair, staring at the gray swirls. It had been weeks since he'd seen any form of precipitation or even an overcast sky. The weather had been so dry and clear, with such a piercing brightness that it hurt his eyes. Now the tables had turned.

He should really go visit his mother, but he couldn't bear the thought of driving through such a heavy snowfall. It would have to wait until tomorrow. Instead he picked up his cell, which was lying on the coffee table, and called Inga, but she didn't answer. That didn't mean anything. She was probably in the communal lounge, talking to somebody. Lance looked at the texts he'd received from Chrissy. He thought about the background noises he'd heard on the phone when he called her yesterday, while he was at the Kozy Bar. They were definitely the sounds of a city bigger than Duluth, so she had to have been somewhere in the Twin Cities. But why had she lied?

At that moment his cell rang. The words "Minnesota Department of Corrections" appeared on the display. Lance felt his mouth go dry.

"Yes?" he said in a low voice.

"Is this Lance Hansen?" asked a woman.

"Yes."

"Is it true that you requested a visit with one of our inmates? Lenny Diver?"

"That's right," said Lance, although his voice was barely audible.

"Your request has been granted. Diver is in the Moose Lake jail."

"So he's willing to meet with me?"

"Your request has been granted," the woman repeated impatiently.

"But doesn't the inmate have to agree to it?"

"I doubt he has other commitments."

"I guess not."

"So now you know."

"Thank you."

She'd already ended the call.

IT HAD GROWN DARK OUTSIDE, but in the glow from the streetlamp down by the hardware store he could see that it was snowing hard. His own hazy reflection against the pelting snow made him depressed—a phantom whose only wish was to get inside. At least he'd managed to accomplish one thing: Andy would no longer lay hands on his daughter. That gave him a good feeling. *And if you leave even one bruise on her body, I'll make it public,* he'd said, knowing full well that Andy knew what he meant by "it." He tried seeing things from his brother's point of view. An abyss instantly opened up before him. For Andy, "it" was probably more terrifying than the possibility that he might be found guilty of murder. Lance would have felt the same. To have "it" exposed in public would mean his life was no longer worth living. The thought sent a cold shiver through Lance's body. What had he done? He'd even lied about knowing what his brother had written on the note he gave to Clayton Miller.

He went into his home office, found Miller's phone number on the Internet, and called the professor and poet in Minneapolis.

"Miller," the man answered, sounding out of breath.

"This is . . . I don't know if you remember me, but we met in Duluth a few days ago."

"Who is this?"

He seemed impatient. In the background Lance could hear traffic and voices.

"Lance Hansen."

"Who?"

"Lance Hansen. We talked about something that happened in high school. You had a fight with my brother, Andy."

"Oh, right. But we didn't have a fight. He attacked me and tried to kill me. What do you want?"

"I'm going to be in Minneapolis tomorrow, and I was wondering if you could set aside some time to meet with me."

Clayton Miller laughed.

"I'm a very busy man," he said.

"I realize that, but it would only take a few minutes."

"Why?"

"I need to know more about what happened back then."

"And of course you haven't talked to your brother about it, have you?"

"No."

"Listen here, I'm really getting fed up with all this nonsense."

"I'm trying to stop my brother from killing himself," Lance explained.

Silence on the line. Nothing but the background sounds of the city.

"Hello?" said Lance at last.

"How well do you know Minneapolis?" asked Miller.

"Pretty well."

"Do you know where Matt's Bar is?"

"The place with the Juicy Lucy burger?"

"Yeah."

"I've been there a few times."

"It's on Cedar Avenue at Thirty-Fifth."

"I know where that is."

"I'll meet you there at one o'clock tomorrow."

"That sounds good."

"Okay, see you tomorrow."

"Thanks a lot," said Lance.

What could he possibly gain from the two meetings? From Miller he primarily wanted to find out what exactly it said on the note Andy had given him. Plus he'd order a Juicy Lucy; it had been a long time since he'd had one of those. When it came to Lenny Diver, things were a lot more vague. Maybe it had to do with looking himself in the eye?

# 27

IT SNOWED the whole way to Minneapolis. The lake had disappeared behind the swirling flakes, but he could still sense the vast space out there. Everywhere he saw people shoveling out buried cars or clearing their driveways. Bowed figures wearing shapeless clothing and moving stiffly. Children played in the snow, dressed in caps and mittens and snowsuits, sliding down hills on their sleds. Snowmen had started to appear in yards and on playgrounds, some with the classic carrot noses and top hats. Lance noted how happy all this made him feel. Minnesota in the wintertime, with a beauty that was only for those who were tough.

After leaving Duluth and Lake Superior behind, he entered the flat, uniform landscape that marked the transition between the forestland of the north and the great plains. Here the woods were interspersed with marshy areas that were visible only as open spaces in which a dead tree or two stuck up.

The farther south he drove, the more the cultivated fields took over. Huge barns loomed, dark and sinister, in the snowdrifts.

Just before noon he crossed the Mississippi. According to the GPS, all he had to do was stay on Cedar Avenue and go past the old cemetery, where the bones of thousands of Scandinavians and Germans lay moldering in the frozen winter ground. A few minutes later he saw the simple stucco building on the corner of Cedar Avenue and Thirty-Fifth Street.

The first time he'd gone to Matt's, Lance had been a young

man attending the police academy in Minneapolis. Later he'd always taken the opportunity to have a Juicy Lucy whenever he was in town. He had a feeling Matt's was one of the few places that hadn't changed at all in the more than twenty years that had passed since then. Here everything was exactly the way it used to be. It was partially this lack of branding and marketing that had made the place so popular. It still functioned as a neighborhood bar, but people from other areas had also embraced it long ago. People like Clayton Miller, for example, thought Lance as he went inside.

Since all the tables seemed to be taken, he sat down at the bar, where a few stools were still vacant. It wasn't yet twelve thirty, but he was starving. Should he wait for Miller to arrive? Yet they hadn't really agreed to have lunch together. And besides, he had a hard time believing a poet and professor would eat in Matt's Bar. Miller probably stopped here occasionally for a beer and discussed with friends how authentic the place was. But a Juicy Lucy? Not likely, thought Lance as he ordered one for himself. Since it was impossible to get anything that tasted even close to a Mesabi Red, he chose a Grain Belt instead.

Matt's resembled a classic American diner, with the long counter and the booths against the walls, which were paneled with dark wood. The red vinyl on the bar stools had cracked to form a fine network of veins. The buzz of voices from the other guests completely enveloped Lance. Most looked to be locals who had dropped by for a bite to eat. The air smelled sharp and damp from the snow that had melted on clothes and boots.

But it was more than just the casual, neighborly atmosphere that made Matt's so attractive. Lance's stomach growled in anticipation as the waitress placed a Juicy Lucy in front of him on the counter. It looked like any decent, ordinary hamburger, but as the name indicated, there was nothing decent about it. A Juicy Lucy was a sinful burger, and that made it dangerous. Lance, who was a man of experience when it came to burgers, let it rest for a few minutes to cool down. When he finally sank his teeth into the burger, melted cheese sprayed out of the meat with explosive force, like yellow lava from a volcano. It burned his hands and face, but not too bad, since he'd allowed it to cool down first. Many a newbie headed to the door with burns on his face after a first encounter with the famous burger. That was because a Juicy Lucy was filled with melted cheese. This was achieved by forming two hamburger patties and then placing a sizable portion of American cheese on one of them. Then the second patty was placed on top of the cheese and the edges of the meat were pressed tightly together all around. Then the burger was put on the grill until it was properly cooked with a piping hot core of melted cheese inside. It was this specialty that was the bar's real claim to fame. Even though it was now possible to get a Juicy Lucy in countless other places in Minneapolis, it was here that the first one was served. At Matt's the cooking grease was scraped off the walls twice a year, an operation that was probably behind the myth that the same grease was constantly reused. And that was purportedly why a Juicy Lucy tasted especially good in this place—because it had been cooked in the original grease from the very first burger.

Lance was almost done with his food when Clayton Miller appeared at his side. He was wearing a heavy, dark coat, a Russian-looking fur hat, and elegant leather gloves, which he proceeded to remove.

"So, here you are, huh?" he said in greeting.

Lance got down from the bar stool to shake hands.

"Have a good drive?"

"Oh, it was okay," said Lance.

They each straddled a bar stool, and Miller ordered a chicken sandwich, mineral water, and coffee.

After taking a sip of the water, he turned to Lance.

"What's going on with Andy?" he asked.

Lance knew that this whole meeting would founder if he tried to sidestep the issue. He needed to get right to the point.

"I'm worried that he's going to try to kill himself," he said.

"For any special reason?"

"I think he might be gay, and he doesn't think he can live with that any longer. I mean, he's married, you know."

"But why did you want to talk to me about this?" asked Miller.

"Because I need to know what it said on that note he gave you."

"What difference does it make?"

"I have to talk to Andy about all this. He's my younger brother, so I feel responsible for him. But first I need to find out if that's really the problem. I don't want to broach the subject if he's not—"

"Homosexual?" Miller finished the sentence for him.

"Yeah."

"Tell me, what do you think it said in the note?"

"That he had feelings for you?" suggested Lance.

Miller smiled.

"It was a poem. And the poem was a declaration of love for me, but I didn't realize that back then. I evaluated its poetic quality, which was so awkward that it made me laugh. It was a terrible poem. Only later did it occur to me what it was really all about, and what it said about Andy. And that's when I was able to understand his reaction."

Lance could hardly believe his ears. Andy had written a poem? He tried to envision his brother as a poet, wearing a beret and holding a pen.

"But what did it actually say?" he asked.

"It was just a bad poem."

"Do you still remember it?"

"I don't think I'll ever forget it."

"Would you recite it for me?"

"Of course not. It would be disrespectful to your brother."

His words were the response of a man who was used to talking to people who were below him in status. It was Clayton Miller the professor who had spoken.

After that they both sat there in silence, waiting for the chicken sandwich to arrive. While Miller ate his lunch, Lance took small sips of his beer and stared at the snow falling steadily outside. So it was true, he thought. Only a few months ago no one could have made him believe such a thing about his brother. But now he knew.

"Are you dreading talking to Andy about this?" asked Clayton Miller when he was done eating. He sounded friendlier now.

Lance nodded.

"I have lots of friends who are gay," said Miller, "and it's my experience that such conversations usually go more smoothly than anticipated."

The situation was so unthinkable that it threatened to overwhelm Lance. This isn't happening, he thought. I'm sitting here in Matt's Bar in Minneapolis and talking to Clayton Miller about Andy's homosexual tendencies.

"It's a different environment than what you're used to," Lance replied. "More masculine."

"So masculine that Andy's thinking of killing himself?"

Lance nodded curtly.

"Is there anyone else, besides you, who happens to know the truth of the matter?"

"No."

"What about his wife?"

"I think it would be totally unimaginable for anyone who knows him."

"Then why isn't it unimaginable for you?"

"I know something that no one else knows."

"Something you want to tell me about?"

"No."

Miller took a cautious sip of the hot coffee.

"Then I don't know how else I can help you," he said.

Lance could hear in his voice that he was getting ready to leave.

"Do you think it might happen?" he hurried to ask. "That Andy might actually kill himself?"

"As I said, I know a lot of gay people, and they've always managed to figure out how to deal with it. You just need to make it clear to him that you know how he's feeling and that he can trust you. That's probably where you should start. But keep in mind that the thought of coming out will seem extremely scary at first. Especially in that kind of environment."

"But do you think it might have the opposite effect? Push him into committing suicide?"

"It's really important that you're completely open with him. Don't make any demands, don't pressure him."

Lance thought with alarm about the scene a couple of days ago. The outmaneuvered brother standing on the front steps of his own house. He must have been really scared.

"But you were the one who . . . ," said Lance.

It took a moment for Miller to understand what he was getting at.

"Well, I never knew where it came from. Maybe because I wrote poetry?"

Lance was about to say something about long, multicolored scarves that Miller had supposedly knit for himself, but he refrained.

"Or maybe because I was so obsessed with clothes," Miller went on.

"No matter what, it was terrible that you ended up with that sort of reputation," said Lance.

"You think so? To be honest, it was kids like you who were behind it. You were the ones who kept the rumors going. Well, maybe not you personally, but others like you. Andy, on the other hand, had something open and seeking about him. He wasn't judgmental, at least not during that one summer when I knew him. But I guess by now he's just like all the rest. I feel sorry for Andy."

Clayton Miller pulled on his gloves and set the big Russian fur hat on his head.

"But not for you," he said.

# 28

THE ROWS OF PLASTIC CHAIRS that were placed back-to-back in the glaring light made the place look like an airport waiting room. Along one wall was a series of small cubicles for visitors. Inside each was a single chair facing a window, and on the other side of the window was a little room with a closed door. Lance was sitting in a cubicle and staring at the door, which he knew would open soon. On the divider to his left hung a telephone receiver that was connected to another receiver on the other side of the soundproof glass. He tried desperately to think of something to say to Lenny Diver, but his mind was blank. Once again he wondered why Diver was willing to talk to him. It couldn't be just because he wanted to be accommodating.

Then the door opened. Lenny Diver came in, holding a bottle of Chippewa mineral water in his hand. Lance noticed at once that he was a small man and that his hair, which he'd worn long and loose in the newspaper photo, had now been cut short. Since he hadn't yet been convicted, he had on his own clothes: black jeans and a faded denim shirt. He moved with a supple ease as he came over to the window and sat down.

They stared at each other from either side of the glass pane. Lance nodded and received a slight nod in return. "Thanks for agreeing to see me," he began.

Lenny Diver put down his bottle of mineral water, then took the receiver from its hook on the wall, and pressed it to his ear.

Lance gestured apologetically and then he too grabbed the phone.

"Thanks for agreeing to see me," he repeated.

"Haven't got much else to do," said Diver. His voice had a metallic sound in the receiver.

Lance was dismayed to feel beads of sweat appear on his face, something that happened only when he was very nervous around other people. He had an urge to wipe the sweat on the sleeve of his jacket, but that would draw too much attention. Yet the more conscious he was of it, the more he sweated. He could feel that a drop of sweat was about to roll down his forehead.

"Nice weather," said Diver.

Lance seized the straw the man had offered him.

"I thought I'd never get here."

"Yeah. It's kind of remote."

"So how are things going?"

Diver raised his eyebrows as he cocked his head to one side.

Lance saw that he found the question irrelevant. "I was the one who found the body," he said.

"I know."

"Georg Lofthus."

"Hmm?"

"That was his name."

"Oh."

"A Norwegian."

"Right," said Diver without interest.

A drop of sweat ran down into the corner of Lance's eye. He set the receiver on his lap and wiped his face with the sleeve of his jacket. This was a mistake. He'd come here in the hope that he'd feel better afterward. As if talking to the innocent man who had been wrongly jailed might somehow absolve him of his sin. But he was the one who ought to do something for Diver, not the other way around.

"I don't know if this is such a good idea," Lance said.

"No?"

"No. I suddenly can't remember why I'm here."

"Maybe you were wondering if I was really the one who did it."

Lance nodded.

"Everybody claims to be innocent, so what's the use?"

"You still maintain that you're innocent?"

"I *am* innocent. But you know what's going to be my downfall?"

"No. What?"

"A baseball bat that I've never seen before, with my finger-prints on it. I was so drunk that night that they could have put my fingerprints on Sheriff Eggum's ass, if they wanted to."

"Eggum has retired," said Lance.

"Christ, I thought he'd stay on forever. What's the new guy's name?"

"Bud Andersson."

"Andersson? Another herring eater?"

"Yeah."

"I was in Grand Marais the whole time that night."

"With a woman you refuse to name."

"So you actually believe me?" Lenny Diver seemed genuinely surprised.

"Because it's true, isn't it?" said Lance. "You know who you were with, but you're refusing to tell."

"Those are your words, not mine," said Diver.

All Lance had to do was open his mouth and say that he knew Diver was innocent and that he knew who had done it. In theory, it was as simple as that. Just a few words, and then every-thing would be set in motion.

"But if you didn't do it," he said, "who do you think did?"

Diver shrugged.

"All I know is that I'm going to be in here for a very long time."

Lance sensed that he wouldn't be able to stand this much longer, sitting face-to-face with Lenny Diver in this building, where no outside sounds penetrated, and doubtless no sounds moved in the other direction either. The jail might just as well have been on the moon. But one thing was perfectly clear: He was the one who should have been sitting on the other side of the window. The one who should have stayed here when the meeting was over, while Diver should have stood up and gone out into the snowy weather to drive north.

"Weren't you married to a woman from the reservation?" Diver asked unexpectedly.

"Where'd you hear that?"

"Oh, you know. It's a small place."

"Well, you're right," said Lance.

"So she was Ojibwe?"

"Uh-huh."

"What's her name?"

He was about to answer when he happened to think about the two young men who had threatened him the last time he was in Grand Portage. They clearly knew something about the situation he was in. They told him that he could save Lenny Diver from life in prison. But how did they know that?

"It doesn't matter," he said.

"And don't you have a son?"

Lance didn't reply.

"Are you scared of me?" Diver was practically sneering.

"Why would I be scared of you?" said Lance.

"I have no idea."

Lance realized that it would be an easy matter for him to find out the names of his ex-wife and son.

"Her name is Mary Dupree," he said.

"Wasn't she a teacher?"

"She still is."

"She was my teacher in junior high."

"She told me that."

"What did she tell you?' Diver suddenly seemed on guard.

"Just that you didn't make much of an effort. And then she said something about a job that you had after junior high, something to do with canoes."

"I was an apprentice with Hank Morrison, who builds canoes in the old way."

"Was it interesting?"

"I liked it."

Lance thought that it was less than ten years ago that Lenny Diver was a young apprentice learning a craft that was a thousand years old. Now he was sitting behind soundproof glass in a jail.

"I've seen birchbark canoes," said Lance. "Beautiful yellow-colored vessels."

"When they're new, yes. It's the inner side of the fresh bark that looks like that."

"'That shall float upon the river / Like a yellow leaf in Autumn,'" said Lance.

"'Like a yellow water-lily,'" Diver continued. "Hank Morrison used to quote 'The Song of Hiawatha' to me while we were working on a canoe."

"But you quit?"

"Other things got more interesting."

"Like what?"

"Partying. Women. Dope."

The same old story, thought Lance. First a few years of hero status among a group of friends, then a life of misery. Sinking ever deeper. As a police officer, Lance was often in contact with men like that. Still, he had to admit that few of them could quote Longfellow.

"Do you have any regrets?" asked Lance. He had a feeling the man sitting in front of him could have become something quite different if he'd made other choices.

"Do you?" asked Lenny Diver.

"Regrets about what?"

"How do I know?"

"Of course I have regrets," said Lance.

It felt good to say that, even though the other man didn't know what he regretted.

Diver took a big gulp of bottled water. "What exactly do you want?" he asked impatiently.

"Maybe I'm looking for some sort of resolution to this case."

"Then you'll have to look somewhere else, but I hope you find it."

"And I hope you find it too."

"Oh, I've already found my resolution," said Diver. "It's happening right now, in the present. But it's a present that will go on for a very long time."

"If you're convicted."

"Of course I'm going to be convicted. They have the baseball bat with the dead man's blood on it, along with my fingerprints."

"And biological evidence that proves the killer had to have been an Indian," said Lance.

"Yeah. That too. Bad luck for me, as usual."

"Why don't you just tell them who you spent the night with?"

He wished that Diver or somebody else would lift the burden from his shoulders, because at this moment it seemed unthinkable to replace this man on the other side of the glass with Andy.

"I was so drunk I can't remember her name or what she looked like," said Diver automatically, as if he'd rehearsed the reply.

"But that means that someone out there could give you an alibi."

"Sure. And there's also somebody out there who knows who the killer is. There are lots of reasons why people choose not to talk."

Lance felt like some heavy object was pressing down on him. His shoulders ached. It was the weight of guilt.

"But maybe someone will finally speak up."

"If they were planning to talk, they would have done it long ago." Diver raised his index finger in warning. "But they're going to be cursed for the rest of their life. That's their punishment."

Lance couldn't stay there even a minute longer. He turned around and craned his neck to get a glimpse of the big window in the waiting room. Outside he saw the snow drifting down in the harsh light from the spotlights.

"I've got a long drive ahead of me," he said.

Diver nodded.

On his way out, Lance again noticed how the place looked like an airport waiting area, but no planes ever took off from here. That much he knew.

# 29

INGA HAD AWAKENED from a dream in which Oscar was sitting at the kitchen table in their house on Fifth Avenue. Behind him, outside the window, she could see a snowbank with the sun shining on it. The light had an April-like glow in her dream. But what she remembered most were his eyes, which were a uniform gray except for the big black pupils. That's not my husband, she had thought as she stood next to the kitchen counter. "I've always had eyes like this," said Oscar, and the second he said that, she knew it was true. She'd just never noticed before.

Now she was trying to figure out where she was. That was not Duluth out there—that much she knew for sure. Duluth never felt this dark. She didn't know what she would encounter if she got out of bed. She might bump into something and hurt herself. For a moment she considered stretching out her hand to find out if there was a night table and lamp close by, but she decided not to, afraid of what she might touch in the dark. All right then. She'd just have to lie here until she discovered where she was. What if she simply fell asleep again? Maybe everything would be clear when she woke up. If so, how would she recall this first awakening? As a dream? And the dream about Oscar as a dream within a dream? Oscar. This probably had something to do with him; it usually did. Then she figured it out. She was staying with Aunt Edna! That's why it was so dark. In Yellow Medicine County the night was as black as the inside of a sack. The vast prairie darkness was what she sensed outside. She'd gone to visit Aunt Edna again. Her childless aunt was asleep in the next room, and outdoors the wash had been hung up to dry on the clothesline stretched between the cherry tree and the rusty hook on the wall of the outbuilding. Their underwear were dancing out there in the night breeze. Inga had to smile at the thought. Yet she realized that it was wrong to run off like this, leaving her husband and children behind. She had done it only a few times before, but that was still too often. She needed to stop leaving them in the lurch. When Oscar was in a certain mood, he couldn't help what he said or did. That was just the way he was, but those episodes didn't last long. Soon everything else inside him would take over, all the good that she loved so much to be near. Just the thought of how he smelled under the bedcovers in the dark, that masculine smell, oh . . . For a moment she felt dizzy, really dizzy, and that hadn't happened to her in years. Why couldn't she just stay with him like an obedient wife? That's what she wanted. But now everything would be different. She would go back home at once and endure whatever the consequences might be. A great sense of happiness flooded over her. Eagerly she reached out her hand, found the lamp on the nightstand, and switched it on. But what was this place—with the knitting on the table and the checked curtains? This was certainly not Aunt Edna's guest room. Where was she?

# 30

LANCE FUMBLED FOR THE CLOCK on the nightstand and turned it around so he could read the red numbers. It was 3:18. What had awakened him? It wasn't because he had to pee. As he was about to turn over to go back to sleep, he realized what it was. He'd left the bedroom door ajar, as he always did to keep the room from getting too stuffy, and through the crack in the door he saw faint flashes of light on the floor. It looked like the flickering light from a television screen. This wasn't the first time that he'd forgotten to turn off the TV before going to bed.

He was already sitting up and moving his bare feet around on the floor to locate his slippers when it occurred to him that he hadn't watched any TV programs that night. He'd driven to Minneapolis, and when he came home, he'd gone straight to bed and fallen asleep instantly. The TV must have turned on by itself, he thought, still only half awake. At last he found his slippers and stuck his feet into them. He stood up and went over to the door. There he paused for a moment to listen, with his hand on the doorknob. Without making a sound, he opened the door and stepped out into the hall, where irregular streaks of light were illuminating the floor and the small table under the mirror. Even as he took the last few steps over to the living room doorway, he knew that something was wrong. And when he caught sight of Andy sitting in the easy chair, he realized that the gun was no longer on the hall table where he'd left it when he came home.

"Tammy loves this show," said Andy with a slight nod at the TV.

It was *The Price Is Right.*

"Come in and have a seat," he went on.

"How did . . . ," Lance began.

Andy raised the gun and pointed it at his brother's knees.

"Sit down," he said.

Lance's legs were shaking as he went over to the sofa and sat down. On the other side of the coffee table sat Andy, wearing a big down jacket and a cap with earflaps.

"That's my service weapon," said Lance cautiously.

"Not anymore," said his brother. "It's mine now."

There was a strange metallic ring to his voice that Lance had never heard before. Had he taken some sort of medicine?

"You're not thinking of shooting me, are you?"

"Of course not." Andy laughed quietly. He didn't sound like himself.

Then he raised the gun and pointed it at his own temple.

"No," gasped Lance.

His brother lowered the gun and laughed.

"So you do care, after all?"

"Could you at least turn off . . ." He motioned toward the TV, where a huge set of dinnerware had just been rolled onto the stage.

"No. Tammy loves this show," said Andy harshly. "And we can't ruin what Tammy loves, now can we?"

Lance didn't dare say a word.

"Now can we?" Andy repeated in that cold, metallic voice.

"No," Lance whispered.

"Speak up so I can hear you."

"No, we shouldn't. We shouldn't ruin what Tammy loves."

"By the way, thanks for leaving the gun out like that. Originally I thought we'd just have a little chat."

"We can still do that," ventured Lance.

"Sure, but a loaded gun definitely changes the terms. Don't you agree?"

"Yes."

"You shot at me at close range," snarled Andy.

"The rifle went off accidentally," said Lance, even though he knew that his brother would never believe him.

"I saw you standing there and taking aim at me only a few minutes earlier, down by the cross," said Andy. "I could tell that I was in real danger, so I got out of there fast. My own brother was aiming at me with a hunting rifle."

"I was just looking at you."

Andy laughed.

"Aiming at me like I was a fucking deer. That's what you were doing. But now the tables are turned. Now it's your turn to be scared."

On the TV the contestants were guessing the price of the dinnerware. Whoever got closest to the actual price would get to take the dishes home.

"What a mess you've made of things," said Andy. "Just because you always have to stick your nose in other people's business. Is it really true that you talked to Clayton Miller?"

Lance nodded.

"How's he doing?"

"I don't know."

"The Professor." Andy snorted with contempt.

"Uh-huh."

"So he told you about . . . ?"

"Yeah."

"I suppose you think it's a fucking big deal. Right?" said Andy. "That it's like night and day. But it's not like that at all. It's possible to forget all about it. It's that simple."

"But when you met those two Norwegians, then you remembered it again?"

"Norwegians?"

"I know that you met them at Our Place over in Finland. That you spent several hours with them."

"Oh, those two. Nice guys. Real nice. It's terrible what happened," said Andy.

"Where exactly is your baseball bat?"

Andy moved so quickly that Lance didn't even have time to raise his arms before he was pinned against the sofa. Andy recklessly shoved the barrel of the gun in his brother's mouth and halfway down his throat. The only thing Lance could hear was the gurgling sound he was making, a sound that filled his head. The gag reflex made his throat muscles tighten painfully around the cold steel, as if it might be possible for him to swallow the gun whole. Above him he saw Andy wearing the cap with the earflaps. In spite of the tears pouring out of his eyes, Lance could see that his brother's face was terribly contorted. Desperately he kicked his legs to show that he was about to suffocate. At the same time, he expected the gun to go off at any moment.

"I'm the one holding the gun now," snarled Andy.

Lance tried to nod, but he couldn't manage it with the gun stuck in his mouth.

"And I'm the one asking the questions now. Understand?"

Lance felt a terrible, searing pain from the sight bead as Andy yanked the gun out of his mouth as brutally as he'd it shoved in. But the next second it was pressed between his eyes, the muzzle wet against his skin.

"Understand?"

Lance tried to answer, but only a whistling sound came out. Instead he nodded as best he could. Andy removed the gun, and Lance toppled over onto the sofa with his hands clutching his throat. He tentatively released a little saliva that fell from his lips onto the sleeve of his pajamas. It was red with blood. He couldn't swallow. His throat felt like it was swelling up inside.

"Sit up," Andy commanded.

Lance managed to push himself into a sitting position. Andy was already back in the easy chair. In the faint light from the TV screen the earflaps on his cap made him look like a cartoon dog.

"So I'm the one asking the questions here," said Andy. "And by the way, you need to do something about the window to the laundry room in the basement. The wood is rotted all around the edges. All it takes is a knife to pop open the latches."

Lance started to cry, not because of the pain in his throat but because the two of them had ended up like this.

"Are you blubbering?" said Andy scornfully.

"What do you want?" Lance managed to say, tears running down his face.

"I want my dignity back."

Andy said the word with a surprised expression, as if he wasn't quite sure he'd actually spoken that word.

"I want to go to my grave with my head held high," he went on. "But if you can't keep your mouth shut, they're going to laugh at me." He rubbed his forehead with the muzzle of the gun. "And I can't let that happen."

Since Lance could no longer swallow, a mixture of blood and saliva was spilling out of his mouth, and he couldn't say a word. All he could do was sit there, huddled up on the sofa, and drool.

"I'm going to tell you one thing, Lance. You're probably the dumbest person I've ever met in my life. A blind buffalo racing across the prairie, that's what you are. And I pity whoever gets in your way."

Andy cast a glance at the TV. A curtain had just been pulled aside to reveal a shiny new car. In unison, the contestants on *The Price Is Right* covered their mouths with their hands. Lance thought about all the times his brother must have watched this show with Tammy.

"If you . . ." Andy waved the gun back and forth, like an admonishing index finger. "If anyone finds out that . . . Then I won't have any dignity left. I want you to tell me how much you think my dignity is worth."

On the TV show the contestants were thinking hard about what the price of the new car could be. The program had reached its dramatic highpoint.

"Didn't you hear what I said?"

Lance realized his brother was serious, but he had no idea what the question meant. Andy raised the gun, holding his arm out straight and aiming at Lance's face.

"Didn't you hear me?" he repeated. "How much do you think my dignity is worth? If you give the wrong answer, I'll shoot you. Or me."

Once again he pressed the gun to his own temple.

"Understand now?"

Lance had no choice but to nod.

"So, how much is my dignity worth?" Andy repeated with the gun pressed to his own head.

Lance desperately tried to think. He looked at the TV screen,

159

as if he might find the answer there, but of course *The Price Is Right* had gone to commercial before the final price was revealed.

"You have to answer," said Andy calmly, with that eerie ring to his voice. "You have to answer now, and you only get one try."

Lance first released a big clot of blood.

"The same as the dignity of Georg Lofthus," he then whispered.

Andy's expression didn't change. He merely sat there with the pistol pressed to his head, but Lance could tell that he was considering what he'd said.

"I'm going to have to accept that answer," he said at last and lowered the gun. "Lofthus. He was the guy who . . . right? I knew at once that they were . . . If only everything could be as good as that, I thought. As good as those two traveling together."

Lance was curled up on the sofa, sobbing. When he glanced up he saw that Andy was on his feet. He was still holding the gun.

"You know nothing about love," he said.

"My gun," whispered Lance.

"Or about pain." Andy practically spat out the last word.

"My service weapon."

"I'm taking it with me. You're not a real policeman, anyway."

Andy quickly strode out of the room, earflaps swaying. Lance didn't move until he heard the front door open and then close quietly, as if his brother was afraid of waking someone. Lance instantly got up, but his legs failed him, and he fell to the floor with a crash. As he lay there, he realized that he hadn't yet heard the sound of a car engine. He managed to crawl over to the window and pull open the heavy curtains, but it was so dark outside that he couldn't see a thing. Where was Andy? He wasn't even sure that he'd left the house. He could have opened and shut the door and then sneaked down to the basement. Or into the bathroom. Or the bedroom. Then a pair of headlights came on down by the hardware store. Of course he'd parked down there. The car headed out along the highway and turned south. Lance kept his eyes fixed on the car lights until they disappeared.

# 31

DEBBIE AHONEN looked up from her magazine and smiled.

"You're back," she said.

Lance went over to the counter, but when he opened his mouth to say hi, only a hoarse sound came out. He'd realized that the pain and swelling in his throat might make it hard for him to talk, but he'd got in the car to drive to Finland all the same. Again he opened his mouth and tried to say something, with no better results.

"Got a cold?" asked Debbie.

At first Lance shook his head, but then he nodded.

"You should get some cough drops," she said, reaching for a little box. But he waved his hand to stop her.

"So, what can I get you?"

He couldn't very well say that what he wanted was her, even though that was the truth. Then she'd just reject him again. But since he had no voice, he couldn't say it anyway. Not wanting to just stand there like an idiot, he picked up a few Dove chocolates and placed them on the counter.

"Is that all?" she asked.

Lance nodded. She was about to ring up his purchase, but then she seemed to change her mind. She moved the chocolates aside and glanced up at him.

"You look worn out. Shall we go into the back room and sit down for a minute?"

He nodded again, and when Debbie got up and walked through the store, he followed. The cramped back room looked the same as before. Once again the sight of the Yahtzee score card and the pen made him wonder if she passed the time by playing Yahtzee on her own.

"Would you like a cup of coffee?" she asked.

"No, thanks," he whispered, putting his hand to his throat in explanation.

Debbie poured a cup for herself.

"To be honest, you really look shitty. Is it anything serious?"

"No, no. Just my throat," he managed to squeak.

She glanced at her watch, which prompted Lance to look at his own. It was only nine thirty.

"Do you know why women like silent men?" she asked.

"No, why?" he whispered.

"Because they don't keep getting interrupted."

He smiled politely.

"Are you working?" asked Debbie. "If you are, you should take off a day or two until your sore throat is better."

Lance grabbed the Yahtzee card and pen.

*I'm on vacation,* he wrote, shoving the pad across the table to her.

"On vacation?" said Debbie, in disbelief.

Lance grabbed the pad and pen again.

*Yes,* he wrote, and handed her the pad.

She laughed that special laugh of hers, which was equally cold and sweet. Lance wasn't sure why she was laughing. Maybe because he was on vacation in this miserable condition, or maybe because he'd taken the trouble to write yes on the pad of paper instead of simply nodding. He'd once seen someone do the same thing on TV, and it had seemed really funny.

The only window in the small room faced the inside of the store. Now the front door opened and a man came in. Lance recognized Richie Akkola.

"Excuse me," said Debbie, jumping up.

Lance stayed where he was, watching the couple out of the corner of his eye. She went behind the counter and leaned forward. Akkola was wearing a big brown jacket that looked even older than he was, and a dark blue cap pulled well down over his ears. So this was the man who had finally won Debbie. He was apparently helping out by taking care of her eighty-year-old mother. Helping financially, thought Lance. And in return, Debbie had agreed to live with him? No, that couldn't be right. But how else to explain their relationship? She couldn't possibly be interested in that scarecrow of a man! Now she was smiling and laughing at something Akkola had said. It was true that Richie was considerably older than Debbie, who was probably about forty-five now, but he hadn't yet reached seventy, and there was something lively and self-confident about the way he moved. Lance had pictured himself playing the role of the knight in Debbie's life, rescuing her from that old geezer, but now he started to wonder whether she really needed to be rescued at all.

After a few minutes Akkola left, without casting a single glance at the man sitting at the window in the back room.

"So," said Debbie as she came in.

*Richie Akkola?* wrote Lance on the Yahtzee score card and then held it up.

"Yeah, that was Richie. Do you know each other?"

He shook his head. Debbie gave him a long look, as if wondering why he'd asked. Then she sat down and lit a cigarette. Lance started to sweat, not because of the smoke, which tore at his injured throat, but because he couldn't think of any reason to keep her sitting here when she was supposed to be working. An awkward silence settled over them, until Debbie abruptly stubbed out her cigarette.

"Well, I guess I'd better . . . ," she began.

Lance stood up and followed her into the store. She went behind the counter and gathered up the heart-shaped chocolates he'd placed there before they retreated to the back room. She rang up the price, and Lance paid for them.

"Always Dove," she murmured as she stuffed the chocolates into a paper bag.

She handed it to Lance, and he was about to leave when he saw that Debbie had thought of something.

"Oh, that's right," she said. "There was something I wanted to show you. Something I found the other day."

She hurried over to the front door to lock it.

"It won't matter," she explained. "There are practically no customers anyway. Only right after they get off work."

Lance followed her down the aisle and over to the door labeled "Stock Room." The air inside was cool, and the shelves on the walls were filled with inventory.

"Come on," she said, motioning him forward.

They went through the storeroom to a door at the other end. When Debbie opened it, a gust of clammy air smelling of brick wafted toward Lance. It reminded him of his childhood, although he couldn't place what the smell came from. It was just one of those familiar smells. When Debbie switched on the light, he saw that they were standing at the top of a steep flight of stairs.

"Be careful," she warned him as she started down.

Lance followed, and soon he could see that they were in the store's junk room. Stowed down here were all those old and unneeded things that they somehow couldn't bring themselves to discard. The hoarding process had undoubtedly been going on for decades. Old lawn mowers, rubber boots, balance scales, snowshoes, several old chainsaws, traps for foxes or wolves, newspapers and magazines stacked so high they nearly reached the ceiling, rows of brown medicine bottles, fridges and stoves, umbrellas, hats, fishing rods, patio furniture, snow shovels, a big poster of President Eisenhower, boxing gloves, electric boot warmers, a couple of vacuum cleaners, ear protectors, hockey sticks, ski equipment, empty milk bottles, a stuffed beaver, one of those long crosscut saws that loggers used before chainsaws, a pinball machine, and much more.

"We could open a junk store with all this," said Debbie.

The room was big and lit only by a bare bulb in the ceiling. A cloud of frost issued from her mouth when she spoke.

"Do you remember these?"

She held up a pair of wraparound sunglasses. The kind that was popular back in the eighties. But it was only when she put them on that it occurred to Lance she'd worn a pair like them during the summer they'd spent together. Good Lord, it was only one brief summer. And now, more than twenty years later, they were standing here in the ice-cold basement of the Finland

General Store, and she was wearing those very same sunglasses again.

"Uh-huh," he whispered.

Debbie smiled as she played with the glasses, sliding them up and down her nose, one moment peering at Lance over the rims, and the next hiding behind the dark lenses.

Lance recalled how almost all the guys wanted to date her back then, but he was the one she'd chosen. Okay, maybe it was only for a summer, but that was still more than the others had been granted. The man he was now could never have managed something like that, could never have won a woman whom all the other men wanted; it was unthinkable. Yet a young man named Lance Hansen had accomplished just that more than twenty years ago, if only for a brief period in the summer. That young man must still be somewhere inside me, thought Lance. Part of the young man, at least.

"But there was something else I actually wanted to show you," said Debbie, putting away the sunglasses.

She squatted down and rummaged through several stacks of newspapers and magazines before she stood up holding an old issue of the *Cook County News Herald*. She leafed through it for a moment and then found what she was looking for.

"Here," she said and handed him the paper open to an article.

It took Lance several seconds to realize what he was looking at. The headline read: *"Eighteen-year-old from Duluth Appointed New Chairman of the Cook County Historical Society."* Underneath was a photograph of the new chairman. Lance knew that the picture had been taken outside his family's house on Fifth Avenue in Duluth. He had a big smile on his face as he looked at the camera, and even though the old, moldy newspaper had been lying down here for close to thirty years, Lance could still see how young he looked.

He read the short article:

*Following the death of the founder and long-time chairwoman, Olga Soderberg, the historical society of Cook County has chosen a new chairman. His name is Lance Hansen. He is only eighteen and lives in Duluth.*

*He is the grandson of Isak Hansen, who opened the
hardware store in Lutsen in 1929. Asked about his
goals as the chairman, young Hansen replied: "To
continue the work of Olga Soderberg. Since the mem-
bership is beginning to age, we also need to attract
younger members." Lance Hansen is a senior at Duluth
Cental High, and he says that he is planning to become
either a police officer or a historian.*

For a short time he had actually contemplated becoming a historian, simply because he'd been chosen chairman of the pathetic
little historical society in Cook County. Fortunately he'd come to
his senses and become a police officer instead.

"When I saw that, I was totally . . ." All of a sudden Debbie
sounded on the verge of tears.

Lance continued to stare at the article. From the yellowing
page of the newspaper his own young face stared back across the
gap of thirty years that had passed since the photo was taken, and
been forgotten. He vaguely recalled seeing the article when it first
appeared. No doubt he'd kept a copy for a while, but eventually it
probably hadn't seemed so impressive, since it was merely a brief
article in a local paper, and he'd thrown it out.

"That was how you looked when we were together," said
Debbie.

"But this was taken seven years earlier," whispered Lance
hoarsely.

"That's still just how you looked."

He glanced up at her and then back at the article before reso-
lutely folding up the newspaper.

"Take it with you," she said.

Neither of them said another word as they stood there, feeling somehow at a loss, in that big cold basement room. Every
time Debbie exhaled, a little cloud of frosty vapor issued from
her lips. He had a strange thought that it was her soul trying to
escape, but each time she sucked it back in. Thousands of days
and nights had passed since they were together, and there was no
more time to lose. Lance always had a pen in his breast pocket,
but did he have any paper? The paper bag would have to do. He

emptied the chocolates into his jacket pocket and then proceeded to write on the stiff white paper, using the old newspaper as a pad underneath. It took a while because the paper had a waxy surface, and he had to go over each letter several times so it could be clearly read, but he finally had a legible sentence. *You are more beautiful than anything else in Minnesota.* His heart felt as if it had stopped beating as he handed the piece of paper to Debbie.

She read what he'd written, then closed her eyes for several seconds. When she opened them again, Lance could have sworn that she looked exactly as she had twenty years ago.

"Oh, Lance," she said.

He took a step toward her, but before he could do or say anything, she turned on her heel and headed toward the stairs. He hurried after her, carrying the folded newspaper in his hand. At the top of the stairs she had to stop and wait for him so she could lock the door to the basement after him. They didn't look at each other as he climbed the stairs to join her. After locking the door, she immediately strode with great purpose through the storeroom and into the store itself. There she took her usual place behind the counter and went back to paging through a magazine. Lance went over to the counter. He didn't know what he was going to say, but he went over to stand in front of her.

Debbie raised her eyes from the magazine and looked up at him.

"Don't you realize that you and I are yesterday's news?" she said, nodding at the paper that Lance was holding.

"No," he whispered in his ruined voice. "You and I—we're like the ravens. They manage to make it through the whole winter up here. The two of us can make it through anything."

Debbie gave him a smile that seemed older than the rest of her. He could see all of her wrecked marriage in that smile, all the years she'd spent in California and the defeat it must have been to come back here.

"We're not ravens," she said. "We're the carcasses they peck at along the road."

# 32

LANCE TURNED ON THE LIGHT and got out of bed, but everything was as normal as it could be after someone had broken in and jammed a gun in his mouth. He opened the curtains just a crack. The only thing he saw outside was the light from his cousin's hardware store and his own reflection against the dark. It was the same old face he'd put on a few hours ago, without a trace of the eighteen-year-old who had looked up at him from the yellowing newspaper page in the basement of the grocery store in Finland.

*You are more beautiful than anything else in Minnesota,* he remembered writing, annoyed. Had he really written something so stupid? Their relationship hadn't lasted more than a couple of months, and Lance feared it had meant more to him than to her. He had to find something that would make all her defenses crumble at the mere memory of it.

In his home office he found Debbie's cell number on the Internet. He sat there, typing various messages on his cell in the hope of finding the right words, but after a while he gave up. It was impossible to keep playing around like this. This time he needed to be smart and use his head.

IT WAS ALMOST NINE by the time he woke up, sitting in his desk chair with his cell phone in his hand, not having written anything. He had a throbbing headache, which was probably because he was so hungry his stomach was rumbling. He realized with alarm that it was almost forty-eight hours since he'd had anything to eat. He'd driven straight back to the North Shore from Minneapolis, and when he came home, he'd been so tired he couldn't muster enough energy to eat anything, even though he was starving. Instead, he'd tumbled into bed, planning to make himself a huge breakfast in the morning. But then the light from the TV had woken him, and in the living room he'd found Andy holding a gun. Lance swallowed, noticing at once that his throat wasn't any better. He still couldn't imagine forcing any solid food down his injured, swollen esophagus. But in the meantime his voice had come back. Maybe not entirely, but he didn't need to use it much anyway.

He poured himself a mug of coffee but let it sit while he had a spartan breakfast consisting of two aspirin, crushed and stirred in lukewarm water. Then he went into the bathroom and took a shower. As he stood there, letting the steady streams of hot water pummel his body, he began to feel better. Suddenly he understood the joy of refusing himself food. A trembling, electric feeling spread upward from his feet to his abdomen, to his stomach and chest, until it reached his head and made him gasp with pleasure. But as soon as he turned off the water and got out of the shower, he legs felt as heavy as lead. And when he stood at the toilet to pee, he began to retch, but without bringing up anything except some white slime, presumably from the aspirin.

Back in the kitchen he leaned against the counter as he drank the now tepid coffee, taking little, painful sips. When he'd finished the coffee, he suddenly realized that he was naked. He brushed off a few dry bread crumbs that had stuck to his butt and then dashed for the bedroom. There he put on some clothes.

Afterward he went into the living room and opened the curtains. Even without any sun, the light hurt his eyes. He turned the easy chair around so it faced away from the window and sat down. It didn't matter that both Swamper Caribou and Andy had sat in this very chair. This whole thing is about the three of us, thought Lance. Somewhere in the house his cell was ringing, but he didn't feel like getting up to look for it. Finally it stopped, only to start up again a few seconds later.

Groaning with annoyance, Lance got up.

# 33

WHEN HE CAME TO, he found himself headed for the shoulder of the road. The car fishtailed as he yanked the steering wheel hard to the left, but after careening from one side of the lane to the other a few times, he finally regained control of the vehicle.

His heart was beating fast, and he had a nervous, flickering feeling inside his chest. Sleep, or whatever it was, had come over him so unexpectedly. It couldn't have lasted more than a couple of seconds, but that had almost been enough. Right now he needed to make his way as fast as possible to Duluth because Chrissy was in danger.

"You have to help me," she'd whispered frantically when he answered his cell.

"What's wrong?" he asked her.

"He's going to kill me."

"What?"

"I found a place to hide, but I think he's waiting for me. He tried to . . . He grabbed me by . . ."

"Where are you?" Lance had shouted, in a panic.

Without really being aware of what he was doing, he had stood in the middle of the living room, shouting into the phone.

"The parking lot at the Last Chance Liquor Store. Honk your horn." And that was the last thing she'd said.

It suddenly occurred to him that a man had attacked Chrissy. Somehow he hadn't fully realized that until now. Lance significantly exceeded the speed limit as he drove the last stretch of road from Two Harbors to Duluth.

THE LAST CHANCE LIQUOR STORE was a small place with a small parking lot. He saw two cars in the lot, and behind the wheel of one of them was a young man who looked like he was waiting for someone. Could that be the guy? Lance honked his horn, giving it two short and two long blasts, which made the young man turn in his direction. As he waited for his niece to show up, Lance looked around distractedly, trying to locate someone who better matched Chrissy's claim that a grown man had assaulted her, but he didn't see anyone. He was about to honk the horn again when Chrissy came running at full speed around the corner of the store, maybe thirty yards away, with her black coat flying out behind her. Lance leaned over to open the passenger door. Out of the corner of his eye he saw the young man jump out of his car and start hurling swear words at Chrissy. He seemed out of his mind with rage and kept punching at the air with his fist.

Chrissy slammed the door shut and threw herself flat, with her head resting on her uncle's lap.

"Are you okay?" he asked, stroking her hair as he drove out of the parking lot and down Sixth Avenue. He had an uneasy feeling that he was being used. That young man didn't fit with what his niece had told him on the phone. It sure didn't look like he was intent on attacking her, thought Lance. For some reason that young man had been furious with Chrissy.

"Maybe you'd better have something to eat," he suggested and he glanced in the rearview mirror to make sure that no one was following them.

Chrissy was still lying on his lap. When he placed his hand between her shoulder blades, he noticed how hard she was shaking.

"Good Lord, honey," murmured Lance, feeling tears rising.

This was Andy and Tammy's little girl lying here. Chrissy, who had been allowed to chase her policeman uncle around the house, from one room to another, shrieking all the way, until she arrested him. Chrissy, who should have been in school right now. The girl was supposed to make something of herself. But here she lay, shaking and sobbing.

"How about some food?" he again suggested.

She sat up, hunched over in what looked like a sitting fetal position.

"Or would you rather have a beer?"

For the first time since she'd thrown herself into the car, Chrissy looked at her uncle. Just a fleeting glance, as if to see if he really meant what he'd said.

"Okay," she replied, still shaking.

Lance drove over to Fitger's Brewhouse, which was close by, and parked.

"You need to pull yourself together," he said as they headed inside.

There were only a few other people in the pub since it was so early in the day.

"What kind of beer would you like?" he asked.

Chrissy seemed far away, as if in a state of shock.

"I don't know," she muttered in that same, unsteady voice. "Something light, I guess."

When the waiter appeared, Lance ordered a Fitger's Lighthouse Golden for his niece and a Mesabi Red for himself. He knew they'd have problems if he had to deal with someone who was a stickler for the rules, but the waiter didn't even cast a glance at the seventeen-year-old Goth girl. He merely repeated their order. Then uncle and niece sat in silence, waiting for the beers. Lance knew it wouldn't look good if anyone they knew turned up, but right now his main concern was Chrissy, and he had a strong feeling that she'd feel a lot better after drinking a beer. She was sitting on the other side of the table with her arms straight down, her elbows locked, as if she were holding on to the seat of her chair, which may have been exactly what she was doing. Her face was even paler than usual, and the dark circles under her eyes were the real thing.

The waiter came back and set the glasses of beer in front of them. No sooner had he turned around than Chrissy grabbed her pint and with trembling hands raised it to her lips. Lance watched in fascination as the young girl's delicate white throat gulped down the beer as if she were an old alcoholic. A moment later she set the glass back on the table, having finished off a good third of the beer. She gave her uncle a wan, apologetic smile.

"Maybe you should have something hot too," said Lance. "Were you lying in the snow?"

"No. In a pile of empty cardboard boxes. I've been in worse situations." She smiled briefly.

"But what are you doing here? You should be in school."

"Please don't ask."

Lance slammed his fist down, making the table jump.

"Don't ask?" he shouted. "You call me up and say that you're about to be . . . I don't know what. So I drive all the way down here from Lutsen, and all you can say is 'don't ask'?"

Chrissy raised her hands, as if to protect herself, and started to cry. A moment later the waiter soundlessly appeared behind Lance.

"Everything all right here?"

"I'm sorry," said Lance. "It won't happen again."

"Good. I hope it doesn't."

And then he was gone.

"If you don't get a grip, we're going to get thrown out," Lance whispered.

"You're the one who pounded on the table."

She drank some more of her beer, but a much smaller amount this time.

"Well, I meant what I said. Since you dragged me all the way out here, you can at least tell me who that guy was in the parking lot."

"Who do you mean?"

Lance gave her a withering look.

"Okay, he was the one who tried to—"

"Don't lie to me. Who was he?"

"A friend," Chrissy said after a moment.

"Not much of a friend."

"You can say that again."

Lance took a sip of his Mesabi Red and instantly began to cough so that foam ran down his jacket. Seeming to rise up out of the floor, the waiter was once again standing next to their table, giving them a professional and politely accusatory glare.

"Okay," said Lance, fuming. "We're leaving."

CHRISSY DIDN'T SAY A WORD as they drove out of Duluth. She sat in the passenger seat, staring straight ahead. The route they took headed inland, through big areas of marsh and bog that were famous for their rich bird life during the summertime. Right now the landscape looked like a lifeless world, which was further enhanced by the naked gray tree trunks that stuck up here and there from the snow. Lance had no idea where they were going, only that they had to get out of Duluth and whatever Chrissy had gotten herself involved in back there. And since the North Shore was not an option, they were driving across the marshlands.

"What's the matter with you?" asked Chrissy after a while. "Are you sick?"

"Haven't eaten in two days."

"Why not?"

"It's something with my throat. Can't swallow."

"So that's why your voice is . . . ?"

"Yeah."

"An infection?"

"Don't know."

"But haven't you gone to the doctor?"

"It'll get better."

Lance wondered what he should do with her. He couldn't just keep driving north toward the Iron Range and Canada. That wasn't much of a plan. She needed to get back to a normal life, which meant school, home, and girlfriends. Not running around in town the way she was doing now.

"What did he want from you?" Lance asked.

"He thought I'd taken something from him."

"And did you?"

"Does it matter?"

"Yes, if by 'taken' you mean 'stolen.' "

Chrissy shrugged.

"Do you realize how scared I was by your call?"

"But he was trying to get me."

"Yeah, because you stole something. That's not exactly the story you told me."

"Sorry."

"I think you'd better tell me what's going on."

"What do you mean?"

"You're telling too many lies. You must be mixed up in something."

"I'm not mixed up in anything."

"Well, you're not the girl I thought you were, at any rate."

"I'm Sad Water. Nobody is building any bridges for me."

She started sobbing quietly. Lance felt dizzy, not just from hunger but also because he was probably dehydrated. Except for that one sip of beer that was still making his stomach rumble, he hadn't taken in any fluids for several hours. And he had no idea where he was going. This road led to the Mesabi Iron Range, with the towns of Eveleth, Virginia, Hibbing, and Babbitt. Why would he and Chrissy go there? Yet at this point, the way back was longer than the way forward, and the lake was farther away than the iron mines. In his sluggish condition, Lance was incapable of making a decision. So he just continued driving through the desolate, snow-covered landscape, with his niece weeping in the passenger seat.

IN THE REMOTE TOWN of Eveleth they stopped at a gas station because Chrissy needed to use the restroom. She was gone longer than normal, and when she came back, Lance had confirmation of what he'd suspected for some time, although he'd never actually put it into words. It wasn't that she staggered or slurred her words. Or talked too much. No, it was more like a fire had been lit inside the body of this girl, which only a short time ago had appeared so cold and worn out. She now seemed enveloped in a sense of well-being, and Lance himself almost felt drawn to the same place, toward the warmth and light from the chemical fire burning inside her. Yet he knew how false that warmth was. As a police officer, Lance knew a great deal about drugs and their effects. Most of it he'd learned in various courses, but he'd also arrested kids who were under the influence, both at campsites in the woods and in Duluth when he was on the police force there. He guessed that Chrissy had ingested cocaine in the gas station restroom. Maybe she'd merely licked her little finger, dipped it in the white powder, and then rubbed it on her gums.

"Could you turn on the radio?" she asked.

Lance complied, and the car was instantly filled with a loud crackling sound. He turned the FM dial back and forth, trying to pick up a station, but the noise didn't stop. Chrissy pressed her hands over her ears and laughed.

"That's all I can get," said Lance after he turned off the radio. "But you know what? We need to call Tammy and Andy and tell them that you're with me and everything's fine."

"Do I have to?" She sighed.

"When's the last time you were home?"

"Yesterday, I think."

"You're not sure?"

She seemed to think hard about the question.

"No," she said at last.

Lance sighed heavily.

"It's not that easy," said Chrissy.

"What isn't?"

"Figuring out where I am all the time."

"Most people seem to manage," said Lance.

Chrissy didn't reply, as if she was scared she'd said too much. Lance took his cell phone out of his pocket.

"What's Tammy's cell number?"

"Why can't you just call our landline?"

"I don't want to talk to your dad," said Lance.

In reality he was worried that Andy would pick up the phone on the second floor to listen in on the conversation.

"Give it to me. I'll do it."

Lance handed his cell to Chrissy. She tapped in the number and handed the phone back to him. Tammy's cell rang and rang, but nobody answered. He was just about to give up when Tammy suddenly picked up, her voice low and urgent, as if she were trying to talk in secret.

"Hi, Lance. Have you heard anything from Chrissy?"

"She's sitting right here next to me."

"Oh, thank God for that."

In the background he could clearly hear the sound of cars driving past. Maybe Tammy had gone outside to take the call when she saw that he was trying to reach her. If so, there was no doubt who wasn't supposed to hear what she said.

"Is she okay?" she asked, sounding worried.

"Fine. We're on our way to Two Harbors now."

"Where was she?"

"You'll have to ask her about that. Not me."

"Okay. But thank you for—"

"Not a problem," Lance said, interrupting her. "We're family, after all."

"So when do you think you'll get here?"

"In about an hour."

"Can I talk to her?"

"No, she's sleeping."

He didn't want her to talk to her daughter when Chrissy was high. Not to spare Tammy, but so that Chrissy wouldn't end up in trouble the minute she got home. The fact that she took drugs was something that had to be dealt with, but it wouldn't help to shout and create a scene.

"Thanks," said Chrissy, giving Lance a radiant smile when he ended the call.

"Nothing to thank me for. I just thought I'd let you handle things yourself."

"It'll be fine," she said. "I'm more worried about you, Uncle Lance. Why don't we stop and get you something to eat?"

"First of all, there's no place to eat around here. We're driving through a wilderness. And secondly, I can't swallow."

"Why not? What's really wrong?"

The memory of the gun shoved down his throat was still extremely vivid.

"When was the last time you saw Andy?" he asked.

"I don't remember."

"So you don't remember, for example, whether you saw him yesterday?"

She didn't answer. Lance almost thought he could hear the

gears of her worn-out brain creaking. And then came the tears.

"Are you crying?" he asked.

Her only reply was a sniffling sound.

"Why are you crying?"

"Could you please stop the car so I can get out for a minute?" she murmured.

"There's a rest area up ahead a little ways. I'll stop there."

For the next few minutes they drove in silence while Chrissy quietly wept. When they reached the rest area, Lance pulled in and parked. Chrissy got out and lit a cigarette. She took a few steps away from the car and stood there with her back to him. Lance wondered whether she wanted to be alone or if he should get out and talk to her. He decided to get out of the car.

"Is everything all right?" he asked, feeling like an idiot.

She turned around. Dusk had begun to set in, and her cigarette glowed in the dim light.

"Where are we?" was her only response.

"Somewhere between the St. Louis and the Whiteface Rivers."

"Shit," mumbled Chrissy, looking around. "What a wasteland."

"Not a lot of people, if that's what you mean."

"That too. Why did our ancestors have to settle in this particular place?"

"I have no idea. But it wasn't easy, I can tell you that," replied Lance. "They worked in the mines. They were loggers. And fishermen. But what our forefathers never did was give up. And you shouldn't either."

"But I'm no longer one of them," said Chrissy.

"Yes, you are. You'll always be one of them, no matter what."

"No. I'm Sad Water. An evil medicine man has cast a spell over me."

# 34

THE WAVES OF HUNGER reminded him of the Northern Lights. The feeling had some of that same trembling, electric movement about it, like when curtains of the phosphorescent green light rippled across the winter sky. But then the feeling was replaced by nausea, and he started to retch, without bringing anything up. He sat hunched in his chair, uttering long, drawn-out grunting sounds that hardly sounded human at all.

When he stood up, the room spun halfway around on its own axis. He took a few short steps, trying to correct his orientation, and crashed right into the wall, but he stayed on his feet. Somewhere far away he thought he heard the sound of breaking glass. He was headed to the kitchen to drink some more water. Ever since he'd returned home after dropping his niece off in Two Harbors, he'd made sure to drink water at regular intervals. He still found it impossible to eat any solid food, but the most important thing at the moment was not to get dehydrated.

In the kitchen he filled a glass with water and proceeded to take small, cautious sips. He'd tried to eat an overripe banana when he came home, but even that proved too much to swallow. It'll be better tomorrow, he told himself. Tomorrow it has to be better.

He just had to make it through the night. And try to get some sleep.

When he went back to the living room, he saw that a

photograph had fallen off the wall, breaking the glass. He knelt down to have a look. It was Andy's high school picture. His face looked splintered behind the shattered glass. That young smile— so big and dazzling white and full of feigned self-confidence—was no longer whole. And one eye had vanished behind a big crack in the glass, while the other was still staring straight at the camera. Lance felt something warm run down his cheek. A drop of blood landed on the photo and immediately dispersed into tiny beads that spread across the front of his brother's shirt. The blood kept on falling. He watched with fascination as each drop struck the photo until Andy's face was practically covered in blood. All that he could see of the smile now was a glimpse of a couple of white teeth amid the red.

Lance was instantly transported back to the woods near Baraga's Cross on that June morning last summer, when he stood staring down at the body of the Norwegian canoeist Georg Lofthus. The man was lying on his stomach, with his face pressed against the ground, and yet Lance could see his teeth. That was what had shaken him the most. A row of pearly white teeth in that repulsive mass of blood and hair, as if his smile had been slammed through his head and out the back. Lance wondered what sort of force had been required to do something like that.

He got to his feet and began looking for his cell phone as the blood continued to run down his face. Where had he left it? He tried to focus, but he just couldn't do it anymore. The headache was back, and every pulse exploded against his skull on the inside. Finally he realized that his cell was in his pants pocket. He sat down in the easy chair and fumbled for a while with the keys before he managed to display the right name and number. How late was it over there? He didn't have the energy to figure it out.

Eirik Nyland answered the phone at once.

"Ja?" he said brusquely.

"It's Lance Hansen."

"Ah. Listen here, I'm a little busy at the moment."

"There's something I have to . . ."

Lance was having trouble formulating the words and putting them in the proper order.

"I'm in the middle of something right now," said Nyland. "Couldn't I—"

"No!" shouted Lance. "No, no, no!"

Eirik Nyland laughed uncertainly on the other side of the Atlantic.

"Okay," he said. "Wait just a minute."

There was a thud as Nyland apparently set down the phone. Then Lance heard him speaking Norwegian in the background, and another man answered.

"Sorry about that, Lance," said Nyland. "I've got a few minutes now. What was it you wanted to talk about?"

"The murder," said Lance. "Georg Lofthus, the way his head was . . . I mean, the degree of . . . His head was smashed almost flat! I was wondering how much force that took. Not just anybody could have done that, right?"

"But Lenny Diver isn't just anybody when it comes to physical strength," said Nyland. "From what I remember, he's a young man who's apparently in good physical condition."

"Yeah. But that's not what's bothering me . . . I just . . . purely theoretically. Who could have done that, and who couldn't have?"

"Tell me, is everything okay with you?" asked Nyland.

"No, it's not. I haven't eaten in days. Some sort of flu, I guess. Fever, and so on."

"Sounds awful. So, you're asking me who could have committed a murder like that? Almost anybody, I'd say. The point is, that when you hit a man in the head once with a baseball bat, he's most likely going to fall to the ground. The rest is . . . Then it's just a matter of continuing to pound on him. It's the weight and length of the bat, meaning the potential force of the murder weapon itself, that's the key. More than the strength of the killer."

"I didn't think of that."

"The bat exerts a tremendous force when it's swung," Nyland went on. "So I'd say almost anyone could have done it. Even a woman could have easily caused the injuries Lofthus sustained. And she wouldn't have to be especially strong. As I said, it's a matter of striking that first blow. After that, the murderer would just have to swing the bat a sufficient number of times."

Lance retched.

"Have you seen a doctor?" asked Nyland, concerned.

"No. I'm sure I'll feel better soon."

"But shouldn't you . . . ?"

"I know. I know."

"Go to bed now, at least. Get some sleep. I'll give you a call in a few days."

"You will?" Lance was surprised.

"Sure. Somebody should be looking out for you," said Nyland. "But right now I've got to get back to work."

"A murder?" asked Lance.

"It never ends."

"No, it doesn't."

"Good night. Or whatever the time is over there," said Nyland.

"Good night," whispered Lance, totally exhausted from the brief conversation.


WHEN HE GOT UP to go to the kitchen to drink more water, his head started pounding so hard that he could barely stay on his feet. After a moment the headache eased a bit, and he made it to the kitchen, where he drank another glass of water, cautiously taking little sips. He retched a few times but managed to keep the water down. There was something obvious that he'd overlooked until now. But no, his brain refused to function. He looked with confusion at the cell phone he was holding in his left hand. When he was done drinking the water, he tapped on the keys until he found the contact list and began scrolling through it, not sure what he was looking for. Chrissy's name and number popped up. Sooner or later he had to have a serious talk with her, but this wasn't exactly the appropriate time. Yet her name remained on the display, as if silently challenging him to call. He considered phoning her until his eyes fell on a name right under his niece's. Debbie! There must be a way into that hard Finnish American heart of hers. Some way to melt it. Melt it like butter. The thought of Debbie Ahonen and melted butter brought a groan to Lance's lips.

Back in the living room he sat down in the easy chair, holding his cell and ready to type in the magic words. But what should he write? Just a few words. Maybe a question? *Do you remember . . . ?* But what was there to remember that could possibly overcome all doubt in her mind? Lance closed his eyes and thought back more than twenty years and immediately pictured Debbie sitting on the shore of Lake Superior, which was enveloped in a fine summer mist. Her blond hair fluttered faintly in the wind. She had tucked up her legs and wrapped her arms around her knees. Now she turned her head to the left, pressing it against the shoulder of the young man sitting beside her. They would end up sitting there for a long time, until the moon rose over the lake. It was one of the first times they were together as lovers, and something special had happened between them on that evening on the rocky expanse near Baraga's Cross. An utter dearth of words that had nothing to do with a lack of anything to say, but for once words were superfluous. They had done nothing but touch each other and look at each other for long, slow moments, just Debbie and Lance, together in something that might turn out to be big.

It could still be something big, he thought, opening his eyes. He blinked several times to clear his vision before starting to type with a trembling thumb: *Do you remember that evening at Baraga's Cross?* This was his last chance. He hurried to press "send" and watched the text message disappear from the display. In a few seconds Debbie's cell would sound. Maybe she was watching TV with Richie Akkola. Lance switched off his cell. He couldn't deal with this now, no matter what her response might be. Somewhere deep inside he knew that he might not get any reply at all.

# 35

FULLY DRESSED, he sat up in bed and listened. There was a sound in the room that he couldn't place. Or was it coming from outside? A sound that made him think of rain. The floor lamp in the corner cast a sickly green glow over the bedcovers and floorboards. He went over to the window and opened the curtains. A faint gurgling of water was barely audible. That must be what had made him think of rain. Silently he glided across the vast deep. With each stroke of the paddle the darkness grew beneath him, the lake opened, and the only thing between him and the depths was the thin birchbark canoe. Far below, on the bottom of the lake, lay the man-sized sturgeons in their semiconscious, semi-alive state, primeval fish that had been here long before any humans and must not be disturbed. They lay in the mud, with their eyes turned upward as they listened. They were all aware that something was happening up above. A birchbark canoe was gliding across the lake. It was night. Lance was paddling into the dark with a feeling of being released from something. Maybe just from the mainland. He could no longer see its contours when he turned around to look. No lights were visible, only the moon casting a wide stripe on the dark surface of the water. He tried to paddle on top of the length of moonlight, but it kept breaking up a short distance ahead of the canoe. Through the dark below him raced great herds of buffalo. The thundering sound of their hooves penetrated the waters under which they were imprisoned.

Down there is the buffalo's realm of the dead, he thought. The second he had that thought, he realized that it was occurring to him in a dream. *I'm dreaming,* said a voice right behind him. He turned around, but there was no one else in the canoe. Below him the thundering of the buffalo herd continued. On the dark prairie down there, no one could reach them. There they were safe, though at the same time they were held captive beneath the unfathomably heavy covering of water.

Far in the distance someone is singing. He opens his eyes, but it's dark, and he sees only treetops silhouetted against the sky high above, and between them a star gleaming. He sits up and breathes in the cool night air. There is a faint smell of smoke; somewhere a campfire is burning. And there's the song again, so far away that it's impossible to distinguish any words or melody, but they are singing. People are sitting around a fire and singing. He closes his eyes and tries to figure out whether it would be dangerous to seek them out, but his mind isn't functioning as it normally does. He is having dream-thoughts, and that's why, in the next instant, he sees an entire armada of canoes moving forward at great speed, rhythmically paddled by men who are singing, big canoes made of hides, each holding ten to twelve men dressed in colorful attire. Some have scarves wrapped around their heads; they are wearing red shirts, blue shirts, hats with long feathers. Sitting in the middle of the paddlers in one canoe is a man wearing an old-fashioned black suit and a small bowler-type hat. He's the only man who isn't paddling. His knees are pressed close together, and on his lap is a leather case that seems to contain important documents from a bank in Europe. The men are paddling with a determination that leaves no doubt that they know where they're headed and that they have important work to do there. High overhead he catches a glimpse of daylight, but it's dark down in the depths where they're paddling. The oars stir up swirls of air bubbles that are flung behind, past the stern of the canoes, and then they disappear into the dark. The flashes of daylight remind him that a world exists above the surface, outside the dream. He reaches out toward it and is on his way up through the light, but then he sees that the glittering ribbon of air bubbles from the oars is already far away, sloping steeply downward into the deep. When he opens his eyes again, it's still dark, and in the distance someone is singing. A heavy rushing sound passes through the branches above him. Down here he feels the wind gently caressing his face; it smells faintly of smoke from a campfire. As he walks through the forest, heading toward the song, which keeps getting clearer, he realizes that he is moving in a dream. Yet he can't remember where in the waking world he is having this dream, and he can't recall who he is. Until he finds out, he won't be able to wake up. He is caught in the dream, and he knows it. Because he is nobody, he feels utterly empty inside as he walks toward the fire. He follows a small stream. The moonlight shoots out in all directions when he treads in the water, raining streaks of light over his boots. The song has ceased, and everyone is looking at the stranger who is coming toward them, taking hesitant steps. Scattered over the ground are books and papers. A black typewriter sits on a rock, gleaming in the light from the flames. The man with the bowler hat stands up. Now he touches his index finger to his chin, feigning an inquiring pose. "You do not know who you are, hmm?" he says with a thick French accent. "Ah, it is a hard nut to crack. Who is this bold young man who has so unexpectedly wandered into the light of our campfire?" He speaks with a certain irony. "Oh yes, he is one of those people who wants to leave the old country. Am I right? You want to travel to the country that is even older. Yes?" And he points toward the darkness, though there is really nothing to see. "Go ahead," he says. "Lac Supérieur!"

That couldn't be phosphorescence, he thinks, noticing the glints of light flickering out there. Nor is it moonlight, because the sky is overcast and rain is pouring down. His hair is soaking wet, and the drops that run down into his mouth taste salty and sour from dirt and sweat. He doesn't know how long he's been hiding behind the lifeboat, or how long the voyage has taken, but now they have reached the land where their dreams will become real. Only now does life begin. The deck is gently rocking, just as it has for a very long time. He can hardly remember a life without the rhythmic rocking from the waves; that's how long they've been traveling. The others have now appeared on deck—black-clad figures; women wearing big hats, with the rain dripping from the brims. It looks as if they've all put on their best clothes. A little girl is standing right next to him, but she doesn't notice him as he huddles behind the lifeboat. He peers up at her and sees that she is crying. Maybe she's afraid because nothing looks familiar. He, on the other hand, feels merely empty, as if everything he once was has been drained away. He has been wrung out and emptied and then sewn back together, but with nothing inside. An empty man. As the rain runs down his face and he surreptitiously watches the little girl who is crying, he notices that something is happening on deck. He doesn't dare look, for fear of being discovered, but suddenly the girl grabs him by the shoulder and says something. He tries to push her away, but she shouts to the adults, and several men wearing heavy boots come stomping across the deck. They are speaking a language that is not like any he has ever heard before. When they seize his arms and haul him out of his hiding place behind the lifeboat, he tries to talk to them, but not a sound comes out of his mouth. The men drag him across the deck toward the rest of the black-clad group, which has practically merged with the surrounding darkness. Then the men force him to take a position among the others. Seated in front are the women with the youngest children; they smell of fish and urine. Anxiously he looks at the men standing on either side of him; he can barely make out their faces in the rain and darkness. They have long, drooping mustaches. Now a ripple of excitement seems to pass through the group; they straighten up, murmuring to one another as the women adjust their hats. Finally they all fall silent. Everyone is staring straight ahead at an indistinct figure standing next to the railing. A man who doesn't look as if he belongs to the group. It's for him that they all straighten their backs. Beside him stands the camera tripod with the dark cloth that photographers always carry. That man must be a photographer from the New World, he thinks. "I'm dreaming," says a voice right behind him. He turns around but sees only an old, stern-looking man who is staring stiffly at the photographer. At that moment the flash explodes in a white *bang!* that totally blinds him. For a long time afterward, a dazzling light hovers before his eyes, hiding the darkness. He can still hear the rain falling on the people all around him. Some of the men start shouting, sounding annoyed, and soon he feels strong hands grip his arms to drag him away from the group. As they press him against the rail and force his arms behind his back, he senses everyone else crowding behind him, black-clad and afraid of the land waiting out there in the dark. They know their own stories are no longer important; what matters are the unknown tales they will never fully understand. When he realizes the after-effects from the flash are gone, he opens his eyes, hoping to catch a glimpse of the new land. And now he sees what all those tiny lights are—the ones he first thought might be phosphorescence. What he sees over there is a glittering town. At that instant men grab him around the waist and by both legs and then lift him over the railing like a black sack.

Slowly he falls through the vast space, his brain taking note of the fact that the night has stayed up there where the black-clad people are probably still standing, waiting for the splash in the dark. He has already forgotten who they are. The big, empty space is filled with a bluish light. Far below, maybe as much as a hundred yards, he sees the bottom. Falling through water is exactly like falling through air, only slower, he thinks, drawing his legs up into a horizontal position. He clasps his hands behind his head and then he is lying there as comfortably as if in a hammock. After a while he looks down to check how far he has gone, and to his surprise he is already passing between the huge blue-shimmering icebergs. The cold settles like a wet blanket over his whole body. He falls precipitously the last few yards, and his chin slams into his knees when he hits bottom. Even before he can get to his feet, he knows that something is seriously wrong. It's difficult to stay upright because the bottom is nothing but ice. Above him tower the pyramid-shaped icebergs. And above them, in turn, is the vast space through which he has fallen. But there is no way back. He attempts to jump, but gets no higher than he would if standing on dry land. It's just as impossible to go from here up to the surface as it is to leap from the ground up to the sky. Terror wraps itself like armor around his torso, shutting off his airways. He can't breathe. He falls onto the shifting ice; he tries to scream in pain, but not a sound comes out. Just as he thinks his body is going to explode from lack of oxygen, the pressure suddenly eases. A series of bubbles issues from his lips, a shiny string of pearls that rises to the surface high above. But then there are no more bubbles. He is no longer hurting, but he's not breathing either. He is cold all the way through, and without a single breath. "I'm dead," whispers a voice right behind him. He turns around, but sees only the icy-blue landscape. "I'm dead," the voice says again, and now he has no idea where it's coming from. The low whispering seems to fill the whole space around him, as if it has become one with the ice and the cold and the bluish light. He can move, but he is no longer breathing, and he's colder than any living person can be. If you die in a dream, you also die in reality—he has heard that said many times. This is the realm of the dead, he thinks, and cautiously begins tottering forward, the ground uneven underfoot. There is nothing for him to wake up to. The world he came from is gone. He no longer really remembers it—something about a boat and falling overboard. The cold gnaws at his bones, but it can't kill him because he's already dead. Yet freezing is painful. His teeth have started to come loose and fall out. He leaves behind an irregular trail of teeth, spitting them out as he walks. White pearls on a winding string laid out on the grayish-blue icy bottom. For a moment he's excited about the idea that he could turn around and follow this trail back. Then he realizes that it wouldn't make any difference if he managed to return to where he'd started. There is no way out of the realm of the dead.

A path is barely visible, climbing the slope between the blocks of ice. Did animals or people go up there? He bends down, trying to discern any tracks, but there's not enough light. No matter what, the path must lead somewhere, so he continues upward. Soon he finds himself in a narrow cleft, no more than a couple of yards wide, between two bare mountain slopes. The cleft appears to be a dead end with not a hint of light up ahead; the dark merely intensifies. But something has to be there, since the path has led him this way. Soon the cleft shrinks to a hole the size of a man. He lies down and peers into the hole, but it's pitch dark inside. Then he begins wriggling his way forward as he feels an ever-growing sense of panic threatening to tear him apart from the inside. He is completely encapsulated in the mountain, like a fossil. Now he can feel both shoulders scraping the sides of the tunnel, and it's almost impossible to move. Yet he can glimpse a faint light straight ahead. Maybe this could be a way out. And now he sees that he's looking at stars. A corner of the night sky.

HE FEELS like he has crossed an entire continent to reach this particular spot. That's how worn out he is as he stands there, looking at the distant lake, which sparkles like a huge gem-stone. Surrounded by darkness, it looks as if it's floating freely in space. Now the terrain gets steeper; great waterfalls drape like bridal veils down the mountainside. Suddenly he hears muted voices. He crouches down behind a bush and peers through the branches. There they come, three men clad in buckskin, wearing colorful caps and scarves around their necks. Each man carries on his back a big pack held in place by a strap around his fore-head. The language they're speaking is not one he knows. One of the men laughs quietly—a warm sound—as they pass the bush that he's sitting behind. Only when he can no longer hear their voices does he get up and continue along the stream, heading in the same direction as the three men. Now he is certain that some-thing is down there, but he doesn't know what it is. The wind has a deserted smell to it, as if there are hardly any people on the entire continent, only a handful here and there, small groups like the one that just passed by. Everything seems so muted, subdued. The noise of the world has not yet been activated; the switch to turn it on has not been touched. Someday all that he now sees— the dark woodland and the huge lake shining in the distance—will echo with the roar of people. But not yet. The night is still quiet. The forest changes the lower he goes. Oaks and maples, with the wind rushing through their crowns. Occasionally he enters a clearing with a view and is able to see the expansive nighttime landscape. Then he knows morning will never come, no matter how long he waits. He glimpses figures going in and out of the circle of light from the campfire, and voices drift toward him on the night breeze. Without fear and without memory he wanders among the tents and makeshift cabins. No one cries out or points at him. It's as if nobody sees him, and soon he realizes it's true.

They can't see him. And someone who's invisible can do whatever he likes. That person has power, he thinks. But in reality it's
merely frightening. He walks around looking at the men in their
colorful garb and the hats with the long feathers. He squats down
in front of them and looks into their faces. Studies every wrinkle
radiating from the corners of the eyes in an old man's face, looks
at the yellow teeth in mouths filled with tobacco spittle, sees their
knives, their rifles with the long barrels. He can look at everything and yet not be seen, but this frightens him. He feels as if he's
dead, while these men are alive. There are many tents and cabins,
many campfires with men seated around them, but everything
is so calm. At a campfire a short distance away a man stands up
and starts toward him, moving slowly, tentatively, as if trying to
take his bearings from a smell or a faint sound. The man wears a
small round hat and a pince-nez. When he gets close, he stops.
It's clear that the man can't see him, although he seems to know
that someone is there. "Ah, you spirit who wanders about in the
dark," he says with a French accent that would seem more appropriate on a music-hall stage than out here in the woods. "How
do you like our little encampment? Attractive, isn't it? Come. Let
me show you what has always been waiting for you." He blindly
stretches out his hand toward the man who is invisible, toward
the spirit wandering in the dark. Then he heads for the lake, taking a muddy path. Soon they are standing on the shore of a small
bay, next to a birchbark canoe. The man with the bowler hat turns
around and smiles at the air. "Each man has his own canoe!" he
says enthusiastically. "Your canoe has been waiting for you. Now
it will take you safely to the other side. Don't be afraid of storms
or monsters; in the realm of the dead no one dies. Bon voyage!"
He bows deeply, making a sweeping gesture with his hat.

THE DARK is almost impenetrable, but Lance forces himself to
keep going between the tree trunks, which are as big and smooth
as marble pillars. Fear is hovering just below the surface, ready to
catch him in its net. Finally the forest opens up, and he is looking
at the enormous lake. The moon has spread a wide stripe across
the water, reaching all the way over to the canoe pulled halfway

up onto the shore. An old-fashioned birchbark canoe. He also notices the smell of smoke. Not far away someone has a campfire going. Following his nose, he heads toward the fire until he's so close he can see the sparks swiftly rising into the air and vanishing in the dark. He thinks this is where he's supposed to be, even though he doesn't know why. This is the place, he thinks. After a moment he starts walking toward the flames, but he stops when he discovers the dark, hunched figure sitting with his back turned, looking as if he has been there a long time. Should he step forward and make his presence known?

Then the man at the campfire raises his hand and calmly motions for him to approach, though without casting even a glance over his shoulder. Lance musters his courage and goes over to him. The man peers up from under the brim of his big, round hat. His face is shiny with grease, or whatever it might be; his eyes are as black as an otter's. "So, it's you," he says, as if he's been waiting for him. "The spirit who wanders in the dark?" It occurs to Lance that he has reached Swamper Caribou's encampment. "Why are you haunting me?" he asks, but the medicine man does not reply. His face is impassive, but his black eyes gleam in the light from the fire. Now Lance notices that Swamper is holding something in his hands, something that is partially hidden in the shadows on his lap. Now and then the flames cast a flickering light over the object, but he still can't see what it is. Suddenly this object commands all his attention. He even manages to overcome his fear of the medicine man to go over and squat down beside him. Up close he sees that Swamper has several cuts on the bridge of his nose. The strands of hair sticking out from under his hat are wet, and water is dripping from the brim. Lance reaches his hand toward the object, but Swamper Caribou hugs it closer, holding it in a tight grip. "You can't have it," he says sternly. "It can't be taken up to the surface." Ashamed, Lance withdraws his hand. The Indian raises the object up to the light from the fire. "This is what you are looking for," he says. At first Lance can't tell what it is, but then he realizes that it's a wooden figure of two people holding hands. Again he reaches for the figure, but cautiously this time, respectfully. As he touches it, the medicine man repeats the words: "This is what you are looking for."

# 36

IT TOOK ONLY A FEW SECONDS after Lance woke up for him to realize he'd been dreaming. He climbed out of bed and went into the home office, where he found a pen and paper and proceeded to write down everything he could remember, all the way up to Swamper Caribou's last words: *This is what you are looking for.*

His throat felt better, so he went into the kitchen to cook bacon and eggs. The smell caused him to produce an excessive amount of saliva that came pouring out of his mouth. He leaned over the sink, spitting, while he did his best to wield the spatula. A couple of times his legs started to buckle. It was now almost three days since he'd had anything to eat.

Lance Hansen's big, hollow-feeling stomach turned somersaults of joy when the food entered his system. His guts rumbled and growled and whined as if about to develop their own language. After washing down the food with a strong cup of coffee, he felt almost human again. He groaned and happily patted his stomach, but the sudden sensation of being full also brought on an acute weariness, even though he'd just gotten up. He went into the living room and stretched out on the sofa, where he instantly fell asleep. When he woke up only twenty minutes later, he was so soaked in sweat that he got up to take a shower.

As he stood under the spray of hot water, it occurred to him that he'd had another dream, but this time it was merely disconnected images dealing exclusively with food and Debbie Ahonen, in the strangest combinations. Oh no, that stupid text message that he'd sent her last night. It couldn't be real. That must be something that he'd imagined because he was so hungry. When he finished showering, he checked his cell and saw to his alarm that he had, in fact, both written and sent the text. And Debbie was the recipient. She hadn't replied. No, of course not. She was probably trying to forget the whole thing had even happened. *Do you remember that evening at Baraga's Cross?* He sounded like an eighteen-year-old boy who'd been dumped.

Yet his first dream in almost eight years had been such a tremendous experience that it overshadowed everything else. The text to Debbie, Andy breaking in, the gun in his mouth, Chrissy's drug use, the two Ojibwe men who had threatened him—they all lost their significance when compared to the fact that he had dreamed.

HE GOT DRESSED and drove to Grand Marais, much too wound up to stay home. On the way north, driving through a light snowfall, he began to wonder whether the dream meant something. He wasn't at all sure whether dreams had meaning. Was there any research on the subject? He pictured in his mind a bumper sticker: *Dream researchers do it in their sleep.* No, the dream had been a chaos of nighttime impressions, a journey that kept leading him to the lake or down into it. He couldn't imagine gleaning any sort of meaning from that. The one exception was the wooden figure Swamper Caribou had shown him. *This is what you are looking for.* There had been something insistent about that specific scene, as if everything else had simply been a long detour on its way to that figure. Two people holding hands. But what did it mean? Debbie and him, perhaps? Was that what he was looking for? In that case, he'd probably ruined the whole thing.

By the time he reached Grand Marais he was hungry again. He parked outside the South of the Border café and went inside. The place was popular with both truckers and locals.

"Hi, Lance. Long time no see," said the waitress when she caught sight of him.

"Hi, Martha."

"Lunch?"

"No, second breakfast," said Lance.

"You don't say?"

"Bacon and eggs and hash browns, rye toast, coffee, and mineral water."

"You got it."

Sitting at the very back, in a small separate section, was Bill Eggum, who had been sheriff of Cook County for twenty-five years until he retired shortly after Georg Lofthus was murdered. Lance went right over to him.

"Mind if I join you?" he asked when Eggum looked up.

"Be my guest," said the former sheriff and then went back to eating his piece of pie.

Lance sat down.

"Nice day," he said.

Eggum replied with a grunt that could mean anything except a desire to chat. So Lance sat and looked out the window. The snow was coming down harder. A couple of cars, their windshield wipers working overtime, crept along the narrow street. It was probably stretching things a bit to call it a "nice day," but he was in an elated mood because of the dream. As he sat there, waiting for Eggum to finish eating, he saw a car he recognized pull into the liquor store lot across the street. Out of the broken-down white pickup climbed the two long-haired guys who had threatened him in Grand Portage. He hadn't got a good look at their faces because they'd deliberately avoided looking at him directly, but now he realized that there was something familiar about them. As they went inside the store, Lance saw out of the corner of his eye that Bill Eggum was wiping his mouth with the back of his hand and pushing the empty plate aside.

"Thought you were in Norway," the former sheriff said.

"I was."

"So how was it?"

"Hmm . . . a little boring, to tell the truth."

"Yeah, well. Why bother to leave the country?" said Eggum. "We've got everything we need right here on the North Shore."

"How do you like retirement?" asked Lance.

"Spend all my time fishing."

"Even in the winter?"

"Yup. Out on the ice. Sit there on a little chair, jigging the line all day long," said Eggum.

"Don't you get lonely?"

"No. I listen to the radio."

"*Car Talk?*"

"Sure. Those guys are hilarious."

"Do you miss the job?"

"Nope. I gotta tell you, fishing is much better."

"I buy my fish in the grocery store."

"Yeah, but that's no way to kill time."

"Guess not," Lance had to admit.

They sat in silence for a moment, sipping their coffee and looking out the window. Then the two long-haired guys came out of the liquor store. Just outside the door, one of them almost dropped the bag he was carrying and had to pause to shift his grip. His pal turned around and said something to him. Suddenly Lance realized these two men were the same ones who had been with Chrissy and her friend in the Kozy Bar.

"Do you know who those guys are out there?" asked Lance.

Bill Eggum leaned forward to look.

"Two small-time crooks from Grand Portage," he replied. "Arrested them a couple of times, but they're mostly just dopers. Why do you ask?"

"Oh, I happened to notice their vehicle in the woods a few times and wondered who the owner was," Lance lied.

The two men got in the pickup and drove off.

"Lou Prodhomme is the name of one of them, but he's called Mist. The other is Duane Kingbird," said Eggum. "Mist and King, two birds of a feather."

"Friends of Lenny Diver?" asked Lance.

"Uh-huh. Those two were supposed to be his alibi the first time he was interviewed, just a couple of days after the murder. Don't you remember? Two friends that he claimed he'd been playing cards with all night, or something like that. It was them. Mist and King."

"Oh, right, I remember now," said Lance. "But tell me, why did the police initially want to interview Diver at all? That was long before they found any biological evidence that indicated the killer had to be an Indian."

"Anonymous tips."

"Somebody called the police about him?" said Lance, surprised.

"And demanded to talk to me," said Eggum.

"What did he say?"

"Just that Lenny Diver from Grand Portage killed the Norwegian at Baraga's Cross."

"Did you check the phone number he was calling from?"

Eggum cocked his fleshy head to one side, looking a bit uncomfortable.

"Is there any special reason you ask?"

Lance automatically reverted to his standard lie.

"I was the one who found the body, you know. And I've never been able to forget it."

"So you're not doing any investigating on your own?" asked Eggum.

"The case was solved long ago."

"True enough. Well, the tip was called in from a phone booth in Duluth."

"And it was a man?"

"I'm not really sure," said Eggum. "I remember thinking the person sounded strange. As if trying to disguise his voice."

At that moment the waitress brought Lance his food.

"You need to watch out for this guy," Eggum told her, pointing at Lance. "He's a sly fox who sticks his nose into everything."

"I always watch out for men who eat two breakfasts in one day," said Martha.

Eggum stared at Lance in disbelief.

"Is that your second breakfast?" he asked.

Lance nodded as he started shoveling food into his mouth.

"Have you gone out of your mind?"

Again he nodded.

# 37

IN THE THREE YEARS since the divorce, he'd never once canceled a weekend with Jimmy, but now that everything around him was spinning out of control, he thought it best to keep a certain distance. On the phone he'd just told his son that he'd come down with a sore throat, but he was sure he'd be fine by next weekend. Now he was standing in the middle of the living room, thinking that he ought to be feeling guilty, but he didn't. One of his first tasks, when this whole thing was over, would be to stop this habit of lying.

When this whole thing was over . . . If he didn't turn Andy in, it would never come to an end. He looked at the broken glass on the framed photograph of his brother, which was still lying on the floor. It actually seemed quite fitting that it was broken, because the Andy he knew no longer existed. It was not the real Andy who had assaulted him, just an evil remnant of his brother that had come to seek revenge. Now Lance understood much better what had happened to Andy as they'd both grown older. And why he had become such a bitter man who almost never smiled or had a friendly word for anyone. No one had known anything. Andy had been forced to bear it all alone.

Lance picked up the photo and a few shards of glass that had fallen out. He carried them into the kitchen and tossed them in the garbage. In the hall he paused to look at the picture of Andy and himself, posing on either side of the big buck. He had made up his mind to take it down on the day he reported to the police the suspicions he had about his brother. What he said would probably lead to Andy being arrested and convicted. When that happened, Lance wouldn't be able to keep a picture showing the two of them together. But for now, the photo was still on the wall. Before he took the last step, he had to make absolutely sure Andy really was the murderer. The worst thing would be if he sent his own brother to prison to serve a life sentence for a crime he didn't commit.

Lance sat in his easy chair, sighing heavily. This was too much responsibility, but he had to deal with it; otherwise he'd never be able to look himself in the eye again. He tried to sum up all the information he thought might be relevant to the case, but he ended up with a tangled mess. One thing seemed to rise above all the rest, and he kept coming back to it. Swamper Caribou saying, *This is what you are looking for.* A wooden figure depicting two people holding hands. As if it held the answer to all his questions, if only he could hear what it said. After sitting there for a while, with the image of that figure repeatedly appearing in his mind, Lance became aware of a great stillness inside him. The confusion ceased, and to his great surprise, he remembered something he'd forgotten.

HE PARKED in front of Willy Dupree's house without giving a thought to what he would say if Mary and Jimmy were there. And they might very well be visiting, since it was only seven thirty on a Friday night.

After pounding insistently on the door a few times, he heard Willy's voice.

"Okay, okay, okay," he grumbled from inside the house.

"Hi," said Lance, when Willy opened the door.

"Oh. Is that you?"

He looked tired, as if he'd been jolted out of a nap.

"Were you asleep?"

"Come on in," said the old man.

After they'd each settled in their usual places and Willy had compelled his visitor to eat a cookie, the first thing Lance noticed was an object on the coffee table that hadn't been there before.

A chic-looking little bottle, maybe three inches tall, with something black inside. He saw that Willy was looking at him with an expectant smile.

"Nail polish," the old man said at last.

"Oh?" said Lance, surprised. But then he got it. "Ah," he exclaimed.

"Your black-clad niece."

"So Chrissy has . . ."

"Drink your coffee while it's hot," said Willy, shoving the plate of cookies closer to Lance. "And have another cookie. You look pale."

Lance did as he was told. Besides, the cookies were good, so he ate a few more.

"Is there something special that you wanted to talk about?" asked Willy after they'd been eating cookies and drinking coffee in silence for a while.

"It's actually something incredible," said Lance. "I had a dream."

"Is that right?" said Willy with interest.

"A long dream."

"Had you been fasting?"

"No, that wasn't necessary. Well, actually, that's exactly what I did. I got a sore throat, some sort of infection, and I couldn't eat anything for three days."

Willy raised his eyebrows. He seemed impressed.

"So that did the trick?" he asked.

"Uh-huh. But what's really amazing, and the reason I'm sitting here, is that I dreamed about the wooden figure, the two people holding hands."

"What?"

He could see that this was going a little too fast for Willy.

"I dreamed about Swamper Caribou, just like you said I would. He was waiting for me in the dream. When I asked him why he couldn't leave me alone, he held up the little figure and said, 'This is what you are looking for.' It was a wooden figure of two people holding hands."

"But that was in a dream I once had," exclaimed Willy in surprise.

"Precisely. That's what I suddenly remembered."

"In my dream I was down by the lake, looking for anything that might have floated ashore," said Willy. "It was after a storm. That was when I found the tree root that looked exactly like two people holding hands. And I remember telling you about it. That must be where you got the idea. But then the figure jumped from my dream into yours. Not all that strange, actually."

"I guess not," said Lance. "But the important part is that Swamper Caribou was holding the figure up toward me and saying that it was what I was looking for."

Willy got up and went over to the old dream catcher hanging from a nail on the wall. He took it down. Without a word he placed it on the coffee table in front of Lance, who hesitantly reached out to touch it. The wood of the teardrop-shaped frame was gray with age, several of the threads in the web had come loose, and only one tattered-looking feather remained of the decoration.

"Did one of your ancestors make this?"

"You know who made it."

"No, I don't," said Lance. But then he realized what the old man meant.

"Swamper Caribou?"

Willy Dupree gave a slight nod.

"I want you to have it," he told Lance.

"Why?"

"You've earned it."

Lance wanted to thank the old man, but he couldn't come up with the right words.

"This is what you are looking for," said Willy thoughtfully, thinking again about the dream. "Did you interpret what he said literally?"

"Yeah, I did," said Lance.

"So you're looking for two people who are holding hands?"

"I guess so."

"Maybe it means you should find yourself a woman," said Willy with a gleam in his eye.

Lance thought about Debbie Ahonen and the text he'd sent her. No matter who the figure represented in his dream, it couldn't be him and Debbie.

"Maybe you're the one who's got a girlfriend." Lance nodded at the bottle of nail polish on the table.

Willy laughed.

"What exactly did she want?" asked Lance.

"She wanted to talk about the fact that all of you have some Indian blood. It seems to have made a big impression on her. She was especially interested in that," he said, nodding at the dream catcher on the table. "Apparently she's suffering from nightmares."

Lance stared at the bottle of nail polish. It was such a glaring presence in the room with the old-fashioned furniture and the oval-framed black-and-white photographs on the walls. Yet he had a strange feeling it somehow belonged here.

"Did she say anything about me?" he asked.

"That you're a man in crisis," replied Willy.

"That I'm what?"

"That you're messing up your own life, like a man wandering through a dark house."

"Jesus," exclaimed Lance.

"That's one smart girl," said Willy.

Lance didn't like the thought of those two sitting here only a few hours earlier, talking about him. The idiot roaming around in the dark, unable to figure anything out.

"What else did she say?" he asked.

"About you?"

"Yeah."

"That she likes you," said Willy.

Without warning a sob rose up in Lance's throat, and tears filled his eyes. Willy noticed and looked away. The next second Lance felt a tear run down his cheek. He wiped it off on the sleeve of his sweater.

"Did she say anything about herself?" His voice quavered.

"She said she's Sad Water."

"She's got problems," said Lance.

"I could tell."

Lance pictured the white-haired Indian talking to the Goth girl, who listened as she put on black nail polish. Those slender white hands of hers still had a childish softness about them. He remembered something she'd once said: *"I've only had one boy-friend, and what I miss most is holding someone's hand."*

"Two people holding hands," he murmured.

"What?" said Willy.

In a flash, as if a sliver of light had opened up in a vast dark-ness, he realized what the figure in the dream meant. Only with great effort could he make himself sit still. It felt like he was fly-ing. *I'm Sad Water. An evil medicine man has cast a spell over me.* Good Lord, how could he not have seen it before? As a police officer, Lance was fully aware that for young girls like Chrissy, it was common practice to get drugs through an older lover who was both a user and a seller. The reason he hadn't thought of this until now had to be that he'd lacked a focal point, but that was exactly what the figure in the dream had given him. And now he saw everything clearly. It had been Chrissy and Lenny Diver the whole time.

"I've got to go," he said, getting up with Swamper Caribou's dream catcher in his hand.

"But you just arrived," said Willy, surprised.

"I've got to go," Lance repeated.

"Chrissy's right," said Willy. "You really are roaming around in the dark, aren't you?"

"No," said Lance. "Just the opposite. I'm turning on the light in one room after the other."

# 38

THAT NIGHT he spent a long time just sitting and thinking. If Chrissy and Lenny Diver had had a relationship, that meant she was either the mystery woman that Diver claimed to have been with on the night of the murder, or else she was the girlfriend that he had been two-timing. If the first instance was true, she would have come forward long ago to give him an alibi, yet for some strange reason Diver hadn't wanted to reveal her identity. But what if she was the jilted girlfriend? The Chrissy that Lance knew would have still done what she could to help someone caught in such a serious situation. So why hadn't she gone to the police and told them about the bloodstained man with the baseball bat who was seen outside Finland only a couple of hours after Georg Lofthus was killed? A middle-aged white man. It was totally implausible that she would have kept quiet. If there was any truth to the story, of course. But there wasn't. It was a lie she'd invented to tell Lance when he showed up unexpectedly, claiming to be working undercover on the Lofthus case. She'd seized the opportunity and made up a story she thought would divert her uncle's attention away from Lenny Diver, hoping it might contribute to setting him free.

Lance fiddled with the old dream catcher. The thought of touching something that Swamper Caribou had touched was soothing, strangely enough.

Maybe Chrissy was the one who had persuaded those two

small-time crooks, Mist and King, to give him a little scare. And it wasn't really surprising that Diver had agreed to meet with Lance, since he probably knew everything about Chrissy's gullible uncle who was working on the case because the police actually doubted they'd got the right man.

Lance put down the dream catcher and got up to go over to the wall where all the family photographs hung, including a picture of Chrissy. It had been taken no more than seven or eight years ago. A girl of ten with long blond hair and blue eyes. Next to it was the conspicuously empty space where the high school picture of her father had been. The only trace remaining was a slightly lighter rectangle on the wall. For some reason it reminded him of the gun Andy had taken from him. When he thought about everything that had happened over the past six months, it seemed unthinkable that they'd ever be able to restore the almost idyllic sense of order that had reigned before the murder of Georg Lofthus. He corrected himself the second he had that thought. There had never been an idyllic sense of order. Chrissy had had a relationship both with Lenny Diver and with addictive substances before the murder. And Andy had been living with his secret. The only difference was that Lance Hansen hadn't known about these matters. That was where the lost sense of order came from. But the period of blessed ignorance was over. Lance had seen the two who were holding hands. Chrissy Hansen and Lenny Diver. He was positive he was right. Now it was just a matter of not making any mistakes.

# 39

TAMMY OPENED THE DOOR, dressed in jeans and a faded T-shirt with a logo from an amusement park somewhere in Wisconsin. Lance hung up his jacket in the hall and followed her into the house.

"Coffee?" she called over her shoulder.

"Sounds good."

She disappeared into the kitchen while Lance stood in the middle of the living room and waited. A moment later she was back, carrying a tray with mugs, a pot of hot water, and instant coffee.

"Go ahead and sit down," she said. "Don't be shy."

Lance sat down. In silence they mixed themselves some coffee.

There wasn't a sound in the house other than the light tapping of the teaspoons as they stirred the coffee in the mugs. Lance had called earlier in the day to ask Tammy if she was home alone and whether he could come over to talk to her about Chrissy. Tammy had been reluctant, maybe because of what had almost happened the last time he'd visited.

Now she set her teaspoon down on the saucer and gave him a skeptical look.

"Why do you want to talk to me about Chrissy?" she asked.

Lance had already decided what to say, since he knew she'd ask that question.

"Actually, this isn't about Chrissy at all," he said. "But it's possible she can help me with something. Have you heard the name Lenny Diver?"

"The murderer?"

"Yeah. That's what those of us on the police force think he is. But now we're afraid that the evidence against him isn't going to hold up. He'll probably get off."

Tammy raised her hand to her mouth.

"And when he goes free," said Lance, "what do you think will be the first thing he wants?"

She stared at him with big eyes, but didn't say a word.

"The same thing all men want if they've been in prison," Lance went on. "Plus dope. Lots of it."

"But he's not going to get out, is he?" said Tammy faintly.

"Most likely he will. And the trial starts soon, so it won't be long before he's back on the North Shore."

"But what . . . What can we . . . ?"

"What can you do?" He finished the question for her. "You can start by telling me everything you know about Chrissy and Lenny Diver. Nothing that you say will be used against Chrissy. Her drug problem will be handled discreetly, and without getting the police involved. I give you my word of honor."

Tammy buried her face in her hands, as if she needed a moment alone. Then she raised her head and looked her brother-in-law in the eye.

"It started almost two years ago," she said. "Chrissy had just turned sixteen. One day I got a phone call from a teacher, who asked me whether everything was okay with her. It turned out that she hadn't been to school in over a week. I had no idea because she left the house every morning, as usual."

She lit a cigarette, inhaled deeply, and paused for a long time before she let a cloud of bluish smoke spill from her lips.

"Andy decided to follow her," Tammy went on. "He found out that a girlfriend who had her own car was waiting for Chrissy down the street. Andy followed them to Duluth, where they disappeared inside a house. He kept an eye on that house all day. I guess there were some real seedy-looking types going in and out. Even back then there were a couple of Indians in the picture. And that really upset Andy."

Lance saw that she suddenly realized what she'd just said,

and who she was talking to, but he waved his hand dismissively before she could apologize.

"So what did the two of you do?"

"Andy said that if Chrissy ever went to see those people again, he'd kill her. He made a horrible scene. But for a while it seemed to have worked. She started going to school again. I checked in regularly with the teachers, and everything was back to normal. After a while she started taking acting classes in the evenings."

"Uh-huh. Sure she did," said Lance.

"That's what I thought too," said Tammy. "So I made up some excuse to call and talk to the drama teacher. It was perfectly legitimate. But something still didn't seem right. I don't know. Every mother thinks she knows her own child and can tell when something's wrong. So one evening I drove over to the school where the drama class was being held. I knocked on the door, and when the teacher appeared, I introduced myself and said that I had to speak to my daughter. He hurried to find her. I almost laughed when I saw the skinny, red-haired girl who was supposed to be Chrissy. But I managed to keep my composure and told the teacher I needed a few minutes alone with her, which of course he agreed to. The girl was so scared she was shaking. I said I'd go straight into that classroom and tell the whole story to the teacher and everyone else if she didn't tell me where Chrissy was and what she was doing. So she told me Chrissy was out driving around with 'a guy.' I demanded to know who he was. That was the first time I heard his name."

"Lenny Diver," said Lance.

"Well, just Lenny to start with."

"How soon did you figure out that she was taking drugs?"

"We suspected it right away. Good Lord, we weren't born yesterday, you know. But it wasn't until the summer that she started coming home high."

"That must have been difficult."

Tammy took a deep drag on her cigarette.

"Difficult is not the word," she said. "It was sheer hell, to put it bluntly. Nobody should have to fight with their own child. And then there's Andy. He gets so mad he lays hands on her. She's had terrible bruises on her arms. He's even pulled her by the hair."

Tammy's eyes were filled with tears, but Lance restrained himself from trying to comfort her by putting his hand on her knee or arm. He wasn't sure what might happen if he did.

"Did you ever meet Lenny Diver?" he asked.

"No. But after a while I realized that it was more than drugs and getting high that attracted her to him. I actually think he was the love of her life. Whenever she talked about him, her whole face lit up like a star."

"So the two of you have talked about him?" said Lance.

"A couple of times. Just Chrissy and me. Well, Chrissy really did all the talking, and I didn't interrupt."

"What did she say?"

"Well, what do you think? She was head over heels in love. It was all about how smart and deep he was. That nobody else saw what was inside him. The usual stuff."

"And the whole time he was supplying her with drugs?"

"That bastard," she muttered.

"You said she started coming home high."

"Uh-huh. The first time was during summer vacation."

"So that was about a year before the murder," said Lance. Tammy nodded.

"What happened during that year?"

"After she started using drugs openly, we managed to get her to quit. She could see for herself that things were really going downhill. As you know, she's always gotten good grades and was determined to make something of herself, so she cleaned up her act. Didn't go out anywhere and worked real hard in school. This was last fall. Right before Christmas we let her go to Duluth to do some shopping since things had been going so well."

"And that's when she started doing drugs again?" said Lance.

"Uh-huh. And she kept at it until Easter. Ran away from home a few times too."

"Why didn't you or Andy tell me?" he asked. "I could have helped you."

"How?" said Tammy hostilely. "Gotten her into a treatment program?"

"For example, yeah."

"But that was exactly what we were trying to avoid. Don't

you see that? We didn't want her to be *officially* labeled a drug addict. What opportunities would be open to her if she's been in rehab? We were thinking of her best interests when we decided not to tell anybody. But around Easter she managed to quit again, and she stayed in her room the whole vacation. She's a smart girl, and she knows how important it is to finish high school. When Diver was arrested for the murder, it was like a gift from heaven. I thought the whole problem would resolve itself. But now I'm scared she's on drugs again."

"I'm afraid you're right," said Lance. "But you said she managed to quit around Easter last year. How long did that last?"

"I don't know exactly when she started again, but it was after the murder and Diver was arrested."

"So she was clean from Easter up until the murder?"

"Yes, I'm pretty sure about that. I've gotten good at noticing when something is wrong," said Tammy.

"On the night of the murder, Chrissy was in Duluth. Is that right?"

"Uh-huh. She had permission to stay overnight with a girlfriend."

"Wasn't that a bit . . . ?"

"Irresponsible?" said Tammy. "I thought that if she was never allowed out, she'd go crazy."

Again Lance thought about the woman Lenny Diver claimed he'd spent the night with at a motel in Grand Marais. If Chrissy was that woman, then why had he refused to say anything? Of course she was a minor, and that was a serious matter, but considering the situation, he risked being convicted of murder. Was Lenny Diver really prepared to spend the rest of his life in prison in order to spare Chrissy the embarrassment if he told the truth?

"What do you think happened on that night?" Lance asked.

"What do you mean?" Tammy seemed nervous.

"How did Chrissy seem when she came back home?"

"She went right to bed."

"In the middle of the day?"

"They'd been up late."

Tammy took another cigarette out of the pack. She didn't

look like she wanted to say any more about that particular subject.

"Andy spent that same night at the cabin on Lost Lake," said Lance. "And the next day he drove all the way to Duluth to pick up Chrissy. Was that something they'd arranged beforehand?"

"Yes." Tammy lit her cigarette.

"Also the fact that he'd stay overnight in the cabin?"

"No, that was something he decided on impulse. All of a sudden he wanted to go fishing. But how is this going to help us get Diver convicted of murder?" she asked, sounding annoyed.

"Chrissy is the only one who can tell me about Lenny Diver's movements," said Lance. "And the best way to get to her is through you. It's a matter of proving that Diver was at Baraga's Cross that night. Or at least make it seem credible. Otherwise, I'm afraid he'll be out again soon, and then Chrissy is the first person he'll want to see."

Lance noticed that Tammy's hand was shaking as she put the cigarette to her lips. She held the smoke in her lungs for a long time before she blew it out through the right side of her mouth.

"Does Chrissy know you're working on the case?" she asked, plucking a shred of tobacco from her lower lip.

"No. This is confidential police work," said Lance. "Nobody can find out about it, least of all the accused man's girlfriend. You can't say a word to anyone. Not even to Andy. I can trust you, right?"

"Of course. I'll do anything to save my child."

Tammy began crying quietly. The tears ran down her cheeks as she continued to smoke.

"Whenever she's gone, we jump every time the phone rings," she said. "We're so scared that one day she'll just . . ."

Lance was on the verge of tears himself.

"You said she went straight to bed when she and Andy came home the day after the murder," he ventured cautiously.

"Uh-huh," said Tammy, sniffling.

"What about Andy? How did he seem?"

"I don't remember."

"Try," Lance insisted.

"He was basically just worried about Chrissy. Said we had to make extra sure she didn't go out at night. From now on, she had to come straight home from school. Things like that. Not really surprising, since a murderer was on the loose."

"But wasn't Andy already like that?" said Lance. "Protective, I mean. She was taking drugs, after all."

"Sure, but after the murder it seemed to take on a whole different dimension. He seemed obsessed."

And yet there was no murderer on the loose, thought Lance. At least not seen with Andy's eyes, if he had, in fact, killed Georg Lofthus. But why had he been so concerned about protecting Chrissy after the murder? Somewhere in the back of his mind a thought was struggling to surface and shout its message. Lance could feel it, but he couldn't manage to bring it all the way up. The thought stayed where it was, down in the dark and the silence.

"I think maybe that's all I need to know right now," he said.

Tammy didn't seem convinced.

"How is this going to prove that Diver was at Baraga's Cross?" she asked.

"Well, first I need to go over everything you've told me and look for connections. That's what police work is, you know. We collect information and look for patterns."

He could hear for himself how phony his words sounded.

"And have you found anything?"

"Not yet, no."

He stood up with an effort as Tammy stayed where she was, smoking her cigarette.

"By the way, how many guns do you have in the house?" he asked.

"Just one, as far as I know."

"The hunting rifle. Right?"

"Uh-huh. Why?"

"I was just wondering," said Lance as he stood in the hall and put on his jacket.

When he was ready, he stuck his head in the door to the living room. "Take care. And take good care of that daughter of yours," he said.

Tammy nodded from a cloud of smoke.

He got into his car and discovered a missed call on his cell, which was lying on the passenger seat. On the display it said, "Lakeview."

# 40

THE TEMPERATURE HAD DROPPED, and along Fifth Avenue in Duluth, the colorful building facades glittered with ice crystals. He drove slowly past his childhood home, which used to be painted blue, but was now a pale yellow. Oddly enough it didn't bother him that strangers now occupied the house. In fact, it made him happy to know that children lived there. That his old room was in use.

This was the second time he'd driven past, yet when he came to the little flower shop at the end of the street, he turned around and drove back. He just wanted to put something behind him. Not his childhood, but something else . . . something more . . . He didn't know exactly what it was, nor did he need to know. Something fell into place as he slowly drove back and forth along his old street. Something drifted to the bottom inside him and settled in the spot where it was supposed to be. It felt right. And it didn't feel sad. Everything else was sad, but not this. In reality that was the most important reason why he didn't want to leave Fifth Avenue yet. He'd found a tiny corner of life where things were the way they should be. That was a big surprise, and he realized it would be over as soon as he drove away. This was not a place in Duluth but a place in life, which meant it would be impossible to return.

When he drove past for the third time, he could tell it was enough. If he continued, the experience would be diminished. He took one last look at the house and then left his old neighborhood without even a glance in the rearview mirror.

CHRISSY WAS WAITING in the lobby of the Lakeview Nursing Home. She had on her usual Goth attire under the ankle-length black coat, but she'd pinned up her hair in a grown-up style. The minute she caught sight of Lance, she ran over to give him a hug. He couldn't return the hug because in one hand he was holding a bunch of new, flattened cardboard boxes, and in the other a roll of garbage bags.

"I've got the key," she said.

Lance looked around the lobby, which he'd walked through so many times over the past few years.

"Well, I guess we should get started," he said.

Neither of them spoke as they rode the elevator up to the fourth floor. Only once did he glance briefly at his niece. He thought he noticed something new in her expression; she had a certain hard or closed-off look in her eye.

Standing in front of the door to room 22, Chrissy burst into tears. She handed Lance the key as if it were a dead kitten that she couldn't stand to look at anymore.

"We just need to get through this," he said as he unlocked the door.

Except for the fact that his mother wasn't there, the room looked the same as always. It seemed as if she'd just slipped out to talk to someone in another room and that she'd soon appear in the doorway behind them, saying, "So there you are, you two!"

"It's so cold in here," said Chrissy, shivering.

She was right. The staff probably turned off the heat to save money whenever somebody died.

"We can't work in this cold," he said. He set the flattened boxes and the roll of garbage bags on the floor and then turned up the radiator full blast.

"Do you really want to help me with this?" he asked Chrissy without looking at her.

"Dad said he couldn't bear it, and I've been here more often than him or Mom."

"If it gets to be too much for you, just tell me."

Lance sat down on the chair that had always been "his." Somehow they were going to have to divide up her belongings. There wasn't really that much. Most of her possessions had been given to family members when she moved here. Only the most personal items remained. Family photographs, photo albums, clothing, and jewelry—all those things that had been part of her daily life. When she moved out of the house on Fifth Avenue, it had felt good to go through her things, but now . . .

"Do you want the picture of the immigrants?" he asked, nodding at the photograph of the Norwegians standing on board the steamer *America* in 1902.

Chrissy sat down on the sofa, and Lance thought to himself that she too couldn't bring herself to sit in Inga's chair.

"No," she said.

"But that's your heritage," he told her. "That ship contains everything that we are today."

"Then I really don't want to have it," said Chrissy.

She had placed her hands on her lap. Lance stared at her slender white wrists sticking out of her sleeves. They looked like they might break if someone so much as touched them. For a moment he pictured again the scene of the crime. He recalled the senseless power radiating from that spot, as if something supernatural had settled in the woods.

"What about the picture of you?" he went on. "Would you like to have it? Inga thought you looked like an angel in that photo. 'The angel from Two Harbors.' That's what she called you. When was it taken?"

"First year in high school."

She leaned back on the sofa, stretching out her legs and closing her eyes. But Lance had a feeling that she could still see him through the narrow slits. Her face was impassive, pale and soft, with a slightly childish look to it. Especially the round, smooth forehead. He saw no trace of harshness, or whatever it was that he'd seen when they were in the elevator. Behind him the radiator was clucking and gurgling.

Here they had sat so many times, he and his mother, talking about family and friends, both living and dead, and about each other while outside the darkness closed in and dusk fell over Duluth. Afterward he would drive back north alone. Bright summer evenings, fragrant with flowers, and winter nights with drifting snow that made it almost impossible to see more than an arm's length ahead.

Lance thought he saw a faint quivering in his niece's nostrils as she reclined in the same position, with her legs stretched out under the coffee table and her hands in her lap. He turned to look out the window. This was the view that his mother had seen every day over the past few years. The buildings and yards were covered with nearly three feet of snow. The gnarled branches of old fruit trees were black against all that white. He saw snow shovels leaning against houses, sleds tossed aside, wood stacked up, and several warmly dressed children off in the distance, running, their shouts inaudible. The low sun cast a warm glow over the old Aerial Lift Bridge, but soon the bridge would be a dark presence looming in the dusk. On the other side of the narrow bay, which was Lake Superior's westernmost point, a low-lying wooded landscape undulated south toward the plains. But to the west and the northeast, there was only a white emptiness to see. The vast emptiness on the edge of which they all lived out their lives.

They had found her sitting in her chair. Presumably she'd been looking at the view when she died, but that was something he'd never know for sure. Or what she was feeling. Maybe it was like being sucked out the window and into everything else.

A sudden, high-pitched snore jolted Lance out of his reverie. Chrissy looked like she was about to wake up, but after a few restless smacking sounds, she dozed off again.

Lance thought it was strange that her parents had let her drive. Why couldn't they have brought her? Okay, he could understand why Andy wouldn't have wanted to see him, but what about Tammy? Chrissy was either high or extremely tired, and yet they had thrown up their hands and left the responsibility to her.

"Chrissy," he said.

She opened her eyes, sighing heavily.

"Were you asleep?"

"No," she lied.

"We need to get started. Let's take everything that's hanging on the walls first."

She nodded.

Lance picked up one of the boxes from the floor and laid it out flat. With a few brisk tugs he had a fully formed box, which he sent scooting across the floor to stop at Chrissy's feet. She got up from the sofa, every movement revealing her reluctance. Her arms hung limply at her sides as she tilted her head to one side and stared at the photos on the wall. Lance studied the back of her neck, which was now visible since she'd pinned up her hair in the new style. He couldn't remember ever seeing it before, since she'd always worn her long hair loose.

Suddenly he heard her gasp. Lance got up, uncertain whether to touch her. He decided to take a cautious hold on her upper arms. In that instant her legs buckled. He didn't try to hold her up, just let her fall to her knees. Then she went down on all fours. She was shaking, but the only thing he heard was her shallow breathing. He didn't know what to do, or whether there was anything to be done at all. Just let her be, he thought, no matter what's going on.

Finally she took a deep breath and then let out a long wail. After a moment it turned into a snarl, a growling sound that eventually faded away. Lance felt his blood go cold, but he didn't touch her or say anything. He just waited. After a while she whispered something. He wanted to ask her to repeat what she'd said, but then he realized she wasn't talking to him. She kept on whispering at the floor, and now he could make out some of the words: ". . . loved her so much . . . loved, loved her . . ."

He squatted down to stroke his niece's back. She was trembling faintly, as if she had a soundless engine inside.

"I did too," he said, his voice thick. "But we can't give up, Chrissy. We have to go on. Somebody has to clear out the room, and you and I are the ones who are going to do it. Let's get up now."

Slowly Chrissy pushed herself into a kneeling position. Lance tried to put his arm around her shoulders, but she pushed it away. Then she stood up, her legs wobbling, and stared at the display of family photos.

"Look how young you are, Uncle Lance." She was pointing at his high school picture.

"Huh. Right."

"What were you like back then?"

"Pretty much the same as I am now," he said evasively.

Chrissy looked at him as if he were a child who had just told a hopelessly impossible lie.

"I wanted to be a historian," he said.

"But you are."

"No. A real historian. An academic." He tried to laugh off his words.

"Well, that would have been a first in our family," she said.

"You need to study hard, Chrissy. You've always gotten such good grades in school."

Without replying, she began taking the photos off the wall. The first one she removed was the picture of herself, the angel of Two Harbors. Then she took down all the rest until there was nothing left but the nails they'd been hanging from. Lance vividly remembered putting the nails in the wall when his mother moved in. He'd been there when she hung up the photos. Only the newest one of Chrissy was put up later. He wondered who had put that nail in the wall for her.

"So, do you want to divide up the pictures?" asked Chrissy, looking at the bare wall.

"For now I'm going to take everything home with me," said Lance. "Then we'll divide up the things later, when . . . after everything is . . ."

Chrissy looked around the room.

"What should we do next?"

"Could you start by emptying the dresser and closet?"

Reluctantly she pulled out the top drawer, where Inga's underwear were neatly folded. Lance looked away.

"Put everything in a bag," he said. "I'll gather up all the loose items in the room."

He was about to pick up a pair of eyeglasses, which lay on the table, but he stopped abruptly, his hand stretched out. The glasses were not folded up the way he imagined they would be

if the person had just died. They had been set down by someone who was tired, or whose eyes hurt, someone who would put
them back on in a few minutes. Inga must have set them there, he
thought. She'd been sitting in her easy chair, staring at the intense
white of the day, and her eyes started to hurt. Not knowing that
this would be the last time, she had taken off her glasses and set
them on the table. Then she closed her eyes to rest. Just for a little
while. And there she had died, in her chair, without her glasses
on. As they lay there, unfolded and ready for her to put them
back on, the glasses revealed to him one of her last conscious
acts. He pictured her taking them off and setting them on the table. In that very spot. Removing them from the room would also
mean erasing her last movement. But he had to do it. The glasses
couldn't stay there forever. He placed them in the box with the
photographs. Then he leaned down and grabbed a stack of magazines from the shelf under the small table between the two easy
chairs. Inga's knitting came with it.

Lance held up the knitting. Something green and white.

"Look at this," he said. "What do you think this was going
to be?"

Chrissy cast a quick glance over her shoulder.

"Probably a scarf," she said.

"I guess we need a separate bag for . . . you know . . ."

"For trash?" Chrissy suggested.

He tore another plastic bag from the roll and put the magazines and knitting inside. After a moment's hesitation he took the
eyeglasses out of the cardboard box on the table and put them in
the trash bag too.

"Here's her purse," said Chrissy. "Maybe you should . . ."

Lance took the black purse that he'd seen his mother carry so many times. He opened it. Inside he found several blister
packs of pills. And a wallet, of course. He hadn't thought about
that. He emptied the contents of the purse onto the coffee table.
Among the medicine bottles, mirror, wallet, prescriptions, hair-
pins, and other items were three postcards that he recognized at
once. He'd forgotten all about them and was totally unprepared
to see his own handwriting.

*Hi Mom!*

*Just arrived in Oslo. A cozy little town. Everyone speaks such good English and is really interested as soon as I tell them about our ancestry. Later I'll go out to Halsnøy, but first I want to see the sights in Oslo. Wish you were here with me! See you very soon.*

*Love,*
*Lance*

"What's that?" asked Chrissy, who had noticed he was reading something.

"Oh, it's nothing."

But the next instant she'd snatched the postcard out of his hand. Lance didn't try to stop her. He just stood there, waiting for her to read what it said.

"How'd you manage to pull that off?" asked Chrissy, handing back the postcard.

"I wrote and addressed the cards and sent them to someone I know in Norway, along with dates when he was supposed to put them in the mail. I needed to convince everyone that I was actually in Norway."

"While you were really working undercover."

"Right."

Lance tried to catch her eye, but she looked away.

"That night," he said. "The night of the murder. You said you were at the cabin on Lost Lake, that you were having a party."

"So?"

Her voice was barely more than a whisper now.

"But your father was at the cabin that night. At least that's what he says. And if he was there, then where were you?"

Chrissy took a step closer and touched his arm.

"Not now," she said.

Lance felt as if all he had to do was hold out his hand and the truth would instantly appear on his palm. That's how close he was. But at that instant everything would fall apart, and he couldn't let that happen. Not now, not here, surrounded by Inga's things. All the rest could wait until later.

Silently they continued packing up the cowboys riding the

little white horses, the hand-painted birds, all sorts of bowls and plates that had never been used for anything; they were just meant to be decorative. Then they moved on to the clothes. After they had emptied the closet, neatly folding up each garment and placing them in a bag, Chrissy said to her uncle, "But who in the family is actually going to wear these clothes?"

They both started laughing. Lance could hear a strained wheezing coming from Chrissy as she tried to catch her breath in between soundless waves of laughter. But he laughed loudly as he gasped for air. Each time he thought of her question, it seemed even more ridiculous. And they'd just made such a point of folding everything up so neatly! After a moment he noticed that Chrissy's laughter had changed to sobs, and then he realized that he didn't know whether he was laughing or crying either. He was just sitting there, on the chair where he'd sat so many times, but without his mother, who had been sucked through the window and into the white landscape outside.

"Good God," he muttered, wiping away the tears.

He looked at his niece, who had covered her face with her hands and was still sobbing.

"I remember once," he said. "I must have been about five. It's one of my earliest memories. Mom was digging potatoes out of the vegetable garden, and I wanted to help. I still remember that cold fall air and those big potatoes that Mom had already dug up. I can see it all so clearly."

Chrissy straightened up and took her hands from her face. There were long streaks of mascara on her cheeks.

"Mom gave me a potato digger," Lance went on. "Sort of a long-handled hoe. It was probably a lot smaller than the one she was using, but it felt big to me. And it was impossible to steer it properly. Since I was so young, it didn't take long for me to get fed up. I started whining and complaining. But Mom didn't get mad at me. She patiently showed me how to use the potato digger. Soon it got easier, and I managed to stick the digger in the ground, but I didn't find any potatoes. Not until the third or fourth try. It was like finding gold. I swung the potato digger over my head as hard as I could and hit Mom in the middle of the forehead."

"Yikes," whispered Chrissy.

"I know. She had just leaned down behind me to pull out some potatoes. A sigh was the only thing I heard, as if the air had suddenly gone out of her. And then the sound of the bucket falling over and all the potatoes tumbling out. When I turned around, she was sitting on the ground with one hand pressed to her forehead. I still remember the look in her eyes. It was so strange. Like she was looking at someone else, not me. She seemed scared. But only for a moment. Then she yelled, 'Good Lord, are you trying to kill me, or what?' I ran inside and upstairs to my room. From the window I could look down into the garden. I remember how she slowly got to her feet. Then she set the bucket upright and began gathering up all the potatoes that had rolled out."

Lance ran his hand over the surface of the small table between the two easy chairs. It was completely bare now. Her eyeglasses were gone. The last thing she'd done.

"But what I remember most," he said. "The reason I've never forgotten that day . . . It must have been at a time when I'd just learned about death. I'd probably started to realize that everybody dies. And my mother had just asked me whether I was trying to kill her. As I stood at the window, hiding behind the curtain and looking down at her, I prayed to God the whole time, begging him not to let it happen. I was so incredibly scared she was going to die."

THEY WERE SITTING IN THE SAME POSITIONS—Lance in his usual chair, and Chrissy on the sofa. He thought she seemed better now. Or at least awake. Even so, he had no intention of allowing her to drive back home. Tammy and Andy would just have to come to Duluth to get their car. It was totally irresponsible of them to have let her drive today.

Chrissy picked up a photo album that was lying on top in one of the boxes. They'd already paged through it once, giving it only a cursory look before going back to work. Now she was studying the pictures on the first page.

"Come look at this," she said.

Lance went over and sat down next to her on the sofa.

"Who do you think this is?" she asked.

At first glance he didn't recognize the people in the photo, but then he realized they had to be his mother and her two sisters, sitting on a blanket at the edge of the water. On the left in the picture the rear of a red car was visible, with the big, bulbous contours of a vehicle from the fifties.

"That's Inga," he said, pointing. "And that's Aunt Laura and Aunt Eleanor."

"Jesus, I didn't recognize her," exclaimed Chrissy. "Look how young she is."

"I think this was before my time, probably in the fifties. She must be about twenty."

They paged through the album, past faces both familiar and unfamiliar, looking at pictures of various excursions and family celebrations. Other photos seemed almost random, as if someone had snapped the shot by accident. Like the blurry and crooked picture of the Aerial Bridge in Duluth. All the photographs in the album appeared to be from before Lance was born. Toward the back the first picture of Oscar showed up. A young man in a police uniform smiling confidently at the camera. In another he was wearing civilian clothes, sitting next to another young man on a bench in Leif Erikson Park. Maybe around 1960, thought Lance. In the background was Lake Superior, the blue of the water so intense and unreal, the way it was only in old color photographs.

Stuck in the very back of the album, between the last page and cover, was a loose picture that Lance immediately recognized as Andy's school photo from his first year at Central High.

"Is that Dad?" asked Chrissy.

"Uh-huh. Sixteen years old."

She turned over the photo. Someone had written a big question mark on the back.

"What do you think that means?" she said.

Lance reached out to take the photo from her. He stared at the question mark, as if he could somehow wrest its secret from the symbol. Who had put that there? Probably his mother. But why? The picture didn't belong in this album, yet she'd stuck it between the back cover and the last page.

"I don't know what it means," he said.

"In a way, it makes sense," said Chrissy.

"What do you mean?"

"If I had to draw a picture of Dad, without drawing a face, this is exactly how I would do it."

Lance flipped the picture over a few times, looking first at the front, then the back. A smiling young face, and a question mark, written in pencil.

# 41

INGA HANSEN was buried on a February day when the temperature was below zero and the wind was blowing in off the lake.

Lance stood with his hand on his son's shoulder as he watched the coffin being lowered between the dark earthen walls that glittered with frost. Jimmy's mother, who stood on the other side of the boy, had placed her glove-clad hand on the back of his neck. They looked like a family. The silent boy's small body trembled, but Lance couldn't tell if it was due to tears or the cold. Only a few yards away stood Chrissy, her head bowed and her face racked with grief, but she didn't utter a sound.

The church had been almost full, and many of the mourners had also come to the gravesite. Not just close family members but old friends and acquaintances from a long life in Duluth. There were quite a few that Lance didn't know.

With a muted thud the coffin reached its end station. They sang "Abide with Me," and with that Lance Hansen's remaining parent was laid to rest. He cast a glance at Andy, who was standing nearby with his family. He looked ill, making a tremendous effort just to stay on his feet. As Lance continued to stare at his brother, Andy's face contorted and he emitted a long-drawn-out gasp that everyone at the gravesite could hear. Tammy looked at him in alarm and then reached out to clumsily stroke his back.

Lance looked away, not wanting to risk meeting Andy's eye.

The mourners who had stood in a semicircle around the grave hesitantly began to leave. Lance heard several people clear their throats to say something, but everyone spoke in quiet, respectful tones. Slowly they headed toward the exit, in pairs or small groups. Still to come was the gathering in the Sons of Norway hall. Lance had taken it upon himself to prepare a brief speech in memory of his mother. He was the one who had made all the funeral arrangements. He had phoned Tammy to tell her that he was taking charge of everything. The alternative would have been to sit home alone, doing nothing. Or to drive around aimlessly, also alone.

He felt suddenly dizzy as he walked between Mary and Jimmy, hearing in all directions the creaking sound of boots on the snow. He felt as if all the blood had drained out of his face. For a moment he thought he might fall, but then the dizziness subsided, leaving behind a faint nausea.

IN NORWAY HALL on Lake Avenue a mural painted in the typical Norwegian rosemaling style adorned one end of the room, while Norwegian and American flags dominated the other. The catering company had set out food and drinks on schedule, and the gathering of thirty to forty guests began helping themselves from the smorgasbord buffet. The long table where they would all be seated was nicely decorated with a white tablecloth and candles in the big candelabra.

Everyone wanted to say something to Lance—about his mother or the funeral or the food or the cold that had settled in, or about the decreasing number of members in the Sons of Norway, or all of the above. Andy sat at the table, silent and unapproachable, leaning over his plate. Tammy had retreated to a corner, and Chrissy was nowhere to be seen. More or less on autopilot, Lance answered all the questions, nodding and putting on a somber expression. More than anything, he wished he could usher everybody out, every single person, emptying the whole place so he could finally be alone. Not just alone, but so far away that nobody could reach him. He wanted to get sucked into the white landscape, merging with it, just as his mother had. It didn't really help that everything related to the funeral would be over soon. It was other things that he found insurmountable. What he should he do about Andy? And Chrissy?

All around him was the muted buzz of voices. Bill Eggum had already sat down and started to eat. People were again talking about ordinary things like the weather and the Minnesota Wild hockey team, but no one had presumed to laugh out loud. The ritual solemnity of the funeral would stay with them until they got in their cars and drove home.

Gary Hansen came over with a cup of coffee in his hand. Gary was Lance's cousin who ran Northwoods Outfitters, a business that sold and rented outdoor gear. The murder victim, Georg Lofthus, and his companion had rented a canoe from him. Lance and Gary had always been good friends.

"My condolences," Gary said as they shook hands.

Lance nodded briefly.

"It's not easy when a parent dies," said Gary.

"No, it's not."

"At least it happened quickly, from what I hear."

"Yeah. She died suddenly, sitting in her chair."

"Was it her heart?"

"Yes."

Gary took a sip of his coffee.

"So, how are you doing?" he asked his cousin.

"Okay," said Lance. "How about you?"

"Well, er . . . You know that we're separated, right?"

Lance shook his head.

"Barb moved out right before Christmas."

"Probably not the best Christmas for you, huh?"

"No, it wasn't," Gary agreed.

"What about your son?"

"He's living with her."

"Ah. Welcome to the club," said Lance.

Gary wasn't sure whether to say thanks or not.

"I thought you were in Norway, by the way."

"I'm back," said Lance.

"Good thing you got home before this happened."

"Uh-huh."

"She must have been thrilled to hear all about it when you came back from the old country."

Out of the corner of his eye Lance noticed that Chrissy had just come into the room.

HE TAPPED HIS KNIFE AGAINST HIS GLASS, and the hum of voices at the table faded. Then he stood up. He had practiced his speech for a couple of days, but he still needed to refer to the key words that he'd written down on a piece of paper.

"It was good to see so many people at the church today," he began. "And it's good to see that so many have joined us here in Norway Hall. I would like to thank all of you on behalf of my family."

His hand holding the notes had now started to shake. He didn't know whether anyone else could hear the paper rustling, but to him it sounded incredibly loud. He took a sip of mineral water and then went on.

"Mom's family was originally from Norway. Nothing unusual about that." Some of the older people sitting at the long table nodded. "I suppose you could say that she was a rather modest person. She didn't exactly like to call attention to herself. But for my part—and I feel certain I can speak for Andy as well, in this regard—I will always be eternally grateful to her for the home she created for us on Fifth Avenue. I know that everyone sitting here has their own memories of Inga Hansen. Whether she was your friend, your neighbor, your mother-in-law, or your grandmother."

He cast a glance at Chrissy, who had found a seat between two elderly men. She was wearing a nice black outfit, with a shawl draped around her shoulders, and her hair was pinned up in a grown-up style. As he was about to take another look at his notes, she smiled at him. A radiant smile that didn't seem appropriate, given the setting.

"But for me, she will always be Mom," he continued. "Irreplaceable. A bond that can never be broken, not even by death. Every family has its difficulties. Problems that cannot necessarily be solved; things that you just have to live with. It was like that in our family too. But because we come from the home she created for us, in the long run all of us will find our way to a safe harbor."

Andy was staring straight ahead, his face pale and drawn.

"Finally, I'd like to share a little story with you. Well, it's not really a story, just something that's a vivid memory for me. About Mom. The last time she and I took a drive together—this was last summer—we headed north along the Shore and talked about the lake. Mom said something like 'I've lived my whole life on Lake Superior, but it's only seldom that I notice it. Isn't that strange?' I don't remember how I replied, or if I even answered at all. But today I know what she meant. That's the way it is when you live so close to something so vast. Most of the time you don't see it. But what if one day it was gone? What if you woke up one morning and the lake wasn't there? Then you would miss it. And that's how I'm missing my mother now. Thank you for everything, Mom."

He sat down, and suddenly he didn't know what to do. So far no one at the table had said a word. No one showed any sign of speaking or continuing to eat. Everyone just sat there, staring down at the tablecloth. Lance wanted to pick up his knife and fork to cut off a piece of the open-face sandwich on his plate, but he couldn't get himself to be the first to break the frozen mood.

Chrissy was the one who did it.

"Woo-hoo!" she shouted so loudly that the elderly man next to Lance cringed. Then she started clapping, turning her smiling face toward her uncle. She was beaming like the sun.

CHAD AAKRE, an old friend of the family and a fanatic birder, had started talking about the eagle population on the North Shore. Lance tried to look interested. He nodded and raised his eyebrows in surprise, interjecting an occasional "exactly" or a "wow, I can't believe it" as he inwardly struggled not to succumb to the weight of the day, which was at last coming to an end.

Finally he excused himself, saying he really ought to circulate and thank people for coming and wish them a safe drive home, and so on. He paused for a moment to take a look around. He immediately caught sight of Bill Eggum and Andy, talking to each other over by the door. He thought about what Eggum had said about the anonymous tip the police had received about Lenny Diver. They had traced the call to a public phone booth in Duluth. A man's voice, Eggum had said. Lance wondered if it was true that the sheriff really hadn't recognized the voice.

Suddenly Chrissy appeared at his side.

"You're so great, Uncle Lance," she said with a smile. "Taking care of everything like this."

At first he felt flattered, but then he noticed the false warmth in her eyes.

"Better to keep busy on a day like this, you know," he said.

Chrissy looked around the room at the rosemaling mural and the Norwegian and American flags hanging on the wall. She rolled her brown eyes, as if she and Lance were pals, sharing a secret.

Over by the door, Andy and Bill Eggum seemed to be concluding their conversation. Lance thought there was something animal-like about the way his brother looked. He was scowling and his lower jaw jutted out slightly—an expression that Lance had never seen before. He thought about the wolf up in Canada that had stood in the road in front of a dead deer. When he saw Andy talking to Eggum, he felt as if a dead body were lying next to him too. At the feet of his brother and the ex-sheriff lay Georg Lofthus, his bashed-in head a bloody mess. But Lance was the only one who could see him.

"Can you give me a lift home?" asked Chrissy.

A glassy film had settled over her eyes.

"I've got to stay and clean up," said Lance.

"I'll help you."

"No. You need to drive home with your parents."

"But I don't want to," she whined.

"Pull yourself together," he hissed. "This is a funeral."

Then he spun on his heel and headed for the door, not because he had any specific purpose in mind. He just wanted to get away from his niece.

Eggum turned to greet Lance.

"Nice speech," he said.

Lance mumbled something, noticing that Andy was looking away.

"Inga was a fine person," Eggum went on. "I remember her so well from the time when your father and I worked together."

Lance felt uncomfortable standing so close to his brother. There was still something odd about Andy's face, but maybe it was just because he was so worn out. Lance felt a wave of exhaustion flood through his body, from his feet to his head.

"It won't be long before Lenny Diver's trial begins," he said.

"That's right," said Eggum. "Are you thinking of attending?"

"Shouldn't we be there? All three of us?" Lance asked.

"Do *you* have an interest in the case?" Eggum gave Andy a surprised look.

"I don't even know what you two are talking about," said Andy.

"The murder at Baraga's Cross," replied Eggum.

"No, that doesn't interest me."

Again Lance pictured Georg Lofthus lying on the floor next to Andy. The image kept growing. Blood appeared on the floor; dark, sticky blood through which people were plodding, wearing their Sunday shoes. He imagined all the bloody footprints in the snow outside Norway Hall.

The guests were starting to say their good-byes. Everyone wanted to shake hands with the two brothers before they left. Chrissy reappeared.

"Can we go soon?' she asked her father.

Andy put his arm around her shoulders.

"We're going now," he said. "Take care."

Bill Eggum and Lance nodded in reply. Then Andy ushered his daughter, gently but firmly, out of the room.

Lance could clearly see the two sets of bloody tracks they left in their wake.

# 42

JUST AFTER DAWN the next morning Lance drove down Baraga Cross Road and pulled into the empty parking lot. With a
heavy sigh he got out, took his snowshoes out of the back, and
put them on. Then he climbed over the high snowbank. Somewhere close by a few titmice cheeped, but he couldn't see them
in the birch forest. Otherwise the only sound was the distant,
snow-muffled rushing of the traffic up on Highway 61. The path
he'd taken on that summer morning was gone, and even wearing
snowshoes his feet still sank a ways into the snow. Soon he could
hear the muted, cave-like sound of water running deep underneath the snow and ice. He emerged from the thickets and saw
the cross and the place where the Cross River emptied into Lake
Superior.

Suddenly it all seemed so simple.

He put on his sunglasses and started walking across the
snow-covered expanse. Every step forward was an effort for his
heavy body until he reached the area where the wind had swept
the ice more or less clean. There he took off his snowshoes and
left them lying on the ground. Then it was only a matter of going
on, without looking back. That was the most important thing.
Not to turn around and see the distance widening. Just keep
moving forward until he disappeared.

Was she part of what now surrounded him? It seemed pointless to think that his mother should be part of the ice and the blue

sky and the low February sun. That sort of thing belonged to . . . He wasn't sure what. Maybe in a poem. Here on the real ice, under the real winter sky, with the real sun on his face, it was impossible to imagine that his mother was part of what he saw before him. She no longer existed. Ever since he'd come back home, he'd given priority to other things instead of going to see her. And worst of all, he knew she had been waiting for him. Waiting and hoping.

Gradually the cold from the ice penetrated the thick rubber soles of his boots and began to lay claim to his body from below. He had a feeling that he was in the process of vanishing. It was a little frightening, but mostly it felt good. Soon he would enter something else and disappear. Disappear from himself too. Since he didn't have a watch, except on his cell phone, which he'd stuffed into his jacket pocket, the sun's position in the sky was his only indication of the time. He tried to avoid looking at it.

The farther out he walked, the greater the silence. When he paused to listen, it was like he was wrapped in thick layers of cotton. Even the ringing in his ears, which usually occurred when everything else was quiet, had gone. He had passed the border for the ringing in his ears and crossed into a place where he'd never been before. This is the beginning, he thought. If I don't look back and just keep on going, it won't be long before I disappear.

His cell phone rang.

He pulled off one glove and dug the phone out of his pocket. It rang again. The sound filled the whole enormous space, resounding between the ice and the sky. Followed by a silence that seemed to drop over him. Before the next ring tone could rip through the silence again, he raised his arm and threw the phone as far as he could. The moment it landed, the phone rang again, but now the ring tone was fainter, as if coming from a great distance.

Lance headed out, wanting to get far away from the sound as quickly as possible. But strangely enough, it didn't seem to get any weaker, no matter how fast he walked, and that made him feel like he hadn't moved at all. For a moment the temptation to turn around and look for the phone was almost overwhelming, but then he would also see how far from land he'd gone. And that would ruin everything.

Finally the phone stopped ringing.


HE HAD CLOSED HIS EYES, swaying as he stood there, as if he were about to fall asleep on his feet. When he opened his eyes, a wolf with bared teeth and raised hackles was standing right in front of him. Fear shot through him, all the way out to his fingertips. For several seconds he was completely paralyzed. Then he spun around and began running toward land, but there was no land to run to, only the same gray endlessness in all directions. Lance turned abruptly, determined to fight, but now there was no wolf in sight. Had it been some sort of vision? The wolf he'd seen in Canada had posed in the exact same way, like an image of everything that refused to budge.

He would just have to go on. As he walked, he thought several times that he could hear the sound of breathing behind him, but when he turned around, nothing was there. He realized no wolf would go this far out on the ice, yet he couldn't help turning to look. Each time he did, he saw once again that there was no land visible in any direction.

After a while he heard the breathing again, but this time he was determined not to look back. He kept on walking, but the sound didn't go away; instead it got louder, and it seemed to have changed. It merged with the rhythm of his pulse, settling like an extra layer of sound on the sound of his own breathing. When he held his breath, the sound behind him stopped too; but the instant he began breathing again, it was there, like a shadow breath. As he continued across ice-covered Lake Superior, he thought the wolf breath slowed, definitely becoming more like the breathing of a human, until there was no longer any doubt. A man was walking behind him. Lance knew who the breathing belonged to. He would have recognized the sound anytime and anywhere. When he stopped short and held his breath, Andy did the same. Utter silence. Then he released the air from his lungs and clearly heard his brother do the same.

LANCE TURNED AROUND, but Andy wasn't there. Nothing else was there either. Making little shuffling movements with his feet, he turned 360 degrees on his own axis, without noticing anything change. The only thing he saw was his own body and the ice on which his boots were moving. Yet Andy kept on breathing, but the sound was no longer coming from a specific direction. It was more like it came from all directions at once, filling the whole space. The huge vault above the lake reverberated with Andy's breathing, as if Lance had walked so far out that he'd at last ended up inside his brother's terrified mind.

Just like the wolf, Andy stood there with his ears flattened and his hackles raised, refusing to budge, and yet he was radiating fear. And right behind each of them lay a blood-spattered body: the dead deer and the dead tourist. The deer is just a carcass the wolf found, thought Lance. The wolf was cleaning up after others. A thought slowly rose to the surface: What if Andy was also cleaning up after somebody else?

ALL AROUND HIM the world was filled with a grayish light that told him nothing about what time of day it was. When he looked up, he didn't see blue sky or clouds, just gray light. It wasn't necessary to walk any farther. All he needed to do was to sit here and wait. He had sat down on the ice, and he could feel how his body was starting to doze off. Whoever had killed Georg Lofthus, it was no longer his concern.

Then he saw Jimmy walking toward him. Lance wanted to go to his son, but when he managed to get to his knees, he saw that he was looking at Jimmy's back; the boy was moving away from him. Jimmy had on a thin summer jacket and no mittens, and no one was holding his hand. Lance realized something terrible: it was not him but his *son* who was about to disappear. Desperately he tried to call out Jimmy's name, but he had almost no voice left. It was like in one of those nightmares when everything depended on being able to shout loudly enough, but it proved impossible. Except that this was no dream. He was really on his knees, way out here on the frozen lake, trying to yell his son's name, but without success.

His legs twinged painfully when he stood up, but he had no choice. He couldn't let Jimmy disappear. By now he could just barely make out the figure of the little boy. He needed to catch up with him and put his hat on, warm up his hands, take off his own jacket and wrap it around his son, carry him back to land. But how could he do that when he couldn't tell one direction from another? He began following the hazy figure as fast as he could, with needles piercing his legs, but soon he lost sight of the boy. For a moment he paused, tempted to sit down and rest his painful legs. Jimmy was gone anyway, and soon he himself would disappear, but something inside him refused to let him sit down. Instead, he started walking again, trying to stick to the same course that Jimmy had taken when he vanished. It was the only chance he had to see his son again.

Not a drop of energy remained in him, other than a tiny scrap of tinder-dry will. Each time he blinked, black spots fell across the ice. Somewhere deep inside he understood what that meant, but he was not afraid. His only thought was to find Jimmy, to give him his hat and mittens, to wrap his own jacket around him. More of the black spots appeared when he blinked. So far they had dissolved whenever he kept his eyes open for a moment, but he could tell that soon they would stay where they were, like black snow.

He stopped and blinked. Black snow swirled into view. He forced himself to keep his eyes open as long as he possibly could. At first the black seemed to have come to stay; he saw nothing but darkness. Then he noticed that it was starting to disperse, the black spots disappeared, but much more slowly than before. He could manage only a couple more blinks. Finally there was only a single spot left on the ice. Lance went over and knelt down. It was his cell phone. He had a hard time getting his hand to obey, but at last he yanked the phone loose from the frosty grip of the ice. He opened the cover and saw the display light up. It was a missed message from Debbie.

*Of course I remember. I can still feel the touch of your hand.*

He blinked again and again, but not a single black spot fell. A thought was slowly forming in his cold head. He'd thrown away the phone a long time ago, when he was still trying not to turn around because he didn't want to see land. After that he must have walked over the ice in a big circle, and now he'd come back to the same place. That meant he couldn't be very far from land even though he couldn't see much more than his own hand and the cell phone. But a voice might be able to reach him from land. And a voice was all he needed to find the right direction.

# 43

SOMETHING WAS MOVING under the ice. A shadow appeared right under his feet, as quick as a darting fish but bigger than a man. It lasted no more than a few seconds, then he lost sight of it, but the fear stayed with him. There was more than just water beneath him. He hesitated, took a couple of steps out. Or was it in? The ice rocked with each step. Then he saw it coming back. The shadow. It came racing toward him under the ice. At that instant the ice broke under his feet, and he fell through. Desperately he tried to lift his arms out of the water to defend himself against the creature speeding toward him.

Lance woke up, soaked with sweat, his chest heaving for air under several layers of woolen blankets. Still panicked from the dream, he cast the blankets aside. In the faint snowy light coming through the gap in the curtains he could see that someone was lying next to him. He leaped out of bed with a shriek and fumbled about in the dark room until he found the light switch over by the door. In his mind, he'd pictured his mother's dead body lying on the bed, but then he realized that it was Debbie Ahonen. She was looking at him with a sleepy, confused expression. Lance's heart was pounding, as if it wanted to leap out of his chest.

"What's wrong?" asked Debbie in a husky voice.

Lance noticed that she was wearing jeans and a T-shirt, but her feet were bare.

"Come back and lie down."

"But what . . . what are you doing here?" stammered Lance.

Suddenly he saw himself sitting in the kitchen, bundled up in blankets, while Debbie tried to get him to drink a mug of hot tea. Was that something that actually happened, or was it something he'd dreamed? But she really was here in his bed right now. And wearing no socks. Or was this also a dream?

"Come on," she said, firmly patting the mattress. "And give me some of those blankets before I turn into a block of ice."

Lance went over to the bed and picked up the woolen blankets he'd thrown off. One by one he placed them over Debbie, covering her up from her toes to the tip of her chin. She seemed to like that. Then he crawled under the blankets, being careful not to touch her.

Neither of them spoke. Lance was trying to collect his thoughts and figure out what was going on, but he couldn't make any sense of it.

"Is it night?" he finally said.

"Almost ten."

"At night?"

"Of course."

As he took another breath, about to ask her what was happening, he suddenly remembered everything. The ice, the gray emptiness out on Lake Superior. He'd thought he was well on his way toward death when he finally heard her voice. Debbie was shouting to him from land. It had taken time to get his bearings, but after a while he'd found the right direction and heard her shouts getting closer, until at last she was standing there, wearing an army-green down jacket, with Baraga's Cross behind her.

"You were mad at me, weren't you?" he said, without looking at her as she lay next to him under the woolen blankets.

"Mad at you?"

"In the car."

"I was yelling your name into the dark, but nobody answered," said Debbie. "All sorts of thoughts were swirling through my mind. I'd almost given up, when you came staggering into view. I think I was more scared than mad."

"So it was starting to get dark?" said Lance.

"Yeah."

"You saved my life."

"Oh, I don't know about that," said Debbie. "If you hadn't got hold of me, I'm sure you would have called somebody else."

"I'd dropped my phone. When I found it again and saw your text . . ."

"Oh, that," said Debbie, embarrassed.

"Is it true that you can still feel the touch of my hand?"

Debbie sighed.

"Is it?" he asked.

"I just meant that . . . I don't know . . ."

"Just meant what?" said Lance.

"You know, don't you?"

"I just want to be sure."

He could hear from her breathing that she was wondering how to put into words what she meant. And he had a feeling that at this moment everything would be decided.

"I'm lying in your bed, aren't I?" said Debbie. "Isn't that proof enough?"

"So it's not just because I got lost and was freezing?"

"No."

"No?" Lance repeated, happily.

"No."

"At first I was scared to see that somebody was lying next to me."

"I guess it's been a long time," said Debbie.

"But then I saw that it was you."

She turned to face Lance, and they kissed. A quiet kiss that went on and on, as if they were trying to build a bridge over the past twenty-five years.

# 44

ONLY WHEN HE SAT UP IN BED did Lance realize he had a cold. He sneezed loudly and got up to go to the bathroom and blow his nose. As he sat on the toilet with his pajama pants around his ankles, a solitary thought came sailing in from the near oblivion of the previous day, effectively turning any rush of happiness to ashes.

*What if Andy was also cleaning up after somebody else?*

There was only one person his brother would be willing to do something like that for. Just as there was only one person Lenny Diver might accept a life sentence for. If Diver and Andy, each in his own way, were protecting Chrissy, nearly everything else fell into place. Such as the fact that Andy's baseball bat was found in Diver's car with the Indian's fingerprints on it. Up until now, this was something that had fit only hazily into Lance's theory that his brother was the killer. He'd assumed that Andy had accidentally come across the drunken Indian and merely exploited the situation. But it was not coincidence that had brought the murder weapon from the Hansen family home in Two Harbors to Lenny Diver's car in Grand Portage. Chrissy Hansen had done that. No doubt her fingerprints were also on the bat, but it was Lenny Diver's prints the police had been looking for, and when they found them, the case was virtually closed. The only way Diver could avoid a life sentence was by denouncing his girlfriend, which was something he was apparently man enough not to do. The fact that Andy had driven down Baraga Cross Road that night, only a few hours before the murder, must have had something to do with Chrissy. Everything he'd done since, all his attempts to keep Lance at arm's length, could simply be explained as his way of protecting Chrissy from the prying eyes of her policeman uncle.

Then doubt came flooding over him. No, not doubt, but the sheer insanity of it all. How could he believe Chrissy was behind the horrifying sight that he'd discovered in the woods that morning? The bashed-in skull. The blood sprayed all over the trunks of the birch trees. But he remembered Eirik Nyland's voice on the phone: *Even a woman could have easily caused the injuries Lofthus sustained. And she wouldn't have to be especially strong.* If someone was high enough, on meth, for instance, no motive was necessary. Drugs could make a person acutely paranoid. As both a drug user and the girlfriend of Lenny Diver, it was almost unimaginable that Chrissy *hadn't* used meth. And she could have been the one who left the blood evidence that had led the police to Diver, since she too had Indian ancestry.

If that was the case, then what had happened? A failed robbery?

*This is what you are looking for.*

He realized now what the wooden figure meant: they were two pieces, with one protecting the other. But then the whole point of trying to get Diver acquitted in court vanished. At any time he could clear his own name and walk out a free man. Yet he was never going to do that, because Lenny Diver was no ordinary small-time crook and drug addict. And that matched perfectly the impression that Lance had gotten the one time they'd met. Somewhere in that jailed man was a huge reserve of strength.

In the shower Lance stood for a long time under the pounding hot water, but he didn't feel any better when he got out. He wiped the steam from the mirror and looked at his face, which he hardly recognized anymore. Gray and doughy. Unshaven too. For more than half a year his life had revolved almost solely around the murder of Georg Lofthus. He wondered if that would ever end.

Seen in this new light, there finally seemed to be an explanation for another relationship. He was thinking of how Andy had tried to keep Chrissy indoors since the murder, even after Lenny Diver was arrested. This had puzzled Lance, because if Diver was guilty, the danger was over once he was in jail. And if Andy was the murderer, Chrissy was in no danger either. So why keep her locked up like the princess in the tower? It seemed inexplicable. Unless it was to protect her from the consequences of something she herself had done. If Andy knew Chrissy had killed Lofthus, he would probably do anything to prevent his daughter from incriminating herself.

But wasn't Georg Lofthus entitled to justice?

Lance saw a similarity between Andy and the gay Norwegian. It was no longer the bloody bond between murderer and victim, but a fellowship of impossible dreams and impossible choices.

He jumped when his cell started ringing in his pants pocket.

# 45

TAMMY'S HAIR LOOKED NEWLY WASHED, and she had on a black blouse that he didn't remember seeing her wear before.

"Thanks for coming," she said. "You have to help me, Lance. If Lenny Diver gets off, my daughter is done for. It's as simple as that. He has a hold on her, both because she's in love with him and because he supplies her with whatever she wants."

Lance had completely forgotten the story he'd made up about how Diver might be acquitted because there wasn't sufficient evidence against him. The truth was that he was already as good as convicted since his fingerprints had been found on the murder weapon.

"There's little we can do about that now," he said.

"But if he's acquitted, won't the case be reopened?" she asked.

"I have no idea," said Lance.

He thought about Diver in the Moose Lake jail. Was he really there because he was protecting Chrissy?

"I was wondering . . . ," Tammy began, and he could hear that she was getting to the real reason for inviting him over. "I thought that you, as a police officer . . . that if you testified and said, for example, that you saw Diver near the cross on that night, something you'd forgotten about but now remembered . . ."

"You mean you want me to give false testimony?" he said.

"No, not false, because we know who did it."

"Do we?"

A barely visible tightening occurred at the corner of her mouth, but Lance noticed it. For several seconds they stared at each other across the coffee table. Then Tammy lowered her eyes.

"An acquittal would be a death sentence for Chrissy," she said in a low voice.

He didn't know what else to say. If he suddenly claimed there was no danger because the evidence against Diver was actually rock solid, it would merely sound like he was lying to reassure her. Yet he also felt a growing annoyance at the way she talked about Lenny Diver. Okay, so he was a crook and a drug addict. But what if he was also the only person standing between her daughter and a long prison sentence?

"Have you heard anything to indicate that Diver was physically abusive toward Chrissy?"

Tammy shook her head.

"Andy, on the other hand . . ."

"Abusive and tender at the same time," Tammy said. "That's Andy in a nutshell."

She stubbed out her cigarette in the ashtray and lit another.

"Have you heard about Clayton Miller?" asked Lance.

His sister-in-law frowned.

"A guy that went to Central High with me and Andy. Now he's a poet and some sort of professor."

"Oh, that's right. Chrissy bought one of his books."

"Andy almost killed him once," said Lance.

She opened her eyes wide.

"If I hadn't stopped him, I think he would have been a murderer on that day."

"But why?"

Lance hesitated.

"I don't know what provoked the situation," he said at last. "Or at least I don't remember anymore. It was so long ago. But Clayton Miller was . . . what shall I say? A slightly girlish boy. Not exactly a fighter. When I showed up, he was lying on the ground with a punctured lung, and Andy was heading for him with a baseball bat."

Tammy got up and ran to the bathroom, not pausing even to close the door behind her. Seconds later Lance heard the contents of her stomach pouring into the toilet with violent force. She continued to vomit, until it turned into dry heaves. Lance had an eerie feeling that he was right on the edge of something very dangerous. When the sounds coming from the bathroom finally ceased, he sat and listened for several minutes before he heard Tammy clear her throat and spit into the toilet a few times. After a moment, she flushed and then began brushing her teeth. He could hear her gargle with mouthwash, but he still noticed the faint smell of vomit when she came back into the living room.

"Sorry," she mumbled.

He looked up at her.

"Maybe I should go."

"No, stay a little longer."

She touched his shoulder in passing as she went over to her place on the other side of the coffee table. She sat down, picked up her cigarette from the ashtray, and took a long drag.

"Shit," she said and laughed nervously.

"Are you sick?"

"No, but the thought of Andy with a baseball bat, just like . . . If Lenny Diver and my husband are just the same, what am I going to do?"

"I don't know who's worse in this story," said Lance.

"Lenny Diver is worse," said Tammy harshly. "Just the thought of that bastard as some kind of drug-addicted Indian brave, with those long braids of his . . . That a man like that could ruin my daughter's life. I refuse to accept it," she cried.

"I know," said Lance.

"That's why we have to stop him from getting acquitted. Don't you see that? No matter what means we have to use. Chrissy is more important to you than your job, isn't she, Lance?"

"Of course, but . . ."

"You're her uncle," Tammy insisted.

"I know that."

"And Lenny Diver is a murderer who deserves to spend the rest of his life in prison."

Lance wondered whether she was really so convinced of Diver's guilt, or whether she too suspected something that was much more horrifying.

"I can't give false testimony," he said. "But I'll do everything I can to find out what really happened at Baraga's Cross that night."

"But we know what happened," she said, sighing with resignation.

"Yes, but I'm going to *prove* it," Lance told her.

Tammy briefly shook her head, giving him a look that he'd never seen from her before.

"It's going to be hours before Andy gets home from work," she said then.

She still smelled faintly of vomit, but oddly enough, Lance didn't mind. He swallowed hard as she got up from the sofa and came over to him. Suddenly her hips were level with his face.

"You know, Andy hasn't . . ." she murmured as she stood looking down at him, but Lance didn't dare raise his eyes because now those slender hands were unbuckling her belt right in front of him.

"He doesn't know how to appreciate . . ." she went on, but then stopped speaking as she swiftly, nimbly unfastened the five shiny buttons on her fly.

A moment later she had wriggled her hips out of both her jeans and her panties and stood there with her dark crotch exposed. Two contradictory forces were struggling to overtake Lance. One wanted to get up out of the chair and leave the house as fast as possible. The other wanted to lean forward and bury his face in her.

He knew which impulse was stronger.

"Don't you think Andy is stupid?" she whispered.

Lance nodded.

"Isn't he stupid, not wanting this?"

"Yeah," he said hoarsely, leaning closer until his face was only inches from her body.

"It's yours now," she whispered.

Slowly he raised his hand to touch what Andy didn't want.

Tammy let out a series of shuddering breaths, as if she'd been holding them in for several minutes.

"Come here," she said, taking his hand.

Lance stood up and Tammy pressed her head against him. He felt her warm breath on his throat.

"Touch me again," she whispered, guiding his hand between her legs. "It feels so good when you touch me."

*I can still feel the touch of your hand.*

In a flash he saw himself and the whole situation as if from the outside, and he tried to wriggle out of his sister-in-law's grasp.

"No, Lance," she said. "Please. I want you."

But he pulled away and fled to the front hall. As he desperately fumbled to put on his boots, she appeared in the doorway. She'd put her jeans back on. Lance was going to apologize for not staying, but that would only make matters worse. Tammy leaned against the door frame, looking at him with big, sad eyes. She didn't seem calculating, just lonely.

# 46

A LITTLE LESS THAN AN HOUR LATER Lance was opening the door to the Kozy Bar. After his conversation with Tammy, he had called Chrissy. She answered the phone with a leaden-sounding voice and had agreed to meet him without even asking why.

As soon as his eyes adjusted to the murky underground light, he saw that she was sitting in the darkest corner, at the same table where he had sat when they met several weeks ago. The only other customer was a gaunt old man sitting at the bar, who barely raised his eyes when Lance asked for a Diet Coke.

An old Madonna video was flickering mutely on the TV screen up near the ceiling.

"Hi," Lance said, sitting down.

His niece gave him a weary smile.

"What exactly are you doing?" he asked her.

She shrugged.

"Shouldn't you be in school?"

"Are you back on the job?" she said in that same heavy-sounding voice, as if something were constricting her vocal cords.

Lance shook his head.

"What did you want to talk to me about?" she asked.

"I'm wondering why you're behaving like this."

"What do you mean?"

"Putting all kinds of things in your body."

Chrissy let her eyes fall shut, but Lance could still see a sliver of those brown irises. He reached out to grab her hand, which was lying on the table, but she pulled away.

"His trial is going to start soon," he said.

She nodded.

"It's guaranteed he'll be convicted."

"He's innocent," she murmured.

"How can you be so sure?"

"Because somebody saw the murderer," she said. "A man holding a bloody baseball bat. I already told you."

"There was never any man with a bloody baseball bat on the side of the road outside Finland," said Lance. "There was never a party at the cabin on Lost Lake either. At least, not on that night."

"But you said you knew who did it," said Chrissy. "Somebody you went to school with. A gay guy, wasn't it?"

"You know as well as I do that I was wrong," he said.

Chrissy looked down at her lap.

"So how can you know Lenny Diver is innocent?" Lance asked again.

His niece looked like she was going to cry.

"Don't you see I'm being torn apart?" she whimpered.

"Yes, I do. But you're the only one who can do something about it."

"No, you have to help me, Uncle Lance. You have to make sure he goes free."

"Not unless the real murderer takes his place in prison," said Lance harshly.

Chrissy leaned forward and hid her face in her arms on the table. Suddenly she looked like a child again. Hesitantly, Lance reached out to stroke her hair. He could see the blond roots amid all that black.

"Don't you think the guilty party should surrender?" he asked.

She looked up from the table.

"Maybe the guilty person is suffering even more than Lenny," she said.

"So the two of you are on a first-name basis?"

"Not really."

"Chrissy . . . I know all about you and Lenny Diver. That he was your boyfriend. Maybe he still is, for all I know. And that he used to get you drugs."

She sat up and looked at him in disbelief. Then it dawned on her.

"Did Mom tell you that?" she asked.

Lance nodded.

"That bitch! She's never wanted me to have anything, not even a boyfriend. She just wants me to have the same miserable life she has. But I'd rather die. She hates Lenny so much it scares me. Just because he's an Indian."

"So it's not because he's a criminal who's been supplying her underage daughter with drugs?"

"No. It's because he's everything they're not."

"I think you should be glad your parents are who they are," said Lance.

Chrissy looked at him with an intense bitterness he'd never seen from her before.

"They're nothing," she said coldly. "And that's why I'm going to be nothing too."

"You're *not* your parents," said Lance. "Part of you is uniquely you, and in that sense, you're in a better position than most people."

"But if I'm going to make something of myself, I need to get out of Two Harbors."

"Yeah. I can see that."

"And away from everything that has to do with this case."

She looked at Lance.

"Away from the murder case?" he said.

"I have to. Otherwise I have no future. You see that, don't you, Uncle Lance?"

They sat there, staring at each other for what seemed to Lance like several minutes, but was probably only seconds.

"Don't you?" she pleaded.

Lance got up without replying.

"I've got to go," he said. "Shall I drive you home?"

"No, I'm going to stay here for a while," said Chrissy.

He was about to tell her what he thought about an underage girl hanging out at the Kozy Bar, but he refrained. Instead, he gave her a little pat on the shoulder and was overwhelmed with tenderness when he noticed how fragile she felt.

# 47

AS HE HEADED BACK NORTH on Highway 61, Lance felt that this burden was too much to bear. Andy, yes. But not Chrissy. The girl had been the closest he'd come to having a child in the years before Jimmy was born. And she'd always had something inside her that pointed beyond where she came from. What exactly it pointed toward was not something he'd ever considered; he just knew it was there. Poetry, possibly, he thought now, recalling her enthusiasm at the poetry reading in Duluth. Maybe she wrote poetry, or she could be studying poems and writing about them. What did he know? What did Lance know about being a talented young person who wanted to escape everything she'd been born into? And who wanted to break away from her parents. He was a middle-aged man who had not only stayed where he was born but had dug in his roots as deep as they would go. He was a policeman like his father, living on the North Shore like the majority of his relatives going back several generations. He was the complete opposite of his strong and courageous niece, who was now carrying the weight of something that was about to drive her into the abyss. For that very reason, he was the one who would have to take away her future. Because even though he could clearly sense that the burden was too great to bear, he knew he would have to do it. It was in his nature for Lance Hansen to shoulder a burden and endure it without complaint.

It was four thirty in the afternoon when he parked outside

the Finland General Store. Through the Santa Claus and reindeer decorations on the window he caught a glimpse of Debbie's blond hair. For a change he also saw a couple of customers inside, probably people who had just gotten off work.

Lance went inside and immediately received a smile from Debbie, who was ringing up the purchases for one of the customers. He took a little stroll through the store as he waited for the others to leave. He glanced at some old, sun-faded postcards with pictures of Finland: a moose crossing the road in front of a car; the St. Urho statue at sunset; a flagpole with the Finnish flag and the motto *We got sisu!* For a moment he considered buying one to send to Eirik Nyland, but he decided not to.

Finally the door closed behind the last customer.

"Afternoon rush?"

"Uh-huh. It always throws me off when both customers show up at the same time."

She got up and came around the counter to give Lance a kiss on the cheek. On the cheek! What's that supposed to mean? he thought. He'd expected a repeat of that long, slow kiss from last night. Well, preferably more than that, so he was taken aback by a friendly kiss on the cheek.

"You've sure got a cold, all right," she said as he snuffled loudly.

"Yeah."

"But you're looking pretty alert, considering what happened."

"That must be because you were the one who rescued me."

Debbie's response was another of those rattling smoker's coughs.

"I need a cigarette," she said when it subsided. "Shall we go in the back room?"

Lance didn't really know what he was hoping to accomplish with this visit, but he felt that the dreary back room would ruin whatever it was.

"How about going for a drive instead?" he suggested.

"But it's almost three hours until I close."

Lance pulled her close and put his arms around her so they were standing chin to chin. He could hear how her breathing was first shallow and hesitant, as if on guard, only to slowly ease, just as her body did, adopting the same rhythm as his own breath until they stood there, embracing each other and breathing as one.

It was a long time before either of them moved.

Finally Debbie drew back, straightened her clothes, and looked around.

"Just close the store," said Lance, "and come with me."

Debbie tilted her head to one side and looked at him. He suddenly remembered that she used to do that during the summer they were together. He wondered whether they were now back together.

"Okay," she said. "But you'll have to take responsibility if I get in trouble."

"I can handle Akkola, no problem," said Lance.


THEY DROVE NORTH along the Baptism River. Lance thought to himself that it had to be twenty-five years since Debbie Ahonen last sat beside him in his car. Everything had been so different. Back then his mother wasn't more than fifty, not much older than he was now. He could never change the fact that he hadn't visited her before she died. It was too late and always would be.

"Is something wrong?" asked Debbie.

"How can anything be wrong when I'm finally out driving with you again?"

"Why did you walk out on the ice?"

"I don't know. Mom died, and . . . Well, there's something happening in my family. It's been going on for a while, and I'm the one who's going to have to do something about it. To be honest, I'm in a real sticky situation."

"Can you tell me about it?" she asked.

"Not yet. But later, after I clear things up."

"Do you promise to tell me later?"

Lance nodded.

"Good," she said.

Then they drove in silence for a while until Lance suddenly thought of something.

"Do you remember what you said about the ravens?" he asked.

"No," said Debbie.

"I said that the two of us were like the ravens, who stay up here all winter. That we're tough. But you said that was wrong. You said we're the carcasses they peck at along the road."

Debbie laughed.

"And you're right," Lance went on. "People like us—we end up like carcasses at the side of the road, and the best we can hope for is that someone will stop and chase away the ravens."

"Then we'll have to do that," said Debbie. "We'll have to chase away the ravens for each other."

Lance didn't reply, just focused all his attention on the winding road through the forest.

"I could use a smoke," said Debbie after a while. "Could you stop as soon as you find a place?"

They came to an open area beside the road where an impressive number of logs had been piled up awaiting the trucks that would carry them away. Lance pulled over, and they got out. The stacked timber towered over them in the dusk. Even in the bitter winter air, he could smell the fresh wood. Debbie lit a cigarette. In the flickering glow from the lighter her face looked smooth and young.

"You have to promise not to disappear again," she said after taking a drag. "Either out on the lake or anywhere else."

"I promise," he said, awkwardly patting her arm. "I promise. You saved my life, after all. You're my hero."

"Heroine," Debbie corrected him. "But I know you would have done the same for me."

Lance thought the best way of saving Debbie's life would be to get her to stop smoking.

"I promise to carry you over even the smallest little bridge," he said, thinking about Willy's story about Otter Heart and Sad Water.

"In that case, you're going to need to start working out pretty soon," said Debbie.

Lance didn't reply. He suddenly remembered something Chrissy had said: *I'm Sad Water. Nobody is building any bridges for me.* But that was exactly what Lenny Diver had done. He had lain down like a human bridge over the abyss that a long prison sentence would be for Chrissy. Yet Lance had no doubt that she was speaking the truth when she'd said that. He clearly recalled the disillusioned, naked sound of her voice. It was the voice of a person for whom no one ever lifts a finger to help.

But what did it mean?

"Look at the stars," said Debbie.

Lance looked up and saw that the stars had appeared in the sky that was already almost nighttime black; only in the west was there a thin brushstroke of light above the forest.

They stood there staring up at the clusters of stars.

"Do you know what's going to be the hardest part?" said Debbie.

"No."

"My mother. I can't expect Richie to keep on . . ."

"I'll help out," said Lance.

"Are you sure?"

"Yeah. I'm sure."

He kept on staring at the stars until his neck felt stiff and he had to look down. That was when he noticed that Debbie was looking at him. In the faint light from the snow and stars it was difficult to read her expression, but he thought she was smiling.


"ARE YOU SURE you want to go back to Finland?" he said a little later when they were on the road again.

"What do you mean?"

"Tonight."

"But I need to close up the store."

"It's closed," said Lance.

"Tally up the cash register."

"Let Richie do that. Just send him a text and tell him you quit."

Debbie giggled.

"And then what?" she said.

"Then we get a motel room," said Lance.

"Really? Interesting. And after we get one?"

"Then it's just the two of us in the whole world."

Debbie didn't say anything. He wondered if he'd moved

too fast, but how likely was that? He noticed that she was doing something as she sat in the passenger seat. When he glanced over at her, he saw that she was texting on her cell phone. After a moment she held it up for him to see. He put his foot on the brake to slow down as he read the message on the display. *I quit. Not coming home. Am with Lance Hansen.* He handed the phone back after reading the text.

"All right," said Debbie, and she pressed "send." "So, that's done. I'm turning it off for the rest of the night."

Lance couldn't think of a thing to say that wouldn't ruin the moment.

# 48

HE SAT ON THE BED, which was covered with a hotel-brown bedspread, and listened to the sound of water pouring over Debbie Ahonen's naked body behind the bathroom door. He thought she'd been in the shower for an awfully long time and wondered whether it was because she dreaded coming back into the room. If that was the case, he could understand, because then it really would be just the two of them in the whole world. Aside from her jacket and cap, which hung next to Lance's on the row of hooks next to the door, she hadn't taken off a single garment before heading for the shower. Not even her heavy white sweater. Lance was also fully clothed as he sat on the bed, wearing a red sweater, jeans on top of long johns, and gray woolen socks on his feet. Only now did he realize what he'd started. Soon it would be his turn to take a shower, and then he'd have to show himself naked to her. The mere thought made his mouth go dry with anxiety.

With a groan he leaned down to pull off his socks, first the thick outer pair, then the thin ones underneath. Then he just sat there, still wearing all his clothes but with bare feet. If he'd had any doubts about whether he really needed a shower, they were now gone. The odor from his feet was anything but conducive to a romantic mood.

The sound of running water stopped abruptly. Then a hair dryer started up. Should he get undressed before she came back, or would that send the wrong signal? As if he was just waiting to throw himself at her? In reality, he was sitting here wishing this wasn't happening. It wasn't that he didn't feel attracted to Debbie, but it had been almost four years since Lance had seen another person naked, not to mention shown his own nude body to someone else. And right now his nervousness was stronger than his desire.

The bathroom door opened and Debbie's bare legs came into view. The rest of her, from just above her knees to the top of her breasts, turned out to be wrapped in a big white towel. She had tucked her clothes under one arm, but now she flung them into a corner before scurrying to the other side of the bed and crawling under the covers.

"Aren't you going to take a shower, Lance?" she said, smiling, with only her head showing.

"Yeah. Sure," he muttered.

He got up and went into the bathroom. As he locked the door behind him, he realized how stupid that must seem, but it would be even dumber to unlock it now, so he didn't. As he took off his clothes he thought about the uncomfortable fact that neither of them would have clean underwear to put on in the morning. Then he stepped into the shower stall, where he found only a scrap of soap that once must have been a big and gleaming bar but had now been reduced to a thin, grayish-yellow square with cracks running through it. One of Debbie's long blond hairs was stuck to it. At least he hoped it was Debbie's.

He soaped up as best he could, using the rock-hard piece of soap, and then took his time rinsing off. For a moment he stood still, letting the water pelt his body. He knew she could hear every sound as she lay in bed, waiting. He'd have to turn off the water soon or it would seem strange. And he'd already done something stupid by locking the door.

Luckily the mirror was covered with steam when he got out of the shower, so at least he didn't have to look at himself naked. When he tried to fasten the towel around his waist his butt stuck out, which would look comical. And if there was one thing he didn't want to be right now, it was comical. Finally he gave up and used his hand to hold the towel closed behind him.

Then, with one hand modestly protecting his rear and at

least forty-five more pounds on his upper body than the last time she saw him without any clothes, Lance Hansen went out to join Debbie Ahonen. She had tossed her towel on the floor, so she had to be stark naked under the covers. He tried to get into bed as fast as possible, without revealing too much, but as he set one knee on the bed, Debbie reached out her long arm and snatched the towel off his body.

WHEN HE WOKE UP, he saw her propped up on one elbow, with her chin in her hand, staring at him. She smiled, as if his face were a story she'd been listening to for a long time and she'd just heard the ending she was hoping for.

"Hi," she said softly.

"Hi." He cleared his throat. "Have I been asleep for long?"

"Don't know. I dozed off myself. But it's really quiet outside, so I think it must be night."

It took him a few seconds to remember where they were. A motel in the little mining town of Aurora, on the Iron Range.

"Nobody knows where we are."

"Mmm. Isn't that nice?"

Debbie laid her head on his shoulder. She smelled faintly of cigarette smoke and soap.

"What made you answer my text message?" asked Lance.

"Oh, it was a very simple question that you asked. Whether I remembered that night at Baraga's Cross. And the more I thought about it, the more I was sure it was the best experience I'd ever had with a man. And I thought that had to mean something."

"Was it really?" he asked in surprise. "The best you ever had?"

"Yes, it was. How awful that somebody had to get killed in that spot. Such an idyllic setting. Do you remember that we drove down there a couple of times and made out in the car?"

"Yeah, I do," he said dreamily.

"But if we'd stayed together, maybe even gotten married, do you think we'd be lying here in bed right now?" she asked.

"I doubt it."

"Maybe everything else had to happen first. Marriage and kids and . . . What do you think?"

"Probably," said Lance. "I just hope it doesn't turn out that there are even more things that need to happen first."

"No," she told him with a big smile. "There aren't."

"So now it's the two of us?"

"That's right."

"And I get to see those beautiful long legs of yours again?"

"You mean now?"

"Yup."

She threw off the covers, and Lance sighed loudly in appreciation.

WHEN HE WOKE UP THE SECOND TIME, he found himself looking right at her slumbering face. Her mouth was relaxed like a little child's, and she'd drooled a bit onto the pillow. Carefully, without waking her, he disentangled himself from Debbie's body and turned onto his back. He lay there, staring up at the none-too-clean ceiling of Room 21 in the Aurora Pines Motel, aware of Debbie's blond hair seeming to light up the pillow as she lay beside him.

It must be almost morning, he thought, although the sun was not yet visible through the orange curtains. Outside the snow was piled high and the temperature was probably at least twenty below. The Iron Range was one of the coldest areas in the States, aside from Alaska. But in here, under several layers of woolen blankets, life was warm and peaceful. Lance had that rare feeling that time was standing still. Everything was here and now, one big silent moment spreading out in all directions, like concentric rings in the water. And he was lying in the middle of those rings with Debbie Ahonen beside him. Outside some big vehicle drove past, probably one of the trucks used in the open-pit mines. The windowpane rattled a bit, but Debbie slept on.

He turned his head to look at her. When she was sleeping, it was even more clear how beautiful she was; as if sleep erased all traces left by time and worry. She looked almost the same as he remembered her from nearly twenty-five years ago. All those intervening years no longer mattered. He thought about how they'd parked a few times at Baraga's Cross that summer when they were together, sitting in the car and kissing. Something about the place attracted couples who could often be seen there, making out.

All of sudden Lance realized what Andy had been doing at Baraga's Cross on that night.

# 49

THE NEXT DAY they went into the gas station in Finland, where Richie Akkola himself was manning the counter.

"You quit?" he said.

"Yep," replied Debbie.

"How am I going to handle this place and the store at the same time?" Akkola grumbled.

"I guess you'll have to find a way," she said.

"So you've found yourself a new guy who can support you and your old mother. Is that right?"

Lance swiftly took a step forward, but the counter blocked his way.

"Well, you can have her," Akkola went on. "Be my guest. Let me tell you what kind of dame she is."

Before he could say another word, Lance jumped up so he was sitting on the counter. Then he swung his legs over the other side. Akkola started for the back door, but he wasn't fast enough, and Lance managed to grab the back of his jacket collar.

"You fucking Finn!" he shouted.

Akkola flailed his arms about, trying to ram his elbow into his assailant, but he was a lightweight of a man and pushing seventy. After a brief scuffle, Lance got him turned around and delivered an uppercut that sent the old man crashing into the magazine rack. Richie collapsed onto the floor and lay there, partially buried under an avalanche of automotive and gun magazines.

Lance looked around for a wrench, a tire iron, anything he could use to make mincemeat of the bastard once and for all. But he caught sight of Debbie, who had raised her hand to her mouth in surprise while at the same time she shook with laughter. And then he realized what he'd done. The area behind the counter looked like a war zone.

"Oi," he exclaimed, which made Debbie double over with laughter.

This time he didn't leap over the counter but instead walked to the end where there was a clear passageway out.

"What's so funny?" he said with a stern expression.

Strange slurping noises were coming from behind the counter.

"Didn't you see that he lost his dentures?" gasped Debbie.

They went over to the counter and peered down at the man who was slowly getting up on all fours. Debbie couldn't stop laughing.

"If you report this," said Lance, pointing a threatening finger at Akkola, "I'll make sure you never get help from the police again. Somebody can rob you blind and burn down your house and hang your cat, but not a single officer will ever lift a finger to come to your aid. Do you hear what I'm saying?"

Akkola merely grunted as he fumbled for his dentures, which were lying on top of a hunting magazine.

# 50

LANCE PAUSED in the entrance to the pub at Fitger's Brewhouse and looked at Chrissy, who was sitting alone at a corner table with a glass of what looked like Coke in front of her. She was wearing her usual black Goth coat, leaning back in her chair with her arms hanging limply at her sides, her eyes fixed on the table. Her face had a pallid glow in the dim light.

As Lance went inside, she looked up and caught sight of him.

"Are you living here now, or what?" he said, sitting down.

"Here?" asked Chrissy in surprise.

"In Duluth."

"Nah."

"Are you still going to school?"

"Not really."

Lance ordered a Diet Coke from the same waiter who had asked them to leave the last time they were there.

"Been home?" he asked when the waiter was gone.

"Since when?"

"Two days ago, at the Kozy."

"Don't think so."

Lance waited to say anything more until after the waiter brought his Coke.

"The trial starts on Monday," he said then. "Lenny Diver is going to get a life sentence. Do you still think somebody else should be serving that time?"

Chrissy used the tip of her tongue to moisten her winter-dry lips.

"Yes. The person who actually did it," she said.

"If Lenny didn't do it, then it had to be you," said Lance.

"What?"

Chrissy's face was filled with fear.

"As you know, I've been working on the case in secret," he said. "Yesterday I got a look at the murder weapon for the first time. And let me tell you, that was a surprise."

Her eyes shifted uneasily.

"I don't know how many times I've seen Andy swing that bat," he went on. "But there it was, lying on the table in front of me. The murder weapon. His initials that he carved into the wood so many years ago . . . a V-shaped gouge from the time I threw down the bat and it hit a rock . . . They were all there."

He gave his niece an expectant look. She was nervously fiddling with a strand of hair.

"Do you think you'll be able to do the time?"

"You need to be very careful what you say," Chrissy told him, but she was only a seventeen-year-old girl, venturing out on ice that got thinner with every word she spoke.

"Really?"

"Yes," she said. "It's a serious thing to accuse someone of—"

"Did you know Lenny Diver's prints weren't the only ones they found on the baseball bat?" Lance interrupted her. "They just never checked them out after finding Lenny's. I assume you'd be willing to give your fingerprints to the FBI, so they could compare them to the prints on the murder weapon. Right?"

Chrissy, who now looked even paler than usual, kept her eyes fixed on the table. It was for her sake that Andy had lied to Lance at the ranger station right after the murder was discovered. He did it to keep his daughter's drug use and her relationship with Lenny Diver from becoming known. And that was when Lance's suspicions had taken hold, because he knew his brother was lying.

"I know that you were there and that Andy showed up. Why don't you tell me what happened?"

Chrissy raised her eyes and scowled.

"Everything?"

"From the very beginning. And the truth this time. Okay?" She sighed.

"I hadn't taken anything since Easter," she began. "That was hard enough, but the worst part was that they refused to let me see Lenny. Mom picked me up at school every day, as if I were a fucking kindergartener. But we talked on the phone, and finally we agreed that I'd try to get permission to stay overnight with a girlfriend in Duluth—Jennifer. She knew about Lenny and me and was willing to help us."

"Is that the same girlfriend who was your stand-in at the drama class?" asked Lance.

"No, that was someone else. Jesus, did you hear about that too?"

"Just tell me what happened," he said.

"First I had to convince Mom that I deserved to go and that everything would be fine. And after that she had to persuade Dad. That's how it's always been. But finally they said yes. It was summer vacation and everything. I think they felt sorry for me."

"Who is this Jennifer?"

"Jennifer Rawlins. Just a girl I know from high school."

"If she lives in Duluth, she wouldn't be going to school in Two Harbors."

"There was some trouble at Central High, so her parents decided it would be best if she switched schools."

"So when did she come over to pick you up?"

"I think it was around eight," said Chrissy. "Mom and Dad said hi to her, and then we got in the car and supposedly headed for Duluth. But we just drove in a big arc around Two Harbors and over to Betty's Pies, where Lenny was waiting. I haven't seen Jennifer since. I called her a couple of times, but she didn't want to talk. Maybe she suspected something. But even if she did, I don't think she's said anything."

"What happened at Betty's Pies?" he asked.

Every detail she could tell him was part of the picture he'd been chasing for nearly half a year. His whole life had been centered on that night: all the comings and goings, car trips, phone calls, lies.

"That's where I finally got to see Lenny again," said Chrissy.

"The love of your life?"

"Yes, he is. He was wearing his hair in two long braids. I'd only seen him do that once before, and that was the very first time we met."

"How did you two meet?"

"At a poetry reading in Duluth."

"Christ," said Lance, surprised.

"You wouldn't have thought that, huh?"

"As you no doubt already know, I visited Diver in jail. He surprised me by quoting Longfellow."

Chrissy smiled sadly.

"That sounds like Lenny," she said.

"So for that poetry reading he'd braided his hair?"

"Yeah. But never after that. Not until that night, as if he knew it might be the last time . . ."

"How did Andy know that you were with Diver?" asked Lance.

"It turned out he knew who Jennifer was. Her father sells snowmobiles, or something, and Dad had seen her at his store. So when she picked me up that night, he recognized her. But he didn't say anything. That jerk."

"Instead he called her father to find out if you were really there?"

"Uh-huh. But Jennifer's little sister picked up the phone. She was home alone. I don't think her parents ever found out about any of this. But Dad knew what it meant."

"And then you met at Betty's Pies . . ."

"We met *outside* Betty's Pies, in the parking lot. Lenny doesn't like going in places like that. Family places."

"I guess not. So when you met there, did he bring any drugs?"

"Uh-huh," she said reluctantly.

"But you didn't take any that night, since you'd been clean since Easter. Right?" said Lance.

"Well, not at first. Lenny was already high when I met him, but he didn't hassle me about taking anything. He never did. It wasn't like he forced me, if that's what you're thinking. Sometimes he even warned me about doing drugs."

"If that's the case, then how did you usually get the stuff?" asked Lance.

Chrissy didn't reply, and he hadn't expected her to. He knew all about how guys like Lenny Diver operated with their young girlfriends. They never pressured them into anything; they were just there, always on hand whenever the urge hit. Since Chrissy didn't look like she was going to answer his question, Lance went on.

"After the two of you met there, did you just drive around, or what?"

"That's what we always did," she said.

"And you got high together. That night, I mean."

"After a while, yeah. First it was just Lenny . . . He didn't want me to . . . But then he decided to let me."

"Meth?"

"Yeah."

"You know it makes your teeth fall out, don't you?" said Lance.

Chrissy didn't reply.

"What time do you think it was when you drove down to the parking lot near the cross?" he asked.

"God, that's so long ago."

"How long do you think it took from the time you parked to when Andy showed up?"

"Maybe half an hour," she guessed.

"So you drove down there around nine thirty. Do you think he knew the two of you were there?"

"No, but you said yourself that it's one of the first places anyone would go."

Lance thought about the nights he and Debbie had sat in that same parking lot. He'd been so in love! A sweetness in his blood flowing through his whole body. Was that what Chrissy had felt too? But possibly with an even greater intensity, since she was high?

"Tell me what happened after Andy arrived," he said.

"Suddenly he was standing there with that fucking baseball bat. Looking insane. But also ridiculous. Lenny could have, like, crushed him with one hand behind his back. Jesus! My dad! He started screaming and swinging the bat around, slamming it onto the hood of the car. Lenny got out and tried to calm him down, but it didn't do any good. Dad shouted at him, said he was going to ruin me, blah, blah, blah. Then Dad opened the door and yanked me out of the car. When I tried to get away, he punched me so hard I landed flat on my face on the ground."

"He did what?" exclaimed Lance.

"What else could he do?"

"Couldn't he have . . ."

"Talked to me?" she said. "I'm afraid that doesn't work so good when somebody's high on meth."

"Good Lord. So how did Diver react?"

"He didn't do anything. I lay there with my scarf pressed to my face and blood pouring out of my nose and mouth. Suddenly Dad seemed to realize that Lenny wasn't going to get involved. He turned his back on him and came over to me. He was still holding the bat in his hand, and I was so scared and high that I thought he was going to beat me to death. But he just tore the scarf out of my hands and threw it away. Then he grabbed me by the arm and dragged me over to his car."

"What happened to the scarf?" asked Lance.

"I have no idea."

"The police didn't find it, at any rate."

"Maybe Lenny took it," she said hesitantly.

"Why didn't he intervene when Andy . . . hit you?"

"He says he didn't want to make me fatherless."

"So you've talked to him since the murder?"

"A couple of times on the phone."

"Was that when you decided to get Mist and King to try and put a scare into me?"

Chrissy hid her face in her hands and groaned.

"I can have you sent to prison if I want to," said Lance harshly.

His niece merely nodded, her face still covered.

"So Andy just drove away with you in his car? Is that it?" he continued in a somewhat gentler tone of voice.

"Uh-huh," she sniffled, wiping away tears and snot. "But first he threatened Lenny, said he was going to come back with a whole gang and beat the shit out of him."

"Did you and Andy go to the cabin?"

"Yes."

"Did you take with you the latest issue of something called *Darkside*?"

"Yeah. It was in my purse. Lenny had bought it for me. How did . . . ?"

"Just forget it. What did you do at the cabin?"

"We had a big fight. Dad tied me to a chair and made me stay there all night. He wouldn't even let me go to the bathroom. I peed on myself, sitting there like that. In the morning he was listening to the news on the old transistor radio, when they said that—"

"Yeah. I was the one who found the body," said Lance.

He pictured Georg Lofthus's friend, who had been sitting at the base of Baraga's Cross, naked and bloody. Suddenly the man had looked up and said something in a foreign language, yet Lance had recognized the sound. He didn't know many Norwegian words, but the naked man had said one of them. A single word had surfaced from the incomprehensible muttering, a word from his Norwegian American childhood. *Kjærlighet.* That was what the man had said. And he repeated it in English. *Love.* Now Lance saw how right he'd been. It was love this whole thing had centered on, from the very beginning. The figure of two people holding hands.

"Uncle Lance?" said Chrissy, her voice thick with tears.

"Yeah?"

"You once talked about a gay guy who had something to do with Clayton Miller when you were in high school. You said he drove down to the cross on that night, just like Dad did."

For a moment neither of them spoke. Lance could hear every breath his niece took.

"So who was that guy?" she asked.

"Just somebody I made up."

Chrissy uttered a little sound. Maybe she said "thanks," but he couldn't be sure.

"What does Lenny Diver say about what happened?" asked Lance.

His niece took in a deep breath and then let it out.

"He says he was wandering around in the woods, high as a kite, and when he came back to the parking lot the baseball bat was gone. He thinks somebody killed the Norwegian and then hid the bat in his car afterward. And it could have happened like that, since his car wasn't locked."

"But his fingerprints were on the bat," Lance pointed out.

"Yeah, but he picked up the bat after Dad and I left. That's what he says, anyway. He was angry and swung it around a few times. Just in the air."

"And the woman in Grand Marais?" said Lance.

"He would have been picked up as a suspect right away if he'd said that he was anywhere near the cross that night. A sky-high Ojibwe, with braids and everything. So he had to come up with a story. At least that's what he told me."

Lance was about to say something, but instead he just sat there, his lips slightly parted as he stared at the snow drifting over the parking lot. At a moment like this, it was important to keep very still and just wait for his mind, all on its own, to find the right door and open it. When that happened, and the door opened, he felt as if someone had blown ice-cold air at the back of his neck, making all the little hairs stand on end.

# 51

A FLUSH quickly spread up Tammy's throat when she saw who was standing on the front steps. The crimson didn't reach her face, but stopped just below her ears and chin. Lance couldn't help staring.

"Can I come in?" he asked.

She bit her lower lip, looking skeptical, then finally stepped aside to let him into the hallway.

"Did you forget something here last time?"

"You might say that," replied Lance as he hung up his jacket.

"Well, I'm still here," said Tammy in a low voice, almost as if she didn't want him to hear what she'd said. She led the way into the living room. Everything looked exactly the same as it had two days ago. The ashtray was even in the very same spot on the coffee table, overflowing with cigarette butts. It looked like she hadn't bothered to empty it since his visit.

"Well?" she said, looking at him.

"There's something I . . . ," he started to say and sat down.

His sister-in-law remained standing. Lance was afraid she'd misinterpret his intentions and think he wanted another chance.

"It's about Lenny Diver," he said.

She sat down on the other side of the coffee table, shook a cigarette out of the pack, and lit it.

"Have you decided to help me, after all?"

"Yes," said Lance.

He saw how relieved she looked. He knew in his heart this was going to be the most difficult thing he'd ever done.

"But first you have to help me with something," he went on.

"Sure. Anything," said Tammy, giving her brother-in-law an expectant look.

"Have you ever met Lenny Diver?" he asked.

She shook her head.

"Right. That's what I thought. So I wonder why you described him as a man with long braids."

Tammy stared at him, uncomprehending. It hadn't yet dawned on her that Lance was not really here to help her.

"As some kind of 'drug-addicted Indian brave, with those long braids of his,'" he said, mimicking her voice. "That was right after you threw up. Remember? You threw up when I told you that Andy had almost beaten a boy to death with a baseball bat when we were in high school."

She still didn't say anything.

"Why did you describe Diver as a man with long braids?" Lance repeated.

"I saw pictures of him in the papers," said Tammy.

"But the papers used the police mug shot of him," said Lance. "And he didn't have braids."

"Who cares about his hair? The man's a murderer."

"It was actually highly unusual for Lenny Diver to wear his hair in braids," Lance continued. "Chrissy saw him like that only twice. Once when they first met. Now if you happened to be there, I'll admit that you could have remembered about the braids. So why don't you tell me where and under what circumstances Chrissy and Lenny Diver first met."

"Well," Tammy began, taking a long, deep drag on her cigarette. "I remember seeing them together, they met . . ."

"I know the answer," Lance warned her.

"At the movies," she said dismissively, but he could hear that she'd given up.

The only movement in the room was the bluish smoke curling up Tammy's wrist and forearm, and the ash growing almost imperceptibly until it formed a white horn curving downward from the tip of the cigarette.

"He'll get out as soon as I call the FBI and tell them what I know," said Lance. "But I don't necessarily have to do that."

Finally Tammy looked at him again.

"What do I need to do?" she asked.

"Tell me what happened when you killed Georg Lofthus. I've spent every waking hour thinking about this case ever since I found his body. If I don't find out what happened, I'm going to go crazy."

"And what happens if I tell you?"

"It'll stay just between the two of us."

"But how do I know I can trust you?"

"Do you have a choice?"

Tammy fixed her eyes on the cigarette drooping from her fingers. She started breathing hard.

"Okay," she sighed at last, without looking up.

"Okay, what?"

"Okay, so I killed him," she whispered.

"But Georg Lofthus didn't have long dark hair in braids."

Tammy raised her arms, her fists clenched, as if holding a baseball bat.

"I hit him as hard as I could," she snarled.

"And then you kept on hitting him?" Lance asked cautiously.

"It felt good," she said, with that same intense snarl.

"Good?"

Tammy's hand shook as she picked up her cigarette from the ashtray, took a deep drag, and blew the smoke out the side of her mouth.

"You would never understand," she said. "You're a wimp, just like your brother. I'm the only man in this family. I was upstairs when I heard Andy phoning somebody, and for some reason I had a bad feeling about it. Probably because Chrissy had gone to Duluth that day, or so we thought. I picked up the extension and listened. He was talking to a little girl who said that Chrissy and Jennifer weren't there. She hadn't seen them at all. I knew what that meant. She was involved in that shit again. And Andy knew it too. From the upstairs window I saw him get the baseball bat out of the garage and put it in his car. Not long afterward, he started talking about going fishing out at Lost Lake."

"But you knew he was going out to look for Chrissy."

She nodded and took another deep drag on her cigarette.

"I drove north, thinking that he might be on his way to Grand Portage to look for them. The strange thing is, I did it to prevent something bad from happening."

"What made you drive down to the cross?"

"That's where everybody goes to make out. I was hoping they might be there and that Andy wouldn't find them. When I was partway down the road, I saw his car. It was a miracle he didn't see me. I backed up almost as far as the highway and pulled onto an old tractor road. While I was walking down to the parking lot, I heard Andy's voice. He was screaming his head off. He slammed the bat on the hood of Diver's car and shouted that he was ruining our daughter and that he'd get him locked up in prison if he didn't stay away from her. Lenny Diver was really calm. It was eerie. I was probably only about fifty yards away. Suddenly Andy hit Chrissy, and she ended up lying on the asphalt. I could hear the impact from where I stood. I was about to run out of the woods to stop him, but fear held me back. The whole situation felt like a bomb that might explode at any second. She lay on the ground for a good long while, holding her face. In the meantime Andy kept on yelling and screaming. Finally he dragged her over to his car as if she was a fucking deer that he'd shot or something. And that horrible man just stood there, watching. If he'd been a real man, he would have defended her. My little girl . . ."

"And then they drove off?" asked Lance.

She nodded.

"So it was just you and Lenny."

"Yes. I stood there, not daring to move. You should have seen that bastard when he picked up the bat and started swinging it around. He kept on doing that while he babbled furiously, like some kind of maniac. I couldn't really make out what he was saying, but I didn't want to know either."

"But Lofthus was killed sometime after midnight," said Lance. "What happened in the meantime?"

"It wasn't hard to guess where Andy was going to take Chrissy. So I drove all the way up to Lost Lake. I don't know what I was thinking of doing. Maybe just talk to them. Tell Andy what

I thought of him hitting Chrissy. I don't remember what I thought. But when I got to the cabin, I saw . . . Through the window I saw Chrissy sitting on a chair, but she looked strange. Then I realized that he'd tied her up. It was straight out of a horror movie. She was crying and screaming, and that cowardly shithead just stood there, looking at her. If it hadn't been for Lenny Diver, none of that would have happened. And I knew Andy wouldn't have the guts to do anything about it. He could hit his daughter, but he'd never dare go after Lenny Diver. So it was up to me.

"I got out of there and drove back down to Baraga's Cross. When I got to the parking lot, I saw the bat was still lying on the ground. It was almost too good to be true. If I hadn't found the bat, I probably would have left, because I had no idea how I was going to kill Diver. But there it was, in the middle of the parking lot, and his car was there too, so I knew he was somewhere nearby. As I leaned down to pick up the bat, I saw Chrissy's scarf. It was drenched in blood. You have to understand . . . that was my little girl's blood, Lance. My only child, my one and only joy. It may seem stupid now, but at that moment it felt right. I wrapped the scarf around my hand and picked up the bat. At that moment I was bound and determined to find Diver and kill him. I wasn't insane or anything like that, but I think I was as scared as anyone could be. If a mouse had run across my path, I would have beaten it flat."

"Wasn't it dark?" asked Lance.

"There was moonlight, almost a full moon, and slowly the sky got lighter. It was the middle of the summer, you know. First I went over to the cross, but he wasn't there. I walked slowly, didn't make a sound. And then . . . somewhere in the woods . . . suddenly I realized a naked man was standing only a few yards away from me."

"Georg Lofthus," said Lance.

"I hit him in the head before I even stopped to think. And when he lay on the ground, I kept pounding at his skull. It felt so good, Lance. You would never understand . . . finally to be totally . . . *free*. But later . . . it was like I came to my senses. And I saw that it wasn't Diver lying on the ground. That was horrible! I thought what I'd done was wasted effort. That I'd killed a man without getting anything out of it. But when I went back to the parking lot, I suddenly knew how I was going to get that bastard after all. His car wasn't locked, so I hid the bat under some junk inside."

"What about your clothes?" said Lance. "They must have been covered in blood."

"When I got home, I took a shower and put on clean clothes. Then I put the bloodstained clothes in a garbage bag and drove to the lake. It was before dawn, so I didn't meet anyone on the way. On the north side of Lighthouse Point, I stuffed some rocks in the bag, tied it up, and threw it as far as I could into the water. It didn't go very far. It's probably still there."

Conclusive evidence, thought Lance.

"After that, it was just a matter of driving home and waiting for them to come back," said Tammy. "Chrissy ran straight up to her room. She looked awful after the beating she'd taken. It was obvious that Andy had hit her at the cabin too. And I was supposed to believe that she'd spent the night with a girlfriend in Duluth! Andy was upset and wanted to know if I'd heard the news. He told me a murder had been committed near Baraga's Cross."

"What did you think when you heard I was the one who found the dead man?"

"I couldn't believe it. Things like that don't happen. That's what I thought. But it did happen."

"Yes, it did," said Lance with a sigh.

The phone on the end table next to the sofa started ringing.

"I'll take it upstairs," said Tammy and stood up.

Lance was surprised at how calmly she walked across the room, as if this was just an ordinary day in her life. Next he heard her running up the stairs, and then the phone stopped ringing. He wondered whether he should pick up the receiver and listen to the conversation, but decided that it didn't really matter who she was talking to.

As he sat there alone, he realized that the blood traces at the scene of the crime, which the authorities had said with a hundred percent certainty had to have come from a person of Native American origin, could have come from Chrissy's bloody scarf, which Tammy wore wrapped around her hand when she killed

Lofthus. Chrissy had the same Ojibwe ancestry as Lance and Andy, after all. Or Andy could have cut himself and bled when he bashed Lenny Diver's car with the bat, or when he punched Chrissy. The blood could even have been Lenny's, just as the police had assumed all along. A small cut on his hand would have been enough to leave blood on the bat when he picked it up. No matter who it belonged to, the blood had been carried into the woods by Tammy, either on the scarf or the bat, and left at the crime scene. The only person out of the four that the blood *couldn't* have come from, was the murderer.

At that moment he noticed how quiet it was upstairs. When he thought about it, he hadn't heard Tammy's voice for a while. Lance went over to the end table and cautiously lifted the phone. But all he heard was a dial tone.

# 52

SHE WAS SITTING ON THE BED with his gun beside her.

"Tammy," said Lance.

As she raised the gun with a trembling hand and pointed it at her temple, he saw that she had something wrapped around her wrist. It took a couple of seconds before he realized she'd kept her daughter's bloody scarf.

"Tammy," he said again, taking a step into the room.

"Don't move," she shouted, fear in her voice.

Lance froze in midstride and stood still as they stared at each other. Aside from Tammy's shallow breathing, there wasn't a sound in the house.

"I don't trust you," she whispered. "You're going to tell."

He heard the familiar scraping sound of a plow moving past. Outside it was just another boring Tuesday in Two Harbors, Minnesota. The kind of day almost nobody remembers afterward, but Lance Hansen would remember it for the rest of his life.

"Who was on the phone?" he asked in an attempt to talk her back from the edge.

"The school. They don't know where she is. Every time the phone rings, I'm afraid she . . ."

"If you kill yourself, Lenny Diver will be the only one she has left," he said.

Looking into Tammy's eyes, he could see she was slowly coming back from that void where she'd gone. Shaking, she put down the gun. Finally he could move, and in three long strides he reached the bed and picked up the weapon. At that instant she collapsed onto the floor, and there she stayed, soundlessly shaking all over.

Lance sat down next to her. He suddenly felt completely drained of all strength. He sat there for a long time, listening to the normal everyday life going on outside the four walls of this house, as he stroked Tammy's hair and thought about all the years in prison that lay ahead of her.

# EPILOGUE

ON A SATURDAY IN LATE MAY, Lance Hansen parked his old
Jeep Cherokee in the lot near Baraga's Cross. Next to him sat Jim-
my, holding the old dream catcher that Lance had been given by
Willy Dupree.

"Are you ready?" asked Lance.

Jimmy nodded solemnly.

Hand in hand they headed across the deserted parking lot.
When they came to the path that led to the cross, they had to
walk single file, and Lance let his son go first. Since Jimmy was
holding the dream catcher out in front of him on the palms of his
hands, he moved slowly through the woods, but Lance thought
that was appropriate. It was as if the boy were carrying a gift or
an offering.

"Should I give it to you now?" Jimmy asked as they emerged
from the woods and saw the lake in front of them.

"You can wait a bit," said Lance.

He put his hand on the back of his son's slender neck, and
then they walked the last stretch over to Baraga's Cross. Lance
leaned against the cold granite and looked out at Lake Superi-
or. He thought about that morning when he found the body of
Georg Lofthus. Since then he'd lost a large part of his family. Inga
was dead, Tammy was in prison, and Andy would never speak
to him again. Down in Minneapolis, Chrissy was in a treatment
program for young drug addicts. He'd been afraid that she would

be drawn to Lenny Diver again once he was a free man, but that hadn't happened. Maybe she'd finally understood how serious things were when she realized that her mother, out of sheer desperation, had tried to kill her boyfriend. But she'd chosen to keep the brown-tinted contact lenses—her Ojibwe eyes. When Lance went to visit his niece, he couldn't help noticing that something had changed between them. Even though Chrissy understood that Tammy had to pay for the murder she'd committed, her uncle would always be the man who had sent her mother to prison.

Yet the most important thing was that he could stand here with his son, without feeling any shame about what he'd done, and without having to lie anymore. On the way here from Grand Portage, he'd told Jimmy about Swamper Caribou, who might have been killed at this very spot long ago. The boy had listened, wide-eyed and happy at being initiated into something that clearly belonged to the grown-up world.

"Okay, you can give it to me now," said Lance.

Jimmy handed him the dream catcher, and together they walked over to the edge of the rocks, where Lance squatted down.

"We're doing this to restore balance to things," he said.

For one last lingering moment he held the sacred object in his hands before he placed it on the water. Swamper Caribou's old dream catcher floated as light as a cork. Lance thought it looked like a funeral wreath as it bobbed up and down on the rippling waves.

**VIDAR SUNDSTØL** is the acclaimed Norwegian author of seven novels, including the Minnesota Trilogy, written after he and his wife lived for two years in Two Harbors, Minnesota, on the North Shore of Lake Superior. *The Land of Dreams* (Minnesota, 2013), the first novel in the trilogy, was awarded the Riverton Prize for best Norwegian crime novel of the year in 2008 and was nominated for the Glass Key for best Scandinavian crime novel of the year. *The Land of Dreams* was ranked by *Dagbladet* as one of the top twenty-five Norwegian crime novels, and the Minnesota Trilogy has been translated into seven languages.

**TIINA NUNNALLY** is an award-winning translator of Danish, Norwegian, and Swedish literature. Her many translations include Sigrid Undset's first novel, *Marta Oulie: A Novel of Betrayal* (Minnesota, 2014). Her translation of Undset's *Kristin Lavransdatter III: The Cross* won the PEN/Book-of-the-Month Club Translation Prize. She was appointed Knight of the Royal Norwegian Order of Merit for her efforts on behalf of Norwegian literature in the United States.